THRESHWALKER

TIMOTHY E. JORGENSEN

First edition

ISBN Paperback: 979-8-9936639-0-6
ISBN Hardcover: 979-8-9936639-2-0
ISBN Ebook: 979-8-9936639-1-3

Published by Veiled House Press

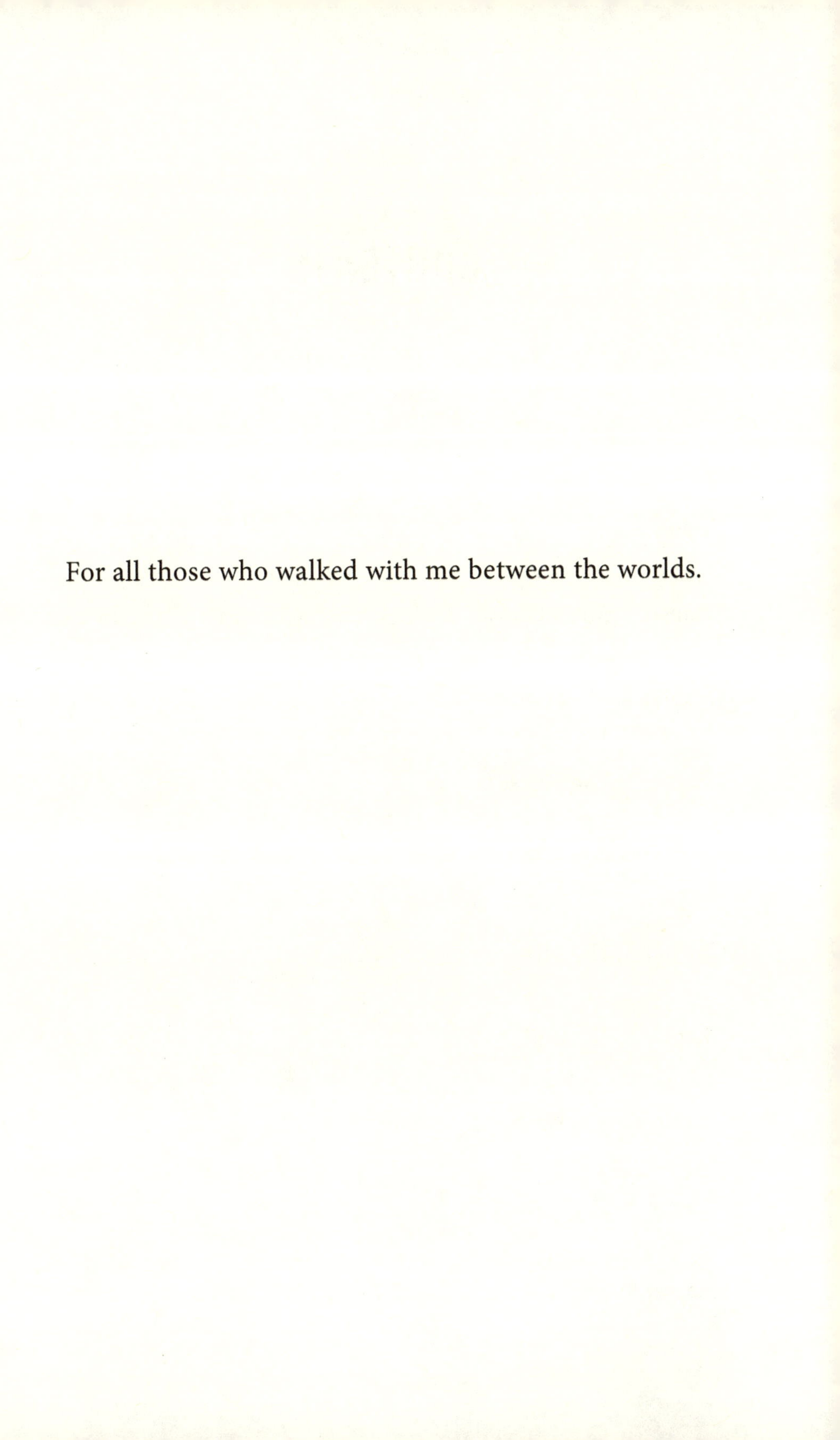

For all those who walked with me between the worlds.

CONTENTS

PROLOGUE

He was coming.

The lock squealed as it scraped against the metal door, wrenching the young woman from her sleep. She shot up, groggy and confused, but scrambled into the farthest corner of the cell on instinct. She tried to become small, just a shadow deep in the corner of the damp concrete wall.

The room smelled of rot, sweat, and something metallic she'd stopped trying to identify long ago. She had never gotten used to it. Even now, it still hit her every time she woke. A constant and instant reminder of the hell she was in. It had been weeks—months, maybe? At first, she tried to keep track, but in that dark, windowless room, time had long since lost meaning. Only the lock and the scrape of the door opening gave her any sense of time passing at all.

She flinched as the door groaned open, allowing the pale light in from the hall. She'd learned to hate it. What used to feel like a reprieve from the darkness was now nothing more than a betrayal of her location in the shadows.

The man always entered the same way. His boots would clunk against the floor with every slow, deliberate step, sending little shocks through her body as each foot fell. He knew. And he enjoyed it.

She never knew right away why he was coming to see her, but it always came down to one of three things: feed her, bathe her, or hurt her. Relief flooded through her whenever she looked up and saw the plate in his hand.

It was the better of the options, though she had learned to hate it just as much as everything else in this place. It was a cruel reminder of the control he had over her. She wished she could refuse it and hurl it back at him, defiantly allowing hunger to kill her before he could. But her body betrayed her. She hated it, and she hated herself more for eating it.

He stopped in the center of the room, tilting his head to look at her. She kept her head down, a lesson she had learned the hard way. He didn't like the way she looked at him, and sometimes, if she didn't engage, he would eventually get bored and leave her alone. She could feel him studying her, his eyes probing and tunneling into her.

Fuck! It meant he was sticking around.

"You should have seen her," he said.

His voice always had a low, almost tender tone to it, with a taint of twisted malevolence held just below it. Her body twitched a bit at every vile syllable that dripped from his mouth.

"She was so perfect."

She squeezed her arms around her legs, digging in to protect herself. They were just words, but there was always a chance it would go further. She dared not respond to the man. There was nothing she could say to improve the situation, and it would only get worse.

"Reminded me of you," he continued. "Well, before you turned into… this."

His insults did little to bother her anymore. Yes, there was shame, maybe even a bit of anger. Hell, sometimes she wanted to scream and claw at his face, but after all he'd put her through, she was more concerned about mitigating an escalation than reacting to his words. So she kept quiet—the only control she had left.

It took a minute, but he eventually tired of her silence, and she heard him sigh. She peeked up just as he shook his head like a disappointed parent.

"You've changed," he said, turning his head away as though he couldn't stand to look at her. "It might be time for you to go."

Those words ripped through her like a shot of adrenaline. She knew better than to assume it meant anything good. But the thought of leaving—of escaping the nightmare of that room, his voice, the… other things—it was a spark she couldn't afford to extinguish. She understood that death was likely the only way out, but in that moment, she thought of her mom's soft smile, her dad's terrible jokes, her brother's teasing laugh. The memories had faded, torn to shreds by time and pain, but they were there, fragile and precious.

"Would you like that?" he asked, turning his head back toward her. "To be with your family again?"

He knew her. He knew exactly what to say to elicit a response. She felt her throat collapse, and she so badly wanted to answer— the word *yes* screaming to come out. But she understood him, too. If she said yes, he would become angry, call her cruel and ungrateful. If she said no, he would berate her and call her needy and obsessive. Both options came with rage and potentially pain. Silence was the only way.

The quiet went on for too long. She could feel him staring at her, enjoying the torment he'd created. He let out a raspy chuckle. "Not speaking to me today? Fine. Have it your way."

He tossed the plate at her feet, scattering food across the cell. She flinched as the plate clanged against the floor and wall and quickly scanned the room to memorize where everything had landed before he could plunge the room back into darkness. The door slammed behind him, and only then did she crawl forward to collect the scraps.

She had just started eating when the door crashed open again, its sound reverberating through the room like a gunshot. She froze, staring directly at his face. He wasn't done.

She had no time to react or retreat. He burst in, grabbing a fistful of her hair, yanking her to her feet. She yelped as the pain exploded through her scalp. She clawed at his wrists, trying to right herself and escape, but it was no use.

"We're done," he snarled as he dragged her into the corridor. She kicked and scraped her feet against the concrete, but all it did was tear the skin from her heels. She wanted to fight, punch, bite, scream, anything, but the pain in her scalp took center stage, and she didn't have the strength.

As they reached the end of the hall, he kicked a door open and threw her into another room. She hit the floor hard—the impact knocking the air from her lungs. Gasping, she pushed herself up, but her body failed her, and she collapsed.

She was no stranger to this room. The bloodstained black and white tiles, the stainless-steel counters, and the chair bolted in the center—its restraints dangling down in front of her. They'd spent many hours there as he worked out whatever aggression or disgust he'd needed to unleash on her before sending her back to her cell.

It felt different this time. It was in his eyes and the way he spoke. She was about to be replaced.

Part of her was glad for it, glad for the torment to finally end. She knew what it meant for whoever followed her, but she was ready for it to be over.

He closed the door behind him and started walking toward her—slowly, like he was trying to savor the moment. She glanced at him and then down at the floor. She knew she was going to die, but then something in her snapped. There was no way she was going to make it easy for him.

In one last surge of defiance, she pushed herself up and planted her feet beneath her. She wobbled and nearly fell but steadied herself against a rolling tray next to the chair, knocking its contents to the floor. As she stood, ready to give him hell, she felt the knife beneath her hand. It was small, but from everything he put her through, she knew it was sharp. Sharp enough to cut deep.

The weight of every bruise and scar, every night she spent alone in the dark, every moment she spent in that room enduring that man pressed down on her, and she realized something. She wasn't afraid anymore. But if it was the end, she'd make damn sure he remembered her. Lyndsay. She raised the knife, holding it out in front of her, ready to start swinging wildly. The man paused and smiled.

"That's my girl. Let's see what you got."

That smile. It was everything about him, and everything she'd endured, all wrapped up in a tight, twisted smirk. As she stood there waving the knife in her trembling hand, she realized even in her defiance, she would give him exactly what he wanted. No matter how hard she fought or how much hate and rage she could muster, deep down, she knew this was the end.

The knife was never about escape—it was about reclaiming some measure of control. But if he was going to enjoy it anyway, maybe there was no point. She pulled it close to her chest, and for the first time in what felt like forever, she had a choice. She could give him what he wanted and fight, or she could take that away from him, the way he had taken everything from her.

She squeezed her eyes shut and let everything fall away. In the moment just before the world went black, she thought she heard a voice calling to her. It was foreign, and yet... somehow familiar, and it seemed to come from every direction. She didn't know what it meant, but she smiled anyway as the voice whispered two final words.

"Find Mac."

CHAPTER 1

MAC'S GHOSTS

Everyone in the room knew ghosts came with the territory—addiction created plenty. Regret, mistakes, failed marriages—memories that wouldn't let go. But whenever Mac walked in, they knew he brought a different kind of ghost with him.

The room was laid out just as it always was. In the center, the chairs were arranged in a large semicircle. A smattering of people, many of whom had been attending for years, stood around chitchatting, quietly laughing, and greeting each other over a cup of stale, slightly burned coffee, the smell of which had permanently stained the air.

It always seemed odd how innocuous it all was on the surface, knowing that every person in that room was haunted by an addiction that had destroyed their lives so completely. Yet there they were, each working, day by day, to pick up the pieces of what they had given up—or lost—along the way. There they were, exchanging pleasantries and enjoying a moment of personal connection before the therapy of it all began.

Mac held the door, and before Daniel got two steps in, Nancy, a former client of Mac's, introduced herself, extending her hand.

"First time?"

Daniel nodded, reluctantly reaching out to shake the woman's hand. Mac understood this was a big moment—one that many who came to these meetings had difficulty getting through during their initial visit. Before that first interaction there was still time to cut and run back to the car. That's why Mac stayed by the door—to ensure Daniel knew that if he wanted to leave, it would mean facing him first. That step was too important.

Nancy held on to Daniel's hand and turned to Mac, giving him a quick nod before taking Daniel to an empty seat in the circle.

"Don't worry," she said. "We've all had a first time. Just sit, drink some coffee, and listen if that's all you're ready to do. There's no pressure here."

"Is he haunted?" a familiar voice asked, sneaking in from behind Mac.

Mac leaned against the wall and crossed his arms, anchoring himself so he couldn't be moved.

"Timothy," Mac replied. "Good to see you. There is something there, yes."

Timothy smiled briefly and looked down at a small stack of pamphlets he was gripping in both hands.

"Feel like joining us today, Mitchel? You know, half these people owe you their lives, and everyone in this room—"

"Today isn't for me," Mac cut in.

Timothy would save anyone who let him, but Mac wasn't interested. And he hated being called Mitchel. Sometimes it felt like he used Mac's first name just to rile him up, though he knew that wasn't Timothy's nature.

"Understood." Timothy patted Mac's shoulder as he started walking toward the group. "Maybe next time," he said with a little disappointment and far too much optimism, forcing Mac to roll his eyes.

As everyone began taking their seats, Mac's attention returned to Daniel, who had planted himself near the edge of the circle, his gaze fixed on the floor. Mac knew what was bouncing off the walls of Daniel's brain. He'd been there many times.

It was the first time Daniel would admit to himself, or anyone else, that he had a problem with alcohol.

A voice Mac knew all too well would whisper how unnecessary it all was. It would tell him to deal with it in secret, keep it private. *You don't really have a problem.*

Daniel shivered and rolled his shoulders. He had a weight on them from years of shame, guilt, and self-disgust. He interlaced his fingers in his lap, like he was holding on to it, not willing to let it go. Like the burden he carried was all he had left. And behind him, a spectral figure took shape, barely visible to Mac.

It rested its hands on Daniel's shoulders, its hollow eyes staring down at him to bear witness to his pain and struggle. It wasn't a comforting touch—rather, a force ensuring he would confront what needed to be faced.

Daniel was haunted, not just by his addiction but by his past, and it was very real. That ghost was the reason Mac was there that day.

"Hi, I'm Jim, and I'm an alcoholic."

"Hi, Jim!" a chorus of voices responded.

Mac was glad that Jim went first. Since Mac had introduced him to the group a couple years back, he'd gained a quiet, steady confidence that put the new folks at ease. He wasn't cocky, but he had self-assurance that only came from fighting the good fight and winning. His voice was steady, practiced, and comforting.

As he spoke about the cycles of drinking—the lies, broken promises, and rage—the newcomer's expression and posture changed. Jim was putting Daniel at ease, and Mac was hopeful that Daniel could share his story and start on a path to removing his burdens.

Mac's attention on Daniel snapped when he noticed the apparition had shifted its gaze and was now staring at him—glaring like it knew what Mac was doing. He stood upright, pulling himself away from the wall. Some spirits welcomed the release, but others fought to the bitter end. He wouldn't allow it to intimidate him. It was a battle of wills, however small.

As others in the group shared, Daniel sat motionless, absorbing every word spoken, every understanding nod, and every quiet "me too." Each chipped away at the wall he had built around himself, opening him up to share his own story.

When it came time for Daniel to speak, he hesitated, but the entire room fell quiet. They all gave him space to either begin or decide to pass. There was no pressure, no expectations. It was all up to him.

His head lifted, and he began, quietly at first, practically whispering, but his voice grew steadier as he went on. He spoke of a broken marriage and how long it had been since he'd seen his kids. He talked about his anger issues and his sadness. There was remorse in his voice and a genuine desire to do better.

"'Asshole' is what she called me," he said. "She was right, of course."

Daniel paused for a moment, reflecting on what he had just admitted to the group. "But I don't think that can be blamed on the alcohol."

This was the moment Mac had been hoping for, and the spirit behind Daniel—still holding on to his shoulders—straightened up, as if it knew what was coming.

"I killed a man," Daniel continued. "Not directly or on purpose," he said. "But I was the reason. I'm sure of it.

"When I was in high school, I had a run-in with a new kid at the school. He was just trying to…" He stopped and shook the thought out of his head. "It doesn't matter what he did, but at that time in my life, it felt like something I needed to retaliate against—just to keep up my, I dunno… reputation, I guess.

"Cooper." He paused for a moment. "God, I haven't said his name in… Anyway, we had swim class together. I was already on the swim team, and he had transferred in midway through the season, so he was doing everything he could to prove he belonged on the roster. I came up with a prank… the specifics don't matter, but it involved brown dye and Cooper's trunks."

Daniel stopped talking. His eyes welled up as he struggled to continue. He looked up at Mac, who nodded his approval and mouthed the words, *Be free of it.*

"I remember," he continued, "the horrified look in his eyes as he saw the stained water floating up around him. It was instant.

Before I could even say anything, one of the other kids noticed and immediately branded him 'Cooper the Pooper,' and the whole class rushed out of the water, screaming in either disgust or laughter."

Daniel's posture and gaze reverted to where he had started. His head shook again. There was shame in his admission. "I never really thought it was that bad, you know? But Cooper never recovered from it. It stayed with him for the rest of high school. A few years later, someone told me that Cooper had killed himself."

The entire room was silent. This was much bigger than most of the stories they were used to hearing, but Mac knew they understood the pain and shame. They listened.

"That was the last day I lived without a drink."

Daniel looked back up at all the concerned faces staring at him. "She was right, my wife. I am an asshole, but not because I drink. I drink because I'm an asshole. Because if I don't, I might look in a mirror and see the boy who killed Cooper."

Mac released a breath he hadn't realized he'd been holding. He knew this moment—he'd seen it before. The confession would either break the spirit's hold... or it would lash out.

Cooper's fingers uncurled, letting go of Daniel like he finally felt it no longer needed to be there. He hesitated, lingering for a second or two before shifting back away from him. The spirit looked over to Mac again, but it was different this time. There was a fullness to his gaze—a quiet look of appreciation. And then it unraveled into nothing, dissolving like a wisp of vapor.

The room stayed silent for a long moment. It wasn't the kind of silence that was empty but more of a shared sense of the collective weight of understanding and care. These were the stories that bound the group—the confessions that reminded everyone why they were there—not for redemption but to survive, to heal.

Newcomers rarely opened up so deeply on their first visit. It surprised them all, even Mac, but it was also amazing. Daniel, now slumped back in his chair, had just shown the sort of courage and complete understanding of his curse that many of them, Mac included, wished they had.

He looked different. It was almost imperceptible, but Mac could see the shift in his posture. Some combination of unburdening himself and Cooper finally moving on had carved out a small space, a tiny relief from the crushing pressure he'd carried for so long.

Nancy reached over and placed her hand on Daniel's knee. "Thank you for sharing that," she said softly, providing an opening for the others, as quiet voices spoke phrases like "So brave" and "We've all been there."

Jim wiped a tear from his cheek. "You can't change the past, Daniel. None of us can. All we can control is how we move forward, and you just took that first step."

Daniel nodded as Jim spoke, still holding his hands in his lap, but he didn't respond. Mac recognized it—that moment when just one more word might cause an eruption of tears.

Mac took a slow, deep breath and let out a long sigh. That was a tough one, even for him. But the ghost was gone, and Daniel was on his way toward true healing. It had been weeks since Mac felt like he might have actually made a difference.

As he stood there, staring at the now-empty space behind Daniel, he caught Timothy smiling at him from across the room, something that became a sort of ritual between them—a way of acknowledging the small victory, as well as Mac's own unspoken battles.

Mac nodded in return and leaned against the wall, crossing his arms again, but this time, he allowed himself the faintest hint of a smile.

The meeting wrapped up, and they each shared final words of encouragement and support before heading off, back to their own routines. Mac stayed until the last of them had gone and tucked his hands into his jacket pockets as he watched Daniel linger near the door, speaking to Nancy. She wrote her phone number for him, offering to be his sponsor and help him on this new journey.

Mac exited the meeting hall and strolled down the steps to the parking lot, taking his time to enjoy the moment. He passed by Timothy, who always waited to shake everyone's hands as they left—something he borrowed from his Sunday sermons.

"You did good today, Mac," Timothy said. He always said that. "We're here for you, too, when you're ready."

Mac nodded and shook his hand but didn't respond as he kept walking to his truck. As he opened the door, he took in one more long breath. There was one less ghost in the world, and Mac was taking one more step forward. It wasn't much, but for now, it was enough.

CHAPTER 2
THE SCREAM

The drive home after a cleansing always felt different. Mac's world was full of ghosts and hauntings, so moments like those—just him, his truck, and a song on the radio—were rare.

He didn't get many chances to feel proud anymore, but there was a quiet satisfaction in knowing he had helped spare someone a lifetime of suffering. And it helped to know there was one less spirit lingering in the world.

His truck was old, thirty years past its prime. Though it rattled and complained the whole way, it got him where he needed to be. And the stereo still worked, which was a plus.

Toto's "Africa" hummed through the speakers, and everything else faded away, allowing him to reflect on the journey he took with Daniel. They'd figured out the haunting was connected to his drinking problem—how both were destroying his life—and that working through one might unravel the other.

It was common for folks dealing with personal hauntings to drink. It was an effective means of dulling the senses, drowning everything out, including those things touching them from the other side. Mac knew this trick well and relied on it every night.

He saw little use in battling his own addiction. He wasn't haunted himself, instead his curse was to witness everyone else's ghosts. No amount of therapy would make that go away. Yet despite it all, in that moment, he found himself happy, truly at peace.

He drummed his fingers against the wheel, letting himself become lost in the rhythm. Then everything exploded.

The deafening *whump* filled the cabin, and a cold gust of air slammed into the space beside him. Something appeared out of nowhere and crashed into the seat with so much force it rocked the truck. His heart seized as he whipped his head around.

A woman took form beside him. Shimmering and translucent, her features were blurry at first but slowly became more human. Her eyes, wide and shocked, met his, and they shared a tiny moment of terror.

The shock hit him like a cold splash to the face. He gasped and jerked the wheel, swerving wildly out of control. The tires skidded across the loose gravel as he slammed down on the brakes, working desperately to avoid tipping over.

When the truck finally settled back onto the road, Mac turned toward the woman, struggling to slow his breathing. He couldn't take his eyes off her, the figure who now sat next to him as if she had been there all along. She watched him, too, equally unsettled, seemingly unsure of what she was doing there—or what had just happened.

"What… who…?" he whispered, the words barely audible over Toto's melody still playing in the background.

Her head tilted as she opened her mouth, trying to speak, but no sound came out. Mac squinted, struggling to make out what her mouth was saying. The movements were too erratic, and the wispiness of her form wasn't helping, but he could swear he made out the words "help me" in all the desperate chaos.

That desperation soon gave way to frustration, and then to something darker. A tremor rippled through her form, and she sucked in a deep, spectral breath. Her face contorted into a raw, primal rage, and then she screamed.

Mac slapped his hands over his ears as the scream tore through the cab like a thunderclap. The sound was human and inhuman—blunt and piercing as it vibrated through him, rattling the very bones of his truck. He squeezed his eyes shut and pressed his hands harder against his ears as the sound reached its peak.

As suddenly as it began, the scream stopped, leaving Mac's pounding heart the only sound remaining. The seat beside him was empty again. The air was still cold and charged with energy, but the spirit was gone.

What the hell was that?

He looked around the truck, checking the mirrors and the truck bed behind him. Everything was normal again.

He grabbed the shifter and took a deep breath before putting the truck in drive, stretching his jaw a few times to relieve the pressure that had built up in his ears.

CHAPTER 3
THE HOUSE

The house loomed at the end of the driveway, a relic of another era, its presence both inviting in its splendor and unsettling because of its age. The once-bright greens and reds had dulled over the years, now chalky and peeling like the remnants of an old oil painting. Tall, narrow windows watched over the property, and a broad porch wrapped around the entire building, its carved wooden details bearing the fine craftsmanship of a bygone age and the undeniable scars of time and neglect.

At the front, a tower reached toward the sky, its conical roof adorned with a small metal cross, like a ghostly crown. The years had washed away much of the color, but the house held an undeniable, eerie beauty despite its decay. If any place was meant to be haunted, it was this one. And haunted it was.

Mac climbed out of his truck, closing the door with one hand while holding a brown paper bag in the other, pinning his phone between his shoulder and cheek.

"I don't know what it was," he said, grabbing the phone with his free hand. "I've never seen a spirit do anything like that."

"Well, it could have been a lot of things. They're rare, but it's not unheard of for a spirit to manifest that way. Maybe a—"

John knew a great deal about the world between the living and the dead and Mac often went to him for help as he encountered new things. Unfortunately, he was as verbose as he was useful. The man truly enjoyed the sound of his own voice, especially when the topic allowed him to lord his knowledge over Mac. He assumed it was John's way of making him feel small, but tonight it mostly just made him feel tired.

As John rambled on, ruminating on all the possible types of spirits he could have encountered, Mac's attention faded. He leaned against the truck and let the day's events settle over him. His gaze drifted as a flicker of movement caught his attention—a spirit drifting across the street, heading toward the wrought-iron fence that bordered his property. Mac kept his eyes on the figure as John continued talking.

"Mac? Are you listening? Maybe a banshee."

"I don't know!" he said. "I wouldn't know what a banshee sounds like—or looks like, for that matter."

The spirit crept closer, seemingly oblivious to Mac and his phone call, its translucent form nearly brushing the iron bars of the fence.

"Hold on a sec…" he said before pressing the phone against his chest to yell at the spirit. "Hey, buddy. You really don't want to cross that fence."

The ghost ignored him and continued forward. Mac sighed, shaking his head. "Seriously, can you hear me? This is not going to end well."

The spirit drifted closer, and Mac waited as it finally passed through the fence like a puff of smoke. He glanced at the house as the familiar low moan vibrated through the air. The sagging electrical lines near the street crackled, and the ghost shuddered as the house drew it in. Its form stretched and flickered, and in a final flash, it was gone, absorbed by the very walls.

Mac rolled his eyes, raising his voice toward the house. "Tried to warn you!" And he brought the phone back to his ear. "Sorry about that. Another one for the house. Hey, look, I'm heading in now. I'll let you know if she comes back."

Pocketing his phone, Mac pulled out his keys, glancing back at the street, where the faintest chill lingered in the air. The old door resisted as he fumbled with the lock, finally giving way with a groan.

Inside, the foyer was a stark contrast to its exterior. It was brightly lit, with walls and floors restored to a modern polish. It looked nothing like the haunted relic that loomed outside. Dropping his keys in a bowl by the door, he walked into the family room, which had yet to be updated like the foyer. He tossed his coat onto the back of a faded couch that faced a large ornate fireplace—clean but unused for decades.

Mac reached into the paper bag and pulled out a bottle of cheap whiskey, unscrewing the cap and tossing the bag aside. He picked up a glass from the floor, where a few drops from last night still lingered, and blew into it, dislodging any dust before pouring himself a full measure. Setting the bottle on the mantel, he walked to the window facing the street, sipping thoughtfully.

The room was a mess of piled books, unopened mail, fast-food trash, and empty bottles. He knew he should clean it up, make it feel more like a home. But what was the point? The only visitors he had these days were wayward ghosts, and the house never let them get close enough to see the mess anyway.

Josie would have had every room in the house fully remodeled and decorated already—completely modernized, but somehow keeping its old Victorian charm. She never would have let it get so messy. Before she died, Josie was a marketing guru—obsessive about detail, borderline pathological about order. She would have made the house amazing. But she would never get that chance.

Most folks who knew him—even the ones who didn't believe in his "gifts"—thought he was crazy for living there. If he really could see ghosts, why live with a poltergeist, one of the most malevolent spirits of them all?

They were different. The typical run-of-the-mill ghost was once human, bound here through unfinished business—a love they never expressed, an action they never took, or in the worst cases, a need for revenge. In a sense, they were haunted themselves.

A poltergeist was something much worse. Born from raw emotion, like pain or rage searing itself into a place like a scar. They didn't haunt so much as they consumed, growing stronger with every spirit devoured or every burst of fear absorbed from the living. They were a living, breathing thing, and power was their only goal.

For Mac, living in a house with a poltergeist meant peace—a dangerous kind, but peace all the same. Most spirits knew to stay away, and any that didn't risked being devoured by the house itself. He thought of the house like a guard dog—something wild and fierce that offered a twisted sort of protection.

As he stared out the window, a form materialized in the street. It was blue, hazy, and it flickered as it slowly coalesced. He waited as it took shape, giving a quick nod to the house.

"Gonna be well-fed tonight, I guess."

The longer he watched the shape coming into its form, the more familiar it became, and his pulse quickened. It was the girl from the truck. Before he knew it, he was frantically tapping on the glass, yelling for her to get away. It wasn't a threat—it was a warning. She didn't seem to hear him either way.

He ran out of the house, not sure why he cared so much. If it were any other ghost, he would just kick back and watch the show. Maybe it was the way she came to him, her attempts to speak… or that scream. Something about this one intrigued him.

By the time he reached the yard, she was already gone. No moans or flickering lights—none of the telltale signs that the house had fed. He sighed, his shoulders relaxing as he looked down at the glass in his hand. He could feel the house behind him, sulking over the loss of its meal.

His phone rang in the distance just as he brought the glass to his lips, jolting him from his thoughts. "Dammit," he muttered before turning back toward the door.

He grabbed his phone off the desk, stumbling past the couch. "This is Mac."

The man on the other end wasted no time, launching into a barrage of reasons he was certain he was being haunted. Scratching noises, banging sounds—all manner of strange things plaguing him and his home. His voice dripped with anxiety, but Mac could also sense a slight note of excitement. The man was convinced already, and he kind of enjoyed it.

Mac leaned back, listening with practiced patience. He'd dealt with clients like this plenty of times before. That kind of enthusiasm usually meant one thing—the "haunting" wasn't real. More often than not, it turned out to be creaky pipes, a family of raccoons in the attic, or an overactive imagination fueled by too many late-night ghost-hunting shows.

But in the end, it didn't matter. Whether it was a poltergeist or a possum, the money spent the same—and he needed it.

"Absolutely," he said, feigning enthusiasm. "But… I'm all booked up tomorrow. I can stop by first thing Sunday if that works for you."

He ended the call and rubbed his temples, enjoying the quiet once again. He looked up at the bottle, still perched on the mantel, and scanned the room for the glass he'd abandoned somewhere. Not that he saw much point in looking for it. It had been a long day, and that bottle would be emptied with or without the glass.

As he reached for it, his eyes lingered on an old photo of Josie, her soft smile shining through the dust and years.

He could almost hear her voice chastising him. *You're better than this*, she would say.

He lifted the bottle to his lips. *Maybe. But not tonight.*

CHAPTER 4

HAUNTED

The morning sun peeked in through the attic window. Mac sat on the floor, sifting through the contents of an old box packed with papers and photographs, mostly just documents from when he bought the house. It wasn't the box he was searching for, but it was still full of memories.

A few years had passed since his first call to cleanse the house. A young couple from Denver had purchased it, dreaming of building a family and spreading out in a home that would have cost them three times as much in the city. They'd lasted barely a month. Strange noises, shadowy figures, and banging pipes had taken their toll—enough to call someone like Mac for help.

He'd done what he could—all the normal stuff: wards, sage, and various rituals he'd learned from John over the years. None of it worked, and that was when Mac first truly understood poltergeists. This wasn't some wayward ghost he could help, bind, or scare away.

It took little for Mac to convince them to sell him the house. His offer was low, but it was fair… and all he had.

He pushed the box away and glanced around, looking for the one he'd come up here to find. He stretched as he reached out, grabbing another box and dug through the contents. His hand found something familiar, and he stopped. Grinning, he pulled out a small wooden jewelry box. It was a simple case, nothing fancy, but the sight and feel of it brought with it a flood of memories.

Flipping the copper latch, he opened it to reveal a small silver bracelet loaded with charms—Josie's bracelet.

Mac sat there, turning it over in his hands, remembering each moment they'd shared as he helped her build her collection of ornaments. His thumb rubbed the face of one charm in particular, a small dangling tree of life, and his mind transported back to the day he'd given it to her. She'd laughed, teasing him for being sentimental but she wore it every day after—until the end.

A few moments later, he wiped the tear swelling in his eye and placed the bracelet back into the box.

"Gotcha," he whispered, pressing the box against his chest before standing.

Mac walked the path with his eyes down and the jewelry box clutched tight in his hand. The cemetery always felt like two worlds. One belonged to the mourners—the families and friends laying loved ones to rest or visiting someone long passed. The other belonged to the ghosts.

He always felt them before he saw them—ghosts and their restless energy itching at the edge of his skin. The place was infested with them. Some hovered near their own headstones, blankly staring off into the distance. Others meandered aimlessly, their spectral forms flickering in and out as they moved.

He ignored them, like he always did. They got all the other days of the week. Saturdays belonged to Josie. So he kept his head down, tried not to make eye contact, and continued until he reached her headstone.

JOSEPHINE MICHELLE CRICHTON
BELOVED WIFE, DAUGHTER, AND SISTER
GONE TOO SOON

He noticed some fresh flowers sitting to one side and assumed her family must have been by. He glanced around, and the ghosts pulled back as he set the jewelry box on the grass, as though they understood it was time to give him a little space.

"Hey, Josie," he whispered. "Found this in the attic… thought you might like to know it's still here."

A nearby ghost drifted closer, a young boy no more than ten or eleven years old. He reached out, but his translucent hand passed through the box. Mac didn't look up, but his jaw clenched.

"Don't start," he snapped. "This isn't for you."

The boy hesitated, sulking back like a scolded cat before disappearing into the mist. Mac sighed and turned his attention back to Josie's grave.

"I miss you," he admitted, his voice barely more than a whisper. "Every day. I haven't really made any progress on the house." He let out a hollow chuckle. "Even with the poltergeist, you'd have had it looking perfect by now."

A flicker of movement caught his eye, and he turned just in time to see another spirit, a middle-aged woman, hovering just out of arm's reach, weeping silently with her hands clasped together in front of her.

"For crying out loud," he grumbled. "Do none of you have boundaries?"

He stood and brushed the dirt off his knees, shaking his head. "You're lucky it's Saturday."

A breeze kicked up, bringing with it a new chill. He tightened his jacket across his chest and turned back to Josie's grave one last time.

"Love you," he said, his voice softer again. "See you next week."

He tucked the box into his jacket and started back toward the path. The ghosts didn't follow him, but he could feel them watching. Not abnormal for Mac, walking that line between the living and the dead, but Saturdays were always the worst.

"Next time, I'm bringing salt," he grumbled.

While Saturdays were hard, the nights that followed were torturous. After spending the day focused entirely on what he'd lost, what he couldn't see, and what he'd never have again, there was only one way Mac had found to keep himself moving forward—drowning it deep in a bottle of cheap whiskey.

The sun was a few minutes from dipping below the mountain horizon when he left the liquor store, crinkling a small paper bag in his grip. There was a sharp chill in the air, hinting at the inevitable first snow of the season. He zipped up his jacket and headed for his truck. The bottle wouldn't be far out of reach tonight.

He pulled himself into the driver's seat and let the door slam shut as he pulled the keys from his pocket. Something flashed in the corner of his eye, and a sharp tinge of dread crept up in his spine. He turned his head slowly, and there she was again. Sitting in the passenger seat, the same young spirit, staring at him like she'd been waiting for him to return.

"You again, huh?" Mac muttered.

He'd never dealt with a spirit like her before. Ghosts usually stayed bound to something—a person, a place, or an object tied to their death. Sometimes, he'd find one drifting toward his house, only to vanish like smoke. This one found its way into the passenger seat of his truck twice in as many nights.

She didn't answer but he could see something in her expression. Frustration, maybe anger. Whatever it was, it didn't feel good. And then, in a voice as clear as his own, she spoke. "Why can't you hear me?"

His heart jolted, and he froze. Ghosts didn't talk. They might moan or rattle chains, maybe shake a pipe or two. But they didn't speak. Not like this.

The words escaped him before he could think. "What… what the *hell*?"

And her face lit up, startled by his reaction, just as he was startled by hers. "Wait… you *can* hear me?"

They stared at each other in silence, both waiting for the other to say something. He'd never been in a situation like this before, and even something as simple as speaking the word *yes* seemed like an impossible leap.

He stumbled over his thoughts, working to piece together something to say. The *what* and the *how* of it all were top of mind, but he had no expectation she would have those answers. Finally, he decided on, "Who are you?"

Her excitement bubbled to the surface, like she didn't know where to start either. "Oh my god, thank you!" she said, reaching out instinctively—her hand passed through his arm as though he wasn't even there.

He jerked back, forgetting for a moment that her touch was nothing more than a chill passing through him. A sad flicker of realization crossed her face, and she let her hand drop. He felt the raw pain in her expression, her unmistakable yearning for connection. He'd seen a lot of ghosts over the years, but something was different. Somewhere deep below the unease, he was feeling something he'd never felt before—sympathy.

"What are you doing here?" he asked.

"I'm not really sure," she answered, glancing around the truck. "Where is here, exactly?"

Confused, Mac squinted. "You mean, like… this liquor store? The town? Earth?"

The look on her face told him a lot. She tilted her head and shot him a disbelieving look. Like it was the dumbest question she'd ever heard.

"Hey!" she said suddenly, startling him. "How are you able to see me? You seem like the only one. I've been all over town, and no one even looked at me."

Mac hesitated. He didn't enjoy talking about his so-called gift. Most folks just assumed he was a bit crazy, until they needed him, anyway. Finally, he sighed. "That's a long story," he said. "I'm Mitchel, but everyone calls me Mac. Do you… do you remember who you are?"

Her face went still as she searched deep into her memories. "Lyndsay!" she blurted out, her expression lighting up with a glint of recognition. But her brows furrowed almost immediately, like the name was just the edge of something much larger.

"Okay," he said. "That's a start. It is nice to meet you, Lyndsay. Do you remember anything else? Anything about… what happened to you?"

He watched as she struggled to dig through her fragmented memory. There were moments he thought she might be onto something, but then nothing would emerge. It was painful to watch and after a long few minutes, he tried to let her off the hook.

"It's okay if you don't—"

"I remember the room," she interrupted. Her voice was distant, like she was speaking through a fog. "It was dark… most of the time."

Her gaze drifted as she spoke, and her words came slowly and in broken fragments. "I remember walking home… and someone talking to me." She hesitated, closing her eyes tight like she was squeezing the image into existence. "I don't…" She sighed. "It was very dark."

A shiver ran through him as she continued. She was mostly talking to herself, like he wasn't there.

"He took me… but he didn't really want me. He wanted me to be someone else."

Her hand twitched as it brushed a phantom strand of hair in front of her face. "My hair… he dragged me." She paused and looked up at Mac as a realization flooded in. "He wanted to kill me," she whispered. "I think he did kill me."

The shiver turned to a chill, and settled deep in his bones. He kept quiet and let her sift through the broken pieces, wondering if this was what it felt like for every spirit he'd dealt with. Even thinking of poor Cooper as he emerged from humanity, struggling to understand what was happening to him.

"Something else happened," she continued. "Something pulled me away, and then I landed here, in your truck, and you couldn't hear me. I felt like you were supposed to hear me, but… and then I was so angry."

The truck was silent as those last words hung between them. He waited, entirely unsure of what to say. As she sat there, staring into him, her eyes pleading for understanding, he knew he had to say something.

"I'm sorry I couldn't hear you before," he said softly. "I'm not sure we're meant to. Something about you is different… I don't know why."

"So what do I do now?" she asked. "Is this… just who I am now?"

"No," he said, trying to keep his voice steady. "You need to find a way to move on. You're in the veil, so to speak—a plane between our world and the next. Something's tethering you here. If you figure out what that is, you might break the tether."

Mac already knew the answer—she was murdered. It was the most common reason spirits couldn't move on. But why wasn't she bound to her killer or a specific place? That part, he didn't understand.

"Will you help me?" she asked, her voice quiet, almost childlike. "You seem to know a lot about this stuff. I don't think I want to be like this."

Part of him wanted to say yes. Maybe because she could speak, or maybe because something about her felt different—less a nuisance, more human. But Mac didn't investigate kidnappings. He didn't hunt murderers. And he definitely didn't help spirits. He helped people get rid of spirits.

Mac glanced at the brown paper bag in his hand. "I'm very sorry… for everything you've been through," he muttered. "If you find out what happened to you, maybe that'll let you go. But I don't know how to help you."

When he looked back up, expecting to see Lyndsay still pleading with him, the seat was empty.

The guilt hit him first—followed by relief. He hated that part of himself. Setting the bottle down on the seat beside him, he started the truck and drove home, ready to numb his gift once more.

CHAPTER 5
THE MISSING

Mac stirred as the morning light peeked in through the drapes, lighting up tiny dust particles in the air. He groaned as he stretched out across the couch to relieve his aching back.

He swung his legs out and stepped down on the floor, tipping his glass from the night before, spilling the last remnants of whiskey onto the already stained rug. The pounding in his head and the surrounding mess were familiar reminders that he'd passed out. A common occurrence for Mac, and always a painful one.

He looked up and let out a long, exaggerated yawn. The clock on the wall read 8:52. Too early for more whiskey, but late enough to realize how behind he was on everything else. He rubbed his eyes free of the leftover sleep as he shuffled into the kitchen, the events of the night before still playing through his mind as he started a pot of coffee.

Even though he didn't want to get involved, thoughts nagged at him—the hollow plea of Lyndsay's voice, the desperation to understand what was happening, and her desire to move on. But even if he wanted to help, he had no idea where to start.

As he poured his first cup of coffee, he couldn't shake the creeping curiosity about the girl in his truck. Her death sounded like more than just a murder, like she'd been kidnapped and held for a bit before meeting her end. If a lifetime of movies and detective novels told him anything, it was that when there was one case, there were probably more.

He took a sip of his coffee and sat at the kitchen table, pulling the laptop toward him. The screen shone back at him, still and waiting while he worked out the best way to start. He typed in the words **Missing Persons Reports** into the search engine and tried sifting through tens of thousands of results from all over the country.

He needed to narrow the search. **Missing Persons Reports in Colorado.** After some digging, he discovered the Colorado Bureau of Investigation's page dedicated to cold cases—a carousel of old, unsolved missing mysteries dating back decades. The sheer number of them, even just in the state, overwhelmed and disturbed him to his core. So many unsolved cases, so many families left without closure or justice.

Mac's own past gave him an understanding of their pain. At least he knew how his wife had died, even if he still didn't fully understand why.

As the faces scrolled by on his screen, one caught his eye. He clicked on the link. The woman, Bonny Herveux, bore a striking resemblance to Lyndsay, but any connection seemed unlikely. Bonny had been in her thirties when she went missing nearly twenty years ago in Denver—far from the wheat and cornfields of Mac's small town.

He found the filter on the page that allowed him to drill down even further to a more reasonable time frame and locale and found several in nearby counties. Like Bonny, many of them looked strangely similar to Lyndsay. But no Lyndsay.

Mac sighed. He didn't have the skills or resources to dig through these cases alone—he needed help. He knew who to call, but he hesitated, knowing exactly how Jason would react to an early-morning call from "kooky" Mac. Groaning, he braced himself as he dialed the number.

"Mac, it's a bit early for you," Jason answered, sounding somewhat annoyed, maybe a little amused.

"I know," Mac said. "This is going to sound like a weird question, but humor me for a sec. Have you gotten any new missing persons cases lately? Anything that stands out?"

There was a pause—just long enough to make Mac brace for what Jason might say. "Some new gig of yours?"

His tone was wary, as usual, but Mac sensed a hint of curiosity as well. He exhaled, choosing his words carefully. "Not exactly. Someone came to me last night, concerned. Thought I'd check, see if there was anything to it."

A sigh crackled over the line. "I didn't tell you any of this," Jason demanded. "There've been a few, yes. Some of them… didn't make it back alive. I got the FBI crawlin' all over the county—it's big, Mac. Like serial big."

Mac leaned back. If this tied back to Lyndsay, it was bigger than just one ghost pestering him for help.

"What do you know, Mac?"

Mac replied quickly, "Nothing. Just someone asking about a relative they haven't seen." His gift had taught him to lie well enough to keep ghosts and other things under wraps. "I'm sure it's nothing, but if anything changes, I'll let you know."

"Uh-huh." Jason didn't sound entirely convinced, but he didn't push further.

Mac hung up, glancing back at the clock. 10:15 a.m. He cursed under his breath. He was late for his appointment. No time for a shower; he grabbed a can of Febreze from the coffee table and gave his clothes a generous spritz of the floral spray. Snatching his keys and a hat from the foyer, he headed for the truck.

Time and weather had not been kind to Mr. Pfeiffer's old house. Mac parked outside and approached the door, catching the man peering out the window like a hopeful child, watching for the ice cream truck to turn down the street.

Before Mac could ring the bell, the door flew open, and he jolted—just a little—stepping back on instinct.

"Mr. Pfeiffer?"

The man opened the door wider and quickly ushered him in. The smell hit him immediately—a strange concoction of tallow, sage, sandalwood, and other herbs all punching at his nostrils. A classic DIY attempt.

"Thank you so much for coming," the man said, wringing Mac's hand. "It's been… unsettling, to say the least."

"Unsettling, how?"

"I hear all kinds of stuff… Like banging and scratching. Sometimes…" He trailed off, lowering his voice to a whisper. "It feels like someone's watching me."

Mac nodded assuredly and followed him through a narrow hallway. He'd done this enough to know the signs of a seriously anxious mind.

He set his bag of tools down as they reached the living room. "Tell me about the noises. When do you usually hear 'em?"

"Nighttime, mostly."

"And you said it's been going on for about a month?"

Mr. Pfeiffer nodded.

"How long have you lived here?"

"Goin' on six months," the man said. "It's coming from the walls, the attic, the pipes… but I know it's not the plumbing." His voice was firm, as if daring him to disagree, but Mac simply nodded again.

It was his first fall in the house and the first time he'd heard how an old place complains when the seasons shift. He knew precisely where this was going to go.

So he pressed his ear against a nearby wall, making sure to let the client watch him closely, hoping his diligence would calm him down. The pipes creaked a bit as the heating kicked in—a familiar sound in older homes.

"It gets way louder than that," the man insisted.

Mac crouched near the baseboard and brushed his fingers along a small pile of sawdust-like debris. Termites, probably—not spirits.

He didn't say that part out loud.

"Mind taking me to the basement?" he asked.

Mr. Pfeiffer nodded and led the way down.

The basement was worse. Cold air, awful lighting, and enough clutter to make it an appealing space for every mouse in the neighborhood. There was a cracked pipe in the corner, insulation sagging from the ceiling, and several cardboard boxes with holes gnawed through them.

He cleared his throat. "Well, I see a couple of things down here that could—"

"The toilet flushes on its own," Pfeiffer blurted. "I'll just be sitting in my living room… no one else in the house and—*whoosh*, off it goes."

Mac had been here before. Clients were often so convinced of their hauntings they'd grow angry if he suggested otherwise. A toilet flushing on its own might seem eerie, but he knew there were ordinary explanations for that.

Resigning himself to the ritual, Mac pulled out a small bundle of herbs and, with a few practiced motions, lit it and murmured calming words. He watched as Mr. Pfeiffer visibly relaxed, and after a few minutes, he clapped his hands together, signaling that the "cleansing" was complete.

"There we go," he said. "Give it a few days… See if it feels better. As for the toilet, it's probably a leaky valve. Contrary to what the movies say, ghosts don't usually flush toilets."

Mac took a piece of paper from his jacket and jotted down the phone number for a local animal shelter, something he memorized specifically for cases like these. "One of the best things you can do to keep disturbances away is to get yourself a cat. Spirits hate cats," he said. It wasn't true, but the cat would help with the pests—and maybe give the lonely man a little company.

Outside, Mr. Pfeiffer seemed more at ease as he handed Mac a check. "Thank you," he said, turning back inside.

Mac packed up his gear, hiding a small smirk. Sometimes the biggest hauntings were in people's minds. Even if this wasn't the "real deal," it kept his mind off Lyndsay and serial killers—and helped him pay a bill or two.

Mac's phone buzzed in his jacket pocket, and as he climbed into the truck, he read the caller ID. It was his mother-in-law. She rarely called him—usually only on his wife's birthday or the anniversary of the accident. This day was neither, which made it worrisome.

"Hello?"

CHAPTER 6
THE CALL

Mac sat in his truck, quietly listening as Maureen's voice trembled on the other end. She was doing her best to keep it together, but he felt the concern in every word spoken.

"It's probably nothing," she said. "But she hasn't been answering her phone. It's just… well, you know how she is." She continued, "It isn't like her, Mac."

Mac leaned back, glancing at Mr. Pfeiffer's house. Joanne was independent, maybe even flighty, but it did seem unusual. She wasn't always great about keeping in touch with friends—or anyone, really—but she never missed a call from her mom.

"She hasn't posted anything on social media?" he asked, already knowing the answer.

"Nothing," she whispered. "I called some of her friends, and no one's seen her since she left work on Friday."

The behavior was out of the ordinary, but he didn't want to add to Maureen's stress. For a moment, he thought about Lyndsay and what Jason had told him earlier, but he shook it off. That was not a thought he would allow to fester in his mind.

"It's probably nothin', like you said."

"Maybe." There was a pause, then she added, "You know Joanne. She's not like Josie…"

Mac tried to focus, but as soon as he heard his wife's name, her words blurred into the background. Josie and her sister were very different. Where Josie was career-driven and book smart, Joanne was carefree and street smart, but for all their differences, they were two sides of the same coin.

"Mac…" he heard her say, but nothing before it. "Are you still there?"

"I'll ask around," he responded, shaking off the memories and regaining focus. "Tell her to call you when I find her."

After the call ended, Mac sat in front of Pfeiffer's house, thinking, worrying. He kept telling himself it was nothing, but something deep in his gut said otherwise. She was younger, free-spirited, independent—but she wasn't one to just vanish.

The more he thought about it, the more he drew connections to his wayward ghost. There were similarities—the age, the dark hair, the slender build—it'd be hard to tell them apart in a dimly lit room.

Mac tried to reassure himself again that it was all likely a misunderstanding. She could've lost her phone, or maybe she was seeing someone new. Whatever the reason, he had to look into it. After Josie's death, her parents moved up to Golden for a change of scenery. They were too far removed from the area to search themselves, and it wouldn't be much to check all her usual haunts.

Mac straightened in his seat and started the truck. Better get started.

Mac spent most of the day slowly driving through town, stopping outside places he knew Joanne frequented: the coffee shop where she sometimes picked up a morning cup, the small grocery where she was on a first-name basis with the cashiers, even the park where she'd meet friends when the weather was just right. With each stop, his concern edged a little higher, the familiar faces around town shrugging with the same uncertainty.

A few people remembered seeing her or chatting with her the week before, but no one knew where she was. Each conversation ended the same way: a polite apology and a promise to let him know if they heard anything.

He kept debating whether to tell Maureen to call the police. Every time the thought surfaced, he shoved it back down, unwilling to accept that it had come to that. The thought of Joanne's face becoming one of the pictures scrolling across the CBI website filled him with a hollow dread. He couldn't let her parents lose another child.

When he arrived at the bar where she worked, the sun was dipping below the horizon. The wooden sign above the door read FRONT 9/BACK 40 and creaked as the evening breeze kicked up. It was early, only about an hour since they'd opened, but it was just coming to life as customers filled in for a cold drink and a break from the day's work.

Mac hesitated at the door, staring at the weathered facade. He told himself it was just another stop, but deep down, he knew it was more than that. Joanne had loved this place, and she'd worked here for years. He'd found his own refuge here after Josie's death, and it was where he'd learned how to drink himself into numbness. It was a hard habit to break, even if, technically, he was still banned.

He pushed open the door, and the scent hit him first—stale beer and fried foods, an all-too-familiar comfort. He stepped inside to the steady hum of small talk, clinking bottles, and a rough-around-the-edges sort of charm that made it a favorite for the local farmers as well as the golfers after building up a thirst on the local course. Mac looked around the room, seeing many of the usual faces, hoping he'd see Joanne behind the bar, pouring a drink for an old farmer with a quiet smile. But she wasn't there.

"I still won't serve you, Mac," a voice boomed from the back of the bar.

Mac looked over to see Caleb, the bar's owner, watching him with a knowing smirk as he leaned against one of the pool tables. Setting his cue in its rack, Caleb met Mac halfway across the room, crossing his arms.

"Not here for drinks, Caleb," Mac replied. "I'm looking for Joanne."

"You and me both." Caleb's expression darkened. "She hasn't been to work in a couple days. Her mom's called like fifty times, but I haven't got anything new to tell her."

Mac sighed as a ripple of unease crept in that he couldn't shake. "She's mentioned nothing?" he asked. "No plans to get out of town or take a break?"

Caleb glanced around the bar like he might spot her mixing in with the crowd and then shook his head. "Last I saw her, she was laughing with some regulars, same as always. If she was planning something, she didn't tell me."

It was a moment when he was supposed to sigh in relief and feel stupid for worrying. The part where Joanne popped up with a story about her weekend road trip or lost phone. None of that was happening, not this time. Whatever reassurance he'd been holding on to was gone. Something was definitely wrong. "Let me know if you hear from her, please."

Caleb nodded. "You do the same."

CHAPTER 7

BAD NEWS

Mac stared out the window of his truck, watching people funnel in and out of the bar as he worked through anywhere else he could look. He wrestled with whether it was time to get the police involved. He probably should've a long time ago, but he was so damned sure he would find her. It didn't matter anymore; the universe decided for him, and his phone rang. The caller ID read "Private Number," which meant it was Jason calling from the station.

He closed his eyes, bracing himself for bad news as Jason's voice flowed through the speaker, calm but with a hint of tension.

"Mac. Joanne's parents called… they filed a missing persons report. That why you called before?"

His heart sank—he had failed. The entire day was spent thinking he would fix it before it got that far, but he should have known better. He wasn't a cop. He was just a guy who talked to ghosts, one who could barely crawl his way out of a bottle.

"Yeah," he said, fighting to force the word out. "Her mother called me earlier… said she was worried."

Mac had gotten used to slightly bending the truth about his gifts and didn't see how muddying the waters with Jason right at that moment was going to help Joanne.

"You should've told me earlier," Jason said. "If I'd known it was about Jo—"

"I know, Jason," Mac interrupted. "I honestly thought I'd find her, and it sounded like you had your hands full."

"Look, Mac, I promise, if this is related in any way… hell, Mac, I don't even want to think about it."

There was a brief pause while neither of them was sure what to say before Jason continued. "These cases are top priority… Everyone, the whole station, county, FBI. We're doing everything we can."

Mac closed his eyes as he listened to Jason's assurances. He knew they were doing their best, but it didn't ease the dread creeping up inside him. It was settling in that Joanne could well be the newest of the cases Jason had hinted at earlier.

"Jason," he started but hesitated as he weighed his words. "Any of 'em named Lyndsay?"

"Lyndsay?" he asked. "Not that I've seen… But these cases are coming up from all over the county. I can check, but why do you ask?"

Mac couldn't find a way to justify the question without revealing too much about her—the kinds of details that spawn eye rolls and a sudden inability to be taken seriously. The silence lingered a little too long, only broken when Jason sighed.

"Mac, is this a ghost thing?"

Mac's hand squeezed a little tighter around the phone as he searched his brain for the right words. Jason's question hung in the air—direct, cautious, and tipped with an uncomfortable familiarity.

"Maybe," Mac admitted. He hated talking about it, even with Jason, who had been one of the few people who even pretended to take him seriously. He had to, though—the stakes were too real to play it coy. If his ability could help find Joanne, he couldn't afford to hold back.

Jason slowly let out a breath. "All right. So… you think this Lyndsay might be connected to Joanne somehow?"

"I've been… seeing someone," he responded carefully, choosing every word cautiously. "A girl. She said her name was Lyndsay and… I think she's one of 'em."

"Mac," Jason said sharply, though Mac could tell he was refraining from pushing too hard. "You know I don't get all this ghost stuff, but if you're onto something… If this girl really is one of the victims… What can you tell me?"

"Not much, yet," he said, reflecting, thinking about his last encounter with her. "She doesn't seem to remember anything coherent. But if there's even the slightest chance I can help her remember, get a lead on Joanne…" He let the sentence hang, his resolve hardening. "I'll do whatever it takes."

"Wild idea," Jason interjected quickly. "Maybe if you come to the station… we could go over some files together. I… I don't know the rules here, but can she, like, I dunno… look over your shoulder and see if it sparks anything?"

A silence stretched between them as Mac chewed on the idea, turning it over in his mind.

"Bring her down there?" he repeated back to Jason. It seemed smart, but he didn't like the idea of showcasing his gift to a room full of strangers. "Where the whole station can witness the freak show talking to his pet ghost?"

But Jason leaned into it. "Look," he said, "we don't have a lot to go on here. We'll keep it discreet. Either way, if you learn anything… anything solid, let me know right away."

"I will," Mac replied as he hung up the phone, failing to say goodbye.

He took a deep breath as his mind churned through what he needed to do. How was he going to help her remember? Joanne's life might depend on him figuring out how to therapize a ghost into reliving her worst memories. But for now, the first problem: He had just sent her away, with no clue how to get her back.

He closed his eyes and cleared his mind of every distraction, focusing on Lyndsay. "Where are you?"

Whatever the next step was, it wasn't going to happen in front of that bar. He put the truck into drive and made a U-turn onto the street to head back home.

As he drove down the dark dirt road leading home, Mac went through all the ways he'd heard of people summoning spirits. Most of them were about as real as the Ouija boards, but every now and then, someone tried a joke ritual and ended up summoning something they didn't mean to.

Personal items usually worked—a piece of jewelry, an old picture, or a diary—something the spirit had a deep attachment to in life. But Mac knew almost nothing about this ghost other than her name. There was no way he'd be able to dig up any of that stuff.

He'd heard about a ritual where you lit a candle in a dark room and said the ghost's name in a mirror, inviting it to appear, but that all sounded a little too Bloody Mary to be real. Then he remembered a story someone told him about deals made at crossroads. People thought they were talking to demons, but in reality, crossroads were often crawling with ghosts from all the accidents that had happened there over the years.

This gave him an idea.

Mac turned the car around and headed back to the place where Lyndsay had first appeared to him. Ghosts often frequented areas where they'd experienced a strong emotional event. Remembering the night she crashed into his truck—it seemed pretty emotional to him.

He pulled up, trying to gauge the exact spot as best he could, and parked. He sat for a few moments, looking around, hoping she didn't crash into him again like she had the first time. His pulse quickened in a mix of anticipation and frustration. This had to work.

Suddenly, his truck shut off, and the radio turned on, once again filling the cab with the sounds of Toto's "Africa." He tried in vain to restart the truck, but it wouldn't turn over.

"I've always loved this song," a voice pierced through the vocals.

Mac turned to find Lyndsay sitting in her spot, staring at him just as she had that first night. It had worked, and his frustration fell away to nervous excitement.

"Although I think I actually prefer Weezer's version," she continued.

"You're here?" he responded, ignoring her thoughts on the song.

"I felt you asking me to be," she said. "But why?"

He swallowed, steadying himself. Despite his relief at seeing her again, a pang of guilt twisted in his chest. He was asking for her help without really knowing what she'd gone through—not to mention the last time they'd met, she asked him for help, and he refused. He had no right to make this her problem.

"Lyndsay," he started, choosing his words carefully, "I think we can help each other… Someone else is missing. Someone close to me."

She raised an eyebrow, something Mac found quite disconcerting, and her gaze shifted back to him. "And you think I can help you find them?"

"I don't know," he admitted. "But I think… whoever took you might've taken her, too."

Her playful expression faded, and her eyes clouded as she looked away. "I don't remember much. It's all scattered. Like… pieces of a dream I can't quite put together."

He leaned toward her so she could see his face. "Anything you remember. Anything at all… a place, a sound… even just a feeling."

Her eyes closed. He watched her process and draw in a breath she no longer needed. "It's a lot of darkness, mostly. And… feeling like I might never see my family again."

"Family?" he repeated. "Maybe we can start there. Do you remember anything from before you were taken? Do you know who you are?"

She opened her eyes again, staring off into the distance like she was searching for something. "Who I am…" she echoed. "There are flashes… kinda like photos in my mind. Faces, laughter, an old porch swing… But when I try to focus, it all slips away."

He waited and observed. Seeing the struggle within her, he didn't want to push and have her disappear again.

"I think, maybe I had a sister? We used to go hiking together… or maybe it was camping."

Her frustration mounted, and it was affecting her physically. The more she dug, the more erratic the outline of her form flickered.

"I remember the smell of pine, and that we'd laugh so much. I don't remember what was funny, just… that feeling."

Mac nodded, encouraging her to keep going. "And before—right before you were taken. Is there anything from that time?"

"I feel cold." Her eyes tightened, and she hugged her arms around herself as if warding off a chill. "Not freezing, just chilly. I think I was walking somewhere… maybe from the grocery store?" she said, her voice uncertain.

Mac watched as she dug through her fractured memories, and he began to fill with rage on her behalf—thinking about her and Joanne, minding their business and getting snatched by some crazed lunatic.

"We *are* going to figure this out." His voice steadied—a quiet promise.

"I'm sorry. That's all I can remember."

"It's a lot more than the other night, and it's a start."

Mac nodded, his mind churning with her fragmented memories—the chill, the smell of pine, laughter with her sister, and that dark, sinking feeling of permanent loss. He squeezed the steering wheel as each memory she shared sharpened his focus. He should have listened to her that first night. If he had, maybe Joanne wouldn't be missing.

"If there's anything else you remember, no matter how small… even just a feeling, I want you to come to me. We'll work with whatever you can recall."

"I appreciate that, Mac." She studied him, eyes searching. "I know you want to help your friend, but thank you for trying to help me, too. I don't think most people would go through the trouble."

"People shouldn't have to go through this alone," he said. "Not in life, and not after."

They sat in silence for a few moments, and as he continued watching her, he recognized something he'd never seen in a spirit before. She wasn't just some ghost trying to brute-force her way toward unfinished business. He saw her as the person she used to be. Still was, in the ways that counted. She was lost, confused, and fractured, but not gone.

She may not be alive any longer, but she was no less human for it.

CHAPTER 8
THE STATION

The station buzzed with activity. Usually, the lot hosted only a handful of police cars and the occasional local filing a report or registering a pet. Today was different. Cars filled almost every space, some marked with county or state insignias, others clearly federal, even without markings. The building itself seemed tense.

Mac looked over to Lyndsay, still staring out the window at all the activity.

"Ready?" he asked himself as much as her.

She nodded, barely looking his way. She seemed just as nervous about entering that place as he was.

He took a deep breath, climbed out, and walked toward the entrance. He could feel his heart pounding, not just in his chest but in his head as well.

Inside, the station looked like the war room of some TV show where the CIA and Navy SEALs were planning an attack or rescue. Officers and plainclothes agents huddled around desks, papers and files spread across every available surface. In one of the glass conference rooms, giant whiteboards and corkboards displayed pictures of people and places—some of which Mac recognized from around town. There was tension in every inch of the room.

Jason spotted him from across the lobby, giving a quick nod before breaking away from a group to meet him. It was odd seeing Jason in a jacket and tie. It had only been a few months since he was stuck wearing the same black on black officer's uniform as every other beat cop.

"Mac," he said. His tone was serious, though laced with an underlying sympathy Mac had grown to despise since his wife's death.

"Jason… Or is it Detective Miller now?" Mac replied, waving at his clothes.

"Only when my boss is around."

"Seems like you're preparing for war in here."

"Feels like it," Jason muttered, gesturing for Mac to follow him. As they walked toward Jason's desk, he lowered his voice. "Still no word on Joanne, but I have something I want you to look at."

Mac glanced at Lyndsay, who had followed him in and was watching everything with a silent, curious intensity.

Jason pulled up a file on his computer and opened an image. "She went missing about a month ago," he said, meeting Mac's eyes. "Her name is Lyndsay Carrington."

He took a deep breath, and Mac could tell he was struggling to even ask the next question. "Is this who you've been seeing?"

Mac instantly recognized her, but before he could react, Lyndsay pushed her way past him. "Hey!" she exclaimed. Her eyes widened as they locked onto the image, and something in her face lit up— just for a second.

She inhaled sharply, and Mac watched her face shift, an unsettled sorrow taking over her features as memories pushed their way to the surface.

"That's… that's me," she whispered, her voice trembling.

Mac watched as the confusion and grief collided in her eyes. She glanced away as if trying to piece together fragments she'd long forgotten.

"I remember my parents… and my brother. He used to tease me. And my mom, she always hated my taste in music…"

Mac kept quiet and allowed her to keep digging through memory after memory, and he noticed a slight shift in the room. A coldness crept in, and it seemed he wasn't the only one feeling it.

Jason shifted in his seat, clearly uncomfortable, as he quietly watched Mac watching Lyndsay. He cleared his throat, breaking the silence, but his voice had a softer, almost fragile edge to it.

"We've had too many cases like this," he said, glancing at the file. "I keep thinking… these families. They're all waiting, hoping for something they may never get. It's just so… unfair."

Mac glanced down. Jason's hands were curling into fists, his knuckles whitening. The lines around his mouth deepened, and his voice trembled with a sadness that felt out of place for Jason. He seemed to be escalating—maybe even spiraling a little.

Jason turned back to the screen. His shoulders sagged, and his voice cracked, the sorrow deepening as he spoke. "Sometimes… I wonder if we'll ever bring any of them home." He hesitated, and Mac noticed his eyes welling up like the dam holding back the tears was about to burst. "How do you… keep going, you know?"

Mac watched him, thrown by the abrupt burst of raw emotion in his voice. He wasn't a cold man, not by any stretch, but this… it wasn't like him. He was usually the one holding everything together, comforting others through their pain or talking them down from their anger. The steady officer Mac knew seemed to be unraveling.

"Hey… Jason. You okay?" Mac asked, keeping his voice steady.

Jason blinked, the fog of emotion lifting. He nodded slowly, a subtle shake of his head clearing away the invisible weight. "Yeah." His voice steadied. "Sorry, I… don't know what came over me. It's been a rough month."

He glanced over. But Lyndsay had vanished, leaving behind only the tension she'd built while regaining her memories. Mac desperately wanted to know what she had just learned about her past.

"So… this one is from the next town over, in Erie," Jason continued, having nearly composed himself. "Her family's still there—parents, a brother—"

"And a sister," Mac interrupted.

"No, it doesn't look like there's a sister."

"Odd," Mac replied, glancing out the window, trying to see if Lyndsay had gone back to his truck.

"Why is that odd? Did she say she had a sister?"

"No," Mac said, the word slipping out faster than he intended. He wasn't sure why he lied. He'd already admitted to conversing with a ghost. Jason couldn't possibly think he was any more bizarre than he already appeared.

Mac pulled out his cell phone and snapped a picture of the photo on the screen. "Hey, thank you for this, Jason. I won't forget it."

"Mac… Be careful. Whoever this is… He's not your ordinary kind of killer." He hesitated a moment, and his voice dropped. "It's evil, Mac. The purest I've seen. If you find anything… anything at all, you call me. Don't go chasing leads on your own."

Mac nodded and started for the door. "Yeah. I'll keep you in the loop."

As he spoke, he knew it wasn't the truth. He couldn't shake the sense that he and Lyndsay were the only ones who could unravel what had really happened.

He trusted Jason to follow the evidence he could see, the cold facts on the file in front of his face. But Mac knew that any evidence he might find with Lyndsay's help would come with a scrutiny he wouldn't be able to defend. "The ghost told me" simply wouldn't cut it.

He looked out at the truck across the lot, but Lyndsay was nowhere to be seen. Disappearing on him was becoming a habit— and it wasn't making things any easier. He turned back to Jason one more time and thought about telling him he appreciated being taken seriously but decided it was a little too sentimental. So, he left, silent and alone in what came next.

Jason lingered a little longer than he'd meant to, watching Mac leave the station. He still felt the ache that crept into his chest a few moments earlier. So much had happened in the past few weeks, and the exhaustion was taking its toll. He didn't get too far into his thoughts before a voice snapped him out of it from behind.

"Who was that?"

He turned to find Special Agent Kane approaching him, taking a sip of his coffee.

"Just a consultant we work with now and then."

Kane raised an eyebrow and tilted his head to get a better look out the front window. "A consultant? Looked like you were discussing something personal."

Jason glanced around the bullpen, ensuring only the right people might be listening in before he lowered his voice. "He has a sort of… unique perspective on these cases."

"Define 'unique,'" Kane said before taking another casual sip of his coffee, his gaze now fixed on Jason.

The sigh that slipped out took even Jason by surprise. He weighed his options, knowing full well Kane wasn't the type to back down, and they'd known each other too long. If he tried to evade the question, Kane would never let it go. Still, the truth of Mac and the relationship he had with the station wasn't something he handed out lightly.

"Mac believes he's a medium," he admitted. He watched, waiting to see how the agent would react—a smirk or roll of the eyes, anything.

Instead, Kane's expression didn't really change—maybe a little thoughtful. "And you?"

Jason shifted. The conversation had taken a turn he wasn't prepared for. "What? What do you mean?"

"I mean," he said, taking a measured step closer, "do you think he's a medium?"

Jason's jaw clenched as his eyes darted briefly toward the floor. He hated this, and he couldn't help but wonder if this was how Mac felt whenever he had to talk about it.

Screw it.

"Honestly, Graham? Yeah, I do."

He waited for the myriad of follow-up questions, or for the agent to eventually burst out laughing, but he just nodded a little, not in disbelief but curiosity.

"Interesting."

"That's it?"

"I mean… sure. Not like I've never seen one before. It's the FBI, Jason."

Kane took another sip of his coffee, and the two said no more on the subject while they stood in silence, as if the conversation had been completely normal. Finally, the agent turned away.

"Let me know if anything he gives you pans out."

Jason watched as Kane disappeared through the crowd of officers and agents, an odd sense of relief washing over him. He couldn't believe he just admitted believing in ghosts to anyone, much less an FBI agent. Turned out, Mac wasn't the only one who needed someone to believe him.

CHAPTER 9

THE PULL

Mac sat in his truck, gripping the steering wheel and staring at the parking lot. Lyndsay was gone—again. He'd thought they'd started to make progress, that maybe she'd stick around this time, but now there was nothing. Just him and his thoughts, churning in an anxious loop.

He rubbed the back of his neck, trying to make sense of what to do next. He could try to find her family—her parents, her brother— but the thought of showing up unannounced made him hesitate. What would he even say? "Hi, I'm Mac, and I've been talking to your daughter's ghost?" Yeah, that would go over great. And he wasn't the police; he had no badge, no authority. Just a gut feeling that he needed answers—and not much of a plan for how to get them.

The truck rumbled to life as he turned the key, deciding to drive into town. Maybe he'd see her. Maybe she was drawn to certain places, like before. There was no telling what she did, or if she even did anything at all, when she wasn't with him. He wasn't ready to stop but also didn't know what to do next.

He drove all across town looking for her, but there was no sign. He was tired and considered heading home. *Just one more pass down Main Street*, he thought.

The streetlights sparked to life as he drove past the quiet storefronts. He kept his eyes split between the sidewalks and alleyways, looking for any sign of his wayward ghost. As he passed the bar, his hands squeezed the wheel just a little tighter, and his foot instinctively hovered over the brake.

Without realizing it, he had pulled the truck over and was idling in front of the bar. The neon sign in the window flickered, each pulse tugging on him to go in. He hated it. It wasn't just a place where Joanne worked; it was where he'd spent too many nights learning to drown himself in a bottle.

He leaned forward and rested his head on the steering wheel. The craving was coming in hard.

It felt like ages since his last drink—keeping active had helped, but now it gnawed at him. With nothing left to keep himself busy, the craving took over. He could almost feel the burn of whiskey in his throat. He closed his eyes tight, trying to fight the urge.

"Mac."

His head shot up, and there she was. No warning. No apology. Just… there. She looked different—agitated, and her movements were jerky, like something was setting her on edge. He rolled down his window.

"Where did you go?" he asked.

She didn't answer. Her focus was locked on the bar, and she seemed confused, frustrated. "This place…" she said. "I think I've been here before."

Mac looked up at the door of the bar. "Here? Are you sure?"

"I… I don't know," she said, pressing her hands to her temples. "It feels… familiar, but wrong. Like there's something here I'm supposed to remember, but I can't. It's just… stuck."

He pulled himself out of the truck, the cool night air brushing against him as he walked to stand beside her. "Let's work it out. Did you work here? Meet someone here?"

She shook her head. "No. Maybe… there's something. I can feel it."

He didn't know if this was an actual lead or just another fragment of her scattered memories, like remembering a sister she didn't have, but the tension in her voice was undeniable. He briefly considered asking about the sister, but she was already agitated, and he didn't want her to disappear again.

"All right, if there's something here that needs remembering, we'll figure it out. Together."

Lyndsay nodded. She didn't say anything, but Mac could feel her unease. As much as he hated the pull this place had on him, there was no avoiding it. If there was anything to be found for either of them, they had to go in.

He pushed the door open and stepped inside, sniffing the air to take in that old familiar smell of bar funk. Most folks found that smell repulsive, but for Mac, it was an old comfort.

As soon as they walked in, Lyndsay's whole demeanor changed. The agitation fell away, replaced by wide-eyed wonder, like someone walking into their childhood bedroom.

"I know this place," she said with excitement as she flitted off toward the bar.

He watched her dart around from one spot to another, eagerly investigating every inch of the space. She ran her ghostly hands over the polished wood of the bar, then turned her attention to the pool tables, her face lighting up as if seeing an old friend.

"I've been here—more than once," she said.

She drifted toward the back, and her attention was drawn to a small stage where they hosted karaoke. As his eyes followed her around the room, he caught a glimpse of Caleb, who was wiping down the bar. Caleb spotted him, sighed, and set the towel down.

"I still haven't heard anything about Jo," he said.

"I know," Mac replied as he walked up to the bar. "I got another question for you."

He pulled out his phone and tapped the screen, bringing up the photo he'd taken of Lyndsay from Jason's computer. He held it out to Caleb, whose expression shifted from curiosity to something more serious.

"This girl," Mac said. "Lyndsay Carrington. Do you remember her ever coming in here?"

Caleb took the phone, squinting at the picture. He rubbed his chin, thinking. "Carrington… name isn't ringin' a bell. But…" He tilted his head, focusing on the image. "I might've seen her. She does look familiar."

Mac leaned forward, his pulse quickening. "Do you remember anything else? Like who she talked to? Did she come here with anyone?"

"Nah, man, I really couldn't say. We get so many people from that damned golf course coming in and out of here, they all kind of look the same to me." Caleb appeared disappointed that he couldn't be of more help. "You know, she kinda looks like Jo."

Mac pocketed the phone and turned to look for Lyndsay, who was now staring at some pictures on the wall, leaning in close as if trying to jog a memory hidden in the faces staring back at her.

He turned to thank Caleb for his help, but before he could get a word out, a loud, shrill voice broke through the background noise of the bar. A couple sitting nearby had escalated from quiet conversation to a full-blown argument in a matter of seconds.

The woman at the table slammed her glass hard enough to shatter it into a hundred tiny shards.

"You never listen to me!" she shouted, her voice cracking as tears streaked down her cheeks. "I keep telling you… but you never listen."

The man shot to his feet, his chair screeching across the floor as he shoved it back. "Oh, give me a break!" he yelled back. "You're making a scene for no reason!"

The noise of the bar suddenly dropped as everyone turned toward the commotion to get a glimpse of the fight. As the couple spiraled into a rage, a few patrons muttered uneasily, shifting in their seats, while others leaned in, enjoying the unfolding drama.

Mac looked over at Lyndsay, but she remained completely unfazed, still hyper-focused on the photos.

Caleb let out a tired sigh. "Excuse me a moment."

He hopped over the bar with surprising agility and hurried over to the couple. "Hey!" he barked. "This ain't the place for that. Take it outside."

The woman glared at Caleb, her eyes shimmering from the tears waiting their turn to shed. "We're leaving," she snapped, clutching her bag as she stood.

The man opened his mouth to argue, but Caleb saw it and stared him down. As they were leaving, their voices trailed off, their heated argument focused on themselves now becoming a condemnation of the bar and Caleb. Caleb shook his head as he returned to his post, muttering something about "free entertainment."

Mac turned his attention back to Lyndsay, who hadn't moved and was completely unbothered by the commotion. She was leaning in close, focusing intently on one photo specifically. Curious, Mac walked over, weaving through the tables until he was standing beside her.

"What are you looking at?" he asked, keeping his voice low to avoid startling her.

She didn't respond at first, her eyes remaining locked on the image in front of her. He leaned in, and the photo came into focus—a picture of a young woman on the bar's small stage, microphone in hand. It was Lyndsay.

"That's me," she whispered.

Her fingers hovered over the photo, as though she wanted to touch it but couldn't bring herself to. "I used to sing here… I remember this."

He felt a chill run through him. This wasn't just a memory surfacing—it was a piece of who Lyndsay had been, something tangible and real.

"What else do you remember?"

"Not much," she said as she straightened herself. "Just that I enjoyed coming here." Her voice wavered, and the joy in her face gave way to a hint of sorrow.

"What is it?" he asked.

"I don't know… I can tell there's something there… just out of reach."

Mac noticed a small timestamp in the corner—September 9th. Just before she vanished. He'd probably driven past the bar that night. She might've still been inside.

"Shit," he muttered.

He looked around the bar, searching for something but not sure what it was. The place that was once his favorite escape now held secrets he wasn't expecting.

"What is it, Mac?"

"This picture… it was taken right before you… you know."

It hit him like a ton of bricks. The realization that both women had been at the bar just before going missing seemed like too big of a coincidence.

He looked around the bar. Faces blurred together. Everyone looked suspicious. Too much interest. Not enough. It didn't matter— his pulse was already spiking.

The killer could have been there. *He could be here right now.*

A bead of sweat formed over his brow. It was too dark in the bar to see everyone clearly, and the dim light casting shadows made everyone look sinister.

A man by the pool tables laughed too loudly, another at the bar glanced his way just a fraction of a second too long. He could feel himself spiraling, but he couldn't stop it.

It felt like someone was watching him, some unseen eye pressing down on him, making the hairs on his neck shoot straight up. He turned, checking the corners of the room, but there was nothing. Just some regulars enjoying their drinks, games, or conversations.

Paranoia, maybe. But the lack of drink, the stress, the impossible situation—none of it helped. Something was there, something dark, crawling along his skin.

He looked back at Lyndsay, who hadn't moved, still focused on the photo.

"I think we should go."

She turned to him, confused.

"But… I feel like I'm really close," she whispered.

He hesitated. The unease hadn't lifted, and he couldn't shake the feeling that someone was watching him. He looked around the room one last time, making mental notes of every face and detail he could before looking back to Lyndsay.

"We'll come back," he said. "But something's not right."

Lyndsay nodded reluctantly, and they retreated to the relative safety of the truck. As they drove away, Mac's eyes darted back and forth between the road and the rearview mirror, half expecting to see someone watching them leave.

Lyndsay's expression shifted, as if she could sense his unease and it was beginning to infect her as well. "What are we running from?"

Mac, realizing that nothing was following them, calmed, his breathing steadying as they got farther away from the bar. He kept asking himself the same question. *What the hell was that?*

"I don't know," he replied. "Something wasn't right."

Lyndsay clearly didn't understand. The look on her face told Mac she was concerned, and maybe she was right to be. Mac felt far out of his depth, and he knew it was starting to show.

"It's fine," he said. "I think I know where to get some help."

CHAPTER 10

HIPPIE-DIPPIE BULLSHIT

Mac pulled up to the curb and gathered his things in his jacket pocket before exiting the truck. When he reached the sidewalk, Lyndsay appeared beside him and followed him toward the shop. She tilted her head to read the bright, colorful hand-painted sign above the door, then chuckled.

"Hippie-Dippie Bullshit?"

"Yep. That would be John Doe," he said. "You'll understand when you meet him."

She looked over at him, and he swore he could see one of her ghostly eyebrows lift. It was the same astonished disbelief he'd felt when he first met John. "His name is actually John Doe?"

"That's what he says."

He stepped inside and held the door for Lyndsay, forgetting that she didn't need it as she floated through the wall. Once inside, she stopped in her tracks, fully entranced by the cluttered interior.

The air inside was thick with the mixed scents of candles and spices, and every inch of the place was crammed with something strange. She bounced from table to table, taking it all in—the crystals, candles, and books piled high on overburdened display cases. Above, dried bats and dream catchers swayed from the rafters.

"This place is wild," she said. "Weird. Kinda creepy."

Kind of creepy. That was his thought the first time he had set foot in the shop. Mac smiled and made his way to the back. As he passed a glass cabinet, something new caught his eye—a jar containing what appeared to be a fetus, suspended in a murky fluid. He grimaced.

"Yuck. Why?"

Before he could dwell too deeply on it, the sound of deliberate, heavy footfalls drew his attention. Mac straightened just as a tall figure emerged from a room in the back.

"Mitchel Anderson Crichton," the man said, emphasizing each word of Mac's name.

"John," he replied, wiping his hands on his jeans as he turned.

John stood in the doorway, his presence as deliberate as his steps. His dark, wavy hair hung just past his ears in an unkempt but effortless kind of way. He was lean—wiry, like someone always ready for action. He had sharp cheekbones and a strong jaw, shadowed with stubble, and dark, hollow eyes.

"What brings you to my shop, Mac? And who is your wispy friend?"

"This is Lyndsay. She's the one I told you about the other night."

Lyndsay turned, floating closer to John. "Wait... you can see me, too?"

As she got closer, John's cocky stoicism shifted, and his fists balled up. "Mac."

The way he said his name sounded like a warning, quiet but insistent. Mac put his hand up in front of Lyndsay, letting her know she should hang back.

"Look, I wouldn't be here if it wasn't important. You know that."

John went pale, and his entire demeanor changed in an instant. Mac had seen that look before, but he caught it too late. Before he could say anything, John reached out.

His fist clenched, as if gripping some invisible rope, and Lyndsay's form jolted midair. Mac had seen that move before—quick, brutal, and unnervingly precise. Whatever magic he had, it wasn't subtle. Her face hovered inches from his, and her form flickered in and out like TV static.

"John!" Mac shouted.

He stepped forward, trying to get between them.

"Who are you?" John demanded. He stared straight into Lyndsay's ghostly eyes. "You don't belong here."

Then, just as fast, something else rose to the surface.

The surrounding air charged with energy, and her shape sharpened, more solid than before. A low hiss spilled into the room as her presence pushed outward, like steam forcing its way through a cracked pipe. Her face contorted with rage, and just like that, the doe-eyed ghost was gone.

"You think you're stronger than me?" John laughed, yanking harder on her ethereal leash.

Her form strained against his pull, distorting at the edges. The space around her warped as a pressure built like a storm rolling through the shop.

John's lip curled up on one side—just a hint of a smirk. "Amateur."

With a sharp flick of his hand, her form collapsed in on itself, then disappeared completely. The room went quiet as the energy and tension dissipated.

"John!" Mac barked. "What the hell did you do?"

John lifted both hands and made a series of precise gestures. The air shimmered as several runes painted on the walls blazed to life in gold and crimson hues. They pulsed, filling the shop with a steady, rhythmic thrum.

"You brought a loose, untethered spirit into my shop?"

John turned to face Mac, nearly as close to him as he had been to Lyndsay. "Why would you do something like that, Mac?"

"Did you…?"

Mac paused, not even sure how to finish the question.

John seemed to sense the worry Mac was holding on to and softened his posture. "She's fine. She'll find her way back in a few hours."

Mac took a deep breath, trying to force his temper under control. John was powerful in ways even Mac didn't fully understand, so he always tried to tread carefully, no matter how much John pissed him off.

"She's not a threat, John. She was murdered. I came here because we need your help."

John crossed his arms and squinted at Mac. "You don't know anything about that thing you just brought in here. And besides, helping them is your thing. They don't want my kind of help."

Mac stepped closer and lowered his voice. "I wouldn't have come to you if I had any other choice. You owe me."

John stared at him, and Mac could tell he wanted to rip his head off, but he didn't argue. Instead, he turned away, his voice trailing over his shoulder. "You'd better have a damn good reason for this… Mitchel."

John liked to use Mac's formal name like a weapon. He knew it grated on him, and when he was particularly annoyed, he'd sting him with it. As he disappeared into the back room, the runes dimmed slowly, leaving the shop in uneasy silence. Mac exhaled and ran a hand through his hair.

"Lyndsay… wherever you are. Stay calm. I'll get you back."

He hesitated a moment before following John into the back room, which was just as cluttered as the front room, though far less decorative. It was a practical workshop lined with shelves holding jars, vials, and instruments Mac couldn't even begin to name. A massive wooden table, scarred and stained from years of use, sat in the middle of the room.

John stood at the far end from the door with his back to Mac, arranging small stones in some weirdly precise pattern. He didn't look up when Mac entered, which Mac assumed was another one of his power plays.

"You got five minutes, Mitchel," he said. "Make them count."

Mac clenched his fists, failing to hold his frustration.

"I don't have time for your theatrics, John. Joanne is missing, and there's a serial killer on the loose. And Lyndsay… was the only lead I had before you sent her to… wherever."

Mac paused, huffing but trying to mask his anger. "I. Need. Your. Help."

John stopped what he was doing and rested his hands on the table. He turned, finally facing Mac. "Okay, Mac. Tell me everything."

Mac sucked in a long breath and launched into the story—Joanne, the unsettling scene at the bar, the connection to Lyndsay, her memory issues, the serial killer—all of it. As he spoke, John listened intently.

When Mac finished, the silence between them stretched. After a minute or so, John leaned against the table and crossed his arms.

"And you've decided that stirring up a half-formed ghost's memories is the best way forward?" His tone was skeptical, but there was no malice in it—just the quiet weight of someone who'd seen too much.

"Exactly..." Mac responded before catching John's phrasing. "What do you mean, half-formed?"

"That's why she has that wispy personality, and why you can hear her. She's not like regular ghosts—she's different. She's something else, something in between... or beyond."

"I don't care about different. Her memories are the key to finding out what happened to Joanne, *before* she becomes like Lyndsay."

John studied him, then shook his head. "Desperation makes fools of us all," he said, pushing off from the table and moving to one of the shelves. He pulled down a battered notebook. As he flipped through its pages, he continued, "You should care, Mac. With the dead, different is never a good thing."

"Good thing I don't have much left to lose," Mac muttered, though his heart sank at the warning. "You made sure of that."

John paused and sighed as he closed the notebook and handed it to Mac.

"This exercise might help. It's a way to anchor her, stabilize her form. If it works, it'll allow her to remember parts of her life she's been suppressing." He locked eyes with Mac. "It's risky. Pull too hard and you might wake something you can't put back to sleep."

Mac snatched the notebook from John's hand. "I don't have a choice."

John's expression darkened, the faintest hint of regret flashing across his face. "You always have a choice, Mac. But if you're set on this…" He let the thought hang, then turned away.

"For what it's worth, I'm still sorry," he said in a quieter tone.

Mac froze, his breath catching. He didn't need to ask what John meant—he already knew. Old wounds pressed on him, but he pushed it aside. This wasn't the time.

"Your sorries change nothing," Mac said gruffly, tucking the notebook under his arm. He turned around and strode out of the store, determined that this was the answer.

He stepped into his truck and looked over at the empty seat next to him. "Hang tight, Lyndsay," he said as he started the engine. "We're not done yet."

CHAPTER 11

VODKA AND GHOSTS

Mac returned home, uncertain how or when Lyndsay might show up again. A part of him worried about what would happen if she tried to come to the house—and how it reacted to ghosts encroaching on its space—but the day had been long, and he needed sleep.

Mac set the notebook down on the kitchen table beside his open laptop and stood there a moment, staring at it. The day's events looped through his mind—so much gathered, but nothing fit together yet. Maybe the notebook was the key to unlocking Lyndsay's memories. Maybe not. Either way, John's warning wouldn't stop echoing.

"He's always so damned cryptic," he muttered.

A glass came out of the dishwasher with muscle memory alone. He opened the fridge, reaching for the water pitcher, but something else caught his eye in the back corner—a bottle of vodka.

Gross.

He couldn't remember the last time he brought vodka into the house—whiskey had long been his drink of choice. He hesitated, then rested his hand on the bottle, testing whether it was solid. The house had a way of materializing objects to mess with him. But it was exactly what he'd hoped, cold and solid. The bottle was real.

He knew he shouldn't, that he needed to stay sharp. Lyndsay could show up at any moment, and he should be ready to move when she got there. For every reason he shouldn't, another whispered why he needed to. There was no energy left to battle that demon.

The movements barely registered—one moment, he was hesitating, and the next, the bottle was in his hand.

He closed the fridge, the glass tucked under his arm as he moved to the living room, snatching the notebook from the table along the way. If he was lucky, he'd read until he found some answers—or drink until he found some sleep.

The shop was dark, the only light coming from a single bulb hanging down from the rafters. John sniffed the air, noticing a subtle change from the usual sage and sandalwood cocktail. A new scent started to take over, something metallic.

The wind chimes near the door rattled softly as a breeze swept through the shop, and the shadows pulled back, shrinking into the corners. Something was coming.

She materialized slowly, and her blue translucent form filled the darkness with new light. It started as just a hint, a faint shimmer, then came her outline—her features were taking shape. Within moments, she stood fully formed, her presence sucking the warmth from the air.

Lyndsay's hands flexed at her sides. Her fingers curled into fists as if she was testing her solidity. She looked around the room, somehow missing John behind the counter.

He waited a moment to ensure that she had calmed down from their last encounter, which she had. She scanned the room—probably looking for Mac.

"Welcome back."

He delivered the line deliberately calm—to not scare her, and to show he'd cooled off, too.

Her head snapped in his direction, and for a moment, it seemed like she wasn't ready to be done with their altercation. He prepared himself for whatever was about to happen and hoped that she wouldn't test him. He owed it to Mac to help, but he would defend himself if necessary.

As the seconds passed, she slowly lost the tension in her form—allowing her fists to relax while her expression shifted to curiosity. She stepped back.

"What did you do to me?"

"What I had to," he said simply. "But I won't do it again… unless you give me a reason."

It was a subtle threat. She was safe, for now, but that was up to her. She shrank back again and turned her attention back to the shop.

"Where's Mac?" she asked. "How long was I gone?"

John pushed off the counter and approached her with slow, deliberate steps. His boots scuffed softly against the worn floorboards.

"Mitchel is probably at home by now," he said, keeping his tone dry. "Sleeping off a bottle of whiskey. And you…" He checked the silver watch on his wrist with a dramatic pause. "You've been gone just over four hours. Actually, a bit longer than I expected."

Lyndsay retreated another step, her gaze darting toward the door. She didn't trust him, which was probably a smart thing.

"That would hurt," he said.

He tried to keep his voice calm but firm.

"The wards are up," he said, motioning around the room. "They don't just keep things like you out. They'll keep you in, too."

"Why are you keeping me here?" she asked. "I just want to see Mac. Please."

He stopped advancing and let out a slow, deliberate breath, relaxing his posture. "There are a couple of reasons for that," he said, intentionally softening his voice. "First, I'd like to know more about you. Mac seems to have taken a liking to you, and I'm not entirely convinced you don't mean him harm."

"I wouldn't… he's helping me," Lyndsay interrupted, her voice trembling. "I'd never—"

"I know," John cut her off, his voice sharp again. "He's helping you solve your murder. Helping you move on." He took another step forward. "That's what Mac does. But he and I… we have a complicated friendship. He's insufferable, a pain in my ass, and he's got this infuriating habit of bringing his problems to my doorstep." He waved his hand toward Lyndsay, and his gaze hardened. "But I owe him. And I'll be damned if this 'gift' that I forced on him… this curse… causes him even one more ounce of pain."

She froze. She appeared to be processing everything he'd just said—she actually seemed to understand, and even care. He could also see that she was still afraid of him and was having a hard time responding.

"You said there were a couple of reasons," she said, her voice barely above a whisper.

John smirked, straightening and spreading his hands in front of him in a gesture of mock surrender. "I did." He lightened his voice a bit, trying to put her more at ease. "The second reason is simple. If I let you flit off to see Mac right now, you'd throw your wispy ass right into the clutches of the poltergeist haunting his house." He raised an eyebrow at her. "That would hurt you. And it would hurt him. And… I can't have that."

The shop fell silent, the weight of John's words and subtle warning lingering between them while she processed it all. Her eyes shifted to the floor.

"I don't understand," she said. "What did you do?"

John tilted his head slightly, studying her, the earlier defiance all but faded. He walked back to the counter, leaning against it again.

"It's complicated," he said finally. "And a very long story."

"You brought it up," she pressed.

John could see her earlier fear had given way to curiosity. She was calmer now, which was exactly what he needed.

"I can't leave," she continued. "You won't let me, so… what else are we going to talk about?"

He smiled at her and crossed his arms again, leaning back as if trying to distance himself from the topic.

"Let's just say I owe Mac more than I'll ever be able to repay. And he's been kind enough to remind me of that every chance he gets."

"What happened?"

He didn't answer immediately. His impulse was to strike out, assert dominance. It was none of her business, and he didn't explain himself to the dead, but he was thinking about Mac, and he owed it to him to keep her safe.

"You really wouldn't understand."

"Try me," Lyndsay said, taking another step forward.

Her voice had softened, almost imploring. She wasn't going to stop asking.

"Why are you so protective of him? What did you do?"

That last question caught him off guard. His breath hitched before he let it out with a slow sigh.

"I did what I thought needed to be done. Mac was… well, he was collateral damage."

Lyndsay tilted her head, waiting. It was clear she would not let it go. He ran a hand through his dark hair, his shoulders slumping slightly.

"It was a long time ago," he said. "Mac wasn't the man you know now. And neither was I."

He paused, glancing at her, trying to decide how much to say. It was hard for him. He'd caused so much suffering that night, not just for Mac.

"The night his wife died… he blames me. And he's not entirely wrong."

He shook his head and pushed himself off the counter, pacing toward the shelf, running his finger over a row of dusty books.

"I had my own demons to battle… One of them, a literal necromancer. In order to win, I… I made a choice that changed both our lives, and no matter what I do now, I can't undo it."

He lowered his head and sighed, shaking off the emotions this conversation was dredging up. The battle had taken its toll, but in the aftermath, for Mac, it had taken everything. He couldn't bring himself to keep talking about it.

"You know what? I think I can let you go now," he said. "Just remember what I said about the house. Wait for him to leave."

He waved his hand, and the wards around the room lit up briefly before fading into nothingness. She must have felt the change, because she vanished before he could say another word.

Mac drifted off as the vodka dulled the sharp edges of his thoughts. He found himself thinking of Josie. It wasn't unusual—she was a constant fixture in his mind—but that night, she seemed closer. He remembered her laughter, the way she sang off-key and didn't care who heard it. Even in the drunken haze, his memory of her was crystal clear.

Unfortunately, the last good memory he had of her was also the worst.

The night started as a celebration. He and Josie had dressed to the nines, ready for a night of light drinking, dancing, and conversation with his co-workers—the firm's annual holiday party. And that year, they had a lot to celebrate: a promotion, some big bonuses. Mac was killing it at work—the kind of success that makes you feel invincible.

Josie was radiant in a deep-green dress that shimmered under the living room lights. Her wild, dark curls were pinned up but still not fully tamed, framing her face. Mac teased her about how her heels made her a full inch taller than him, and she'd laughed, calling him a sore loser.

On the drive to the venue, Toto's "Africa" came on the radio, and Josie cranked the volume up before belting out the first line with all the enthusiasm of someone performing at a sold-out concert. She loved that song, knew every word, and proved it loudly whenever she could.

Mac played the joker, as usual. "I wonder what Toto sounds like when they sing it," he joked. And in response, she sang louder and prouder, and even more off-key.

In truth, he loved it when she sang. Loud, imperfect, a little feral even—she was unapologetically alive, and it was one of the things he loved most about her. She never cared if she was hitting the notes wrong. She lived every moment to the fullest, and being with her made him feel like he could, too.

The city lights blurred as they cruised down the busy street, laughter filling the car and spilling out into the chilly Denver air through the cracked windows. Mac tapped the steering wheel in time with the beat and snuck a glance at Josie.

"Eyes on the road, mister," she teased. "Can't have you crashing before I get to show off my dancing moves."

"Yes, ma'am," he said before turning his attention back to the road.

As soon as they turned onto Broadway, the traffic thickened— typical for the city's main road. He knew it well, but it seemed busier that night—slower than normal.

The traffic came to a stop just past 10th Street—the start of a two-block stretch of clubs and small shops. He squinted at the new construction up ahead, trying to make out the handwritten sign above the door.

HIPPIE DIPPIE BULLSHIT.

He chuckled as the light ahead turned green and started inching forward when he felt something change in the air—a static charge sending all the tiny hairs on his body to attention. He glanced over to Josie, who was still singing her heart out, seemingly oblivious to whatever he was feeling.

"Do you feel that?" he asked.

She studied him, tilting her head. "Feel what?"

But before he could answer, a flash of blue light erupted from the storefront he had just been admiring. It ripped through the glass windows like a horizontal bolt of lightning arcing out from the construction. The energy of it cracked and hissed, lighting up the street in a blinding cascade of sparks.

"Mac!" Josie screamed, pointing at a bus in the right lane just ahead of them.

The blast hit the bus with a deafening crack, rolling the massive vehicle across all four lanes, where it landed on a row of parked cars.

Mac yanked the wheel, veering sharply to the left to avoid the bus and whatever was coming out of the shop. But it was not enough. The energy rolled over them, slamming into the car with a force that ripped the breath from his lungs. They flipped violently, over and over, the world turning into a whirlwind of sound and blurred motion—glass shattering, metal groaning, and Josie screaming.

They rolled once, twice, three times before smashing into the side of a building. The car came to a stop right side up, though the roof had caved in from several impacts with the street, and the windshield was barely more than a jagged hole.

For a moment, there was only silence.

Mac blinked as he came to, trying to clear the blur, and winced as he reached up to feel his head—pain radiating from everywhere. His hands groped for the seat belt as he remembered to breathe again.

"Josie?"

His voice cracked, barely audible over the ringing in his ears. "You okay?" His heart seized as he turned toward the passenger seat. Josie wasn't there.

Her seatback lay flat against the rear seats, the force of the accident having broken the welds that bound it to the floor. Panic set in as he clawed at his seatbelt release and cranked his neck, looking through the jagged glass of the rear window.

"Josie!" he screamed, his hands fumbling, slick with blood, and shaking too hard to grip anything. He finally released the belt and forced the door open, crawling out and falling to his hands on the ground.

Though he hadn't noticed, broken glass cut into his palms as he staggered to his feet. He looked around at the chaos—cars stopped in every direction, some with headlights still shining and others completely darkened. Smoke billowed from the overturned bus, and the air smelled like burnt rubber and gasoline.

Despite the mayhem, there was an eerie silence—no screams or calls for help—just Mac, his heavy breaths, and his heartbeat pounding in his ears.

Then he saw her. She lay there, in the middle of the street, her dark curls fanned out against the pavement, outlined by a puddle of blood. Too much blood, he thought.

"Josie..."

His voice broke as he stumbled toward her, each step hurting more than the last. He dropped to his knees beside her and paused as he moved his hands over her, too afraid to touch her.

"Josie," he repeated. "Wake up," he whispered.

He watched her, silently pleading to whatever god might be listening. He gently placed his fingers on her neck, checking for a pulse that he wouldn't find. He listened to her chest, searching for a breath she wouldn't take. He looked around for help but found none.

"Please, baby, wake up."

The light was gone.

A sob roared out from his throat as he bowed his head, and bloodstained tears fell onto the fabric of her dress. He couldn't move, think, or breathe until the sound of shuffling footsteps broke through the deepening despair.

Mac lifted his head. "Please help her," he yelled before knowing who he was asking. As he looked out, he watched as people began emerging from the wreckage. Ten, maybe fifteen of them, no more than silhouettes in the darkness.

"Can anyone please help?" he screamed again, louder this time, but no one answered.

As he stood to his feet, he noticed one person walking in his direction from the nearby bus, and relief surged through him.

"Hey!" Mac called out. "Help us! My wife, she needs..."

The man didn't respond or even appear to hear Mac. His eyes were fixed straight ahead, empty and unfocused.

Mac stood, waving his arms as the man got closer. "Hey! I'm talking to you," he said, but the man kept walking, ignoring Mac's plea.

When they were close enough, Mac reached out, grabbing for the man's shoulder, but his hand passed right through him like smoke.

Mac staggered back, and his breath caught in his throat. "What the hell…"

The man's empty eyes stared through him, and Mac was beginning to understand. These weren't survivors. Mac didn't know it yet, but the energy that came barreling out of John's shop had killed his wife and replaced her with a curse.

CHAPTER 12

THE PAST

Mac jolted awake, and his heart hammered as the last fragments of the dream faded. It took him a moment to get his bearings, as the smell of vodka and old books didn't match the metallic tang of the crash site that still lingered at the edge of his senses.

He grabbed the couch cushion beneath him as his eyes adjusted to the light pouring in from the window, and there she was.

Lyndsay's pale face became clear, just inches away. Her wide eyes and tilted head made her look eerily focused, like she was studying him a little too closely.

"Jesus Christ!" he shouted, scrambling upright and nearly toppling off the couch. His heart, already pounding from the dream, threatened to beat its way clear out of his chest.

She moved closer, studying him intently.

"You were dreaming."

Mac dragged a trembling hand down his face, trying to steady his breathing. "Yeah, no kidding. What the hell are you doing here?"

His voice came out rougher than he expected—probably from the mix of adrenaline and the vodka hangover. Not that it mattered, since Lyndsay ignored the question entirely.

"If you could see all those ghosts after the crash… how come you didn't see Josie?"

Mac froze, his mind stuttering over the words like a record skipping over a scratch. He must've asked himself the same question a million times since that night, but why was she asking?

"How do you know about that?"

"I saw it," she said simply as she straightened herself, her ethereal form shimmering faintly in the light. "The crash, the ghosts, you." Her eyes narrowed. "I don't know how, but I could see what you were dreaming."

Mac stared at her as his thoughts scrambled to catch up.

"Wait, hold on…"

He stopped mid-sentence as the realization hit him like a slap to the face. She was here, inside. It should have been impossible. The house had never let a spirit get fully past the fence line before swallowing it up.

"How the hell are you in my house?"

"What do you mean?"

Mac gestured to the walls around them. "This house doesn't really let ghosts in. Any spirit who gets close enough ends up… well… eaten."

His eyes narrowed as he took her in, his initial fear morphing into suspicion. "How are you here?"

Lyndsay glanced around the room, then shrugged.

"I don't know," she said. "I haven't felt like I was being eaten."

Mac leaned back against the couch, his breathing still unsteady. "Interesting," he muttered. "Keeps getting better."

"John told me about that night," she said, shifting the subject back to the dream. "But he didn't tell me everything."

"No," he said, pushing himself off the couch. "I wouldn't expect he would." He stopped, listening to the stillness of the house—much quieter than normal. "Curious," he muttered, still off-kilter from the jarring awakening.

"Did you see her?" Lyndsay pressed. "After… I mean."

Mac didn't enjoy talking about Josie under normal circumstances, and having the conversation with a ghost who had just delved into his subconscious didn't make it any easier. He considered telling her to mind her own business, but something forced the truth to the surface.

"No," he said, more curtly than he intended. "Not that night and not since," he continued, his voice edged with bitterness. "Another perk of John's gift. Everyone gets to be haunted except me."

"Until me, you mean," she said.

Mac stared at her for a moment, blinking as her words registered. Something inside him unclenched, and in spite of himself, he laughed—not at her joke but at the strange comfort he found in the idea.

"I guess you have a point."

Lyndsay's gaze shifted to the notebook lying splayed out on the floor in front of the couch. Mac grabbed it and headed to the kitchen, Lyndsay floating behind him.

"John said that would help me remember."

"Sounds like you two had quite the conversation. Honestly, I'm surprised he let you leave," he said, tossing the book onto the dining table before filling a glass with water.

"I don't know if I want to remember. What if it's worse than not knowing?"

Mac leaned on the kitchen counter, gripping the edge tightly, trying to find the right words.

"I get it," he said, softening his tone. "I know it must be terrifying… but this might be the only way to find out what happened to you. To stop it from happening to Joanne."

"I know what's at stake, but what if I remember and it's… awful? What if I remember every second of what he did to me and it doesn't even help? What if it's just pain?"

Mac could feel her fear. He wondered if it was selfish to ask this of her, but thoughts of Joanne loomed, and in the end, Lyndsay would need this to move on as well.

"I can't promise it'll help," he admitted. "I wish I could. But what I do know is that not knowing… that's killing you, again. It'll keep you here, stuck… in this limbo."

Mac paused, allowing her to process his words before continuing.

"Even if it doesn't give us all the answers, even the smallest clue is a step forward. For you. For Joanne. For everyone this guy has hurt."

"And if it's just pain?"

Mac struggled to answer. He had no idea what to expect. He wished he had something more to offer her.

"I don't know. It could be. But knowing has to be better than this. Right? And for what it's worth, you don't have to carry it alone."

She softened, her posture relaxing as her grip on her arms loosened.

"I guess… we should get started?"

Mac nodded. "Let's do it."

He stopped, glancing past Lyndsay at the rest of the house. It wasn't quite right—no scratching in the walls, no pipes knocking, no low moaning sounds that usually crept into the silence. Just stillness. Too much stillness.

"You better not have broken my house," he muttered. "I paid a lot for this poltergeist."

He smiled faintly as he grabbed the notebook off the table and flipped it open to the page with the ritual. "We need salt."

CHAPTER 13

THE RITUAL

The pages were old—yellowed and brittle, and the faded ink was barely legible enough to make out the instructions. The steps were clear, though the actual phrases for the ritual were from a language he'd never seen before.

Mac worked at the pronunciation as best he could, muttering the words under his breath repeatedly until they felt right, stumbling over some of the syllables. The whole thing sounded like gibberish.

"This reads like a lunatic wrote it," he said, glancing at Lyndsay.

She was sitting and watching him fumble through it. She seemed ready, focused, but seeing her like that gave him second thoughts.

"Yes, I'm sure," she said, smiling.

She must have seen it in his eyes, because she knew that was the question he was about to ask. He smiled and took a deep breath, holding it for a moment before exhaling as he lit the last candle and motioned for her to step inside the salt circle.

"Here goes nothing," he said.

He started chanting, slow at first, focusing on every syllable. The longer he went on, the more naturally the words flowed until it felt like they were pulling themselves from his lips. The room turned colder, and the candles flickered as though caught in a breeze, despite the air in the room being still.

Lyndsay peered down at the bowl in the circle as it began to glow. She looked determined but worried.

"What if it doesn't work?" she asked.

"Then we're no worse off than we were twenty minutes ago."

He pointed at the bowl, motioning for her to lean in closer.

"Just focus on the water."

She stepped forward, and her hands trembled as she hovered over the bowl. They both watched as the water's surface rippled and shimmering images took form—a sidewalk, her own reflection in a window, the headlights of a car.

She was still, expressionless, as she locked in on the shifting images. A scene emerged, showing her walking down a dimly lit street with a bag slung over her shoulder. Someone was following her, nothing more than a face in the water. It was hard to make out the features, but it didn't feel familiar. Judging by her lack of reaction, she didn't seem to recognize it either.

Mac felt his chest tighten as the image shifted abruptly to something that was familiar—the cemetery. Then it flashed again, this time focusing on the sign above the bar's door: *FRONT 9/BACK 40.*

The brighter the bowl glowed, the dimmer Lyndsay became—like the ritual was drawing power from her energy to keep it going. She must have felt it, but she never wavered.

He stepped back and glanced down at the book, trying to focus on the next line of the incantation, still muttering under his breath. The air in the room felt heavier, like it was thickening and pressing down. He ignored it and kept his focus tight until a sudden rattling behind him made him flinch.

He spun around to find a few jars clanking against each other as a shelf on the wall shook. The room was colder, like the temperature had dropped twenty degrees in an instant, and a low groan bellowed through the house.

"Is this supposed to happen?" Lyndsay asked.

"Maybe?"

The house shook. A shudder so violent, a picture fell off the wall, scattering shards of glass across the floor. The flames of the candles were stretching sideways, as if caught in a windstorm.

"Okay… maybe not?"

Mac grabbed the table's edge to steady himself as the vibrations intensified. He felt something ripple through the floorboards, and his heart pounded. A low scratching crept across the ceiling, like something being dragged across the floor in the bedroom above him.

"Should I stop?" Lyndsay asked, her voice trembling now.

"It'll be fine!" he replied unconvincingly. "Just keep going—focus on the bowl."

Another groan ripped through the house, louder this time, as a chair near the table tipped over. The air electrified, and he dug his fingers into the table, desperate to keep standing as the surrounding house tried to shake him loose.

"It's fine," he muttered, more to himself than to her. "John would have told me if this would upset a poltergeist… right?"

"I'm tied up. I think I'm in the trunk of a car," Lyndsay whispered suddenly, her voice distant and trembling. "Someone else is in here with me. She looks like me… but I don't know who she is." Her eyes stayed locked on the water, wide with fear. "He's pulling her out of the trunk. Mac, I don't think she's alive."

The rattling intensified, and something crashed in the kitchen with a deafening noise. Mac cursed under his breath, whipping around to see cabinet doors swinging open, plates spilling out and shattering on the floor.

"Um… I'm starting to think the house doesn't like this," Mac muttered. "If it throws a fridge at us, I'm calling it quits."

"I don't think it's the ritual," Lyndsay said suddenly, looking up from the bowl. "I think it's reacting to me."

"You mean the house?"

"I can feel it tugging at me, like it's trying to pull me out of the circle," she said. "I think we need to hurry…"

He clenched his fists, alternating his focus between Lyndsay and the house, which felt like it was ready to tear itself apart.

"Fine," he said. "Let's finish it. You saw him… what else? What else did you see?"

She turned back to the bowl and steadied her focus as the images in the water flashed rapidly. "It's… it's all kinda the same."

"Lyndsay," he urged as he stepped closer. "If there's nothing else to see, we need to stop this before the house stops it for us."

"I see his face. I know him… I just can't make it out."

The words had barely left her when the glow from the bowl exploded in a blinding flash. A blast of cold air rippled the room, extinguishing every candle. Mac staggered back, shielding his eyes as the light vanished, plunging the room into darkness.

The groaning and shaking subsided, and the house settled. The shadows retreated as the sunlight filtered in through the windows. Mac lowered his arm and took in the aftermath—shattered glass everywhere, and none of his furniture was where it had been at the beginning.

"Jesus."

Lyndsay still stood in the circle. Her form seemed weak, like a light not getting enough energy to stay bright. She turned to him, quiet for a moment, exhausted, but with a grim sort of determination on her face.

Mac swiped away a small section of the salt and motioned for her to follow him. "I think we should get you out of the house," he said, keeping his voice low as he scanned the room, half expecting the house to retaliate.

"I remember."

They sat in silence at the end of the driveway, broken bits of glass from his shattered windows still clinging to Mac's jacket. He rested his hands on the wheel, staring out the window, replaying the events in his head.

Lyndsay was recovering in the passenger seat. Her form was stronger, though not back to its usual hue yet. She, too, stared out the window, likely replaying the visions, trying to make sense of it all.

"That was… intense," Mac said, breaking the silence.

She turned to him for the first time since getting into the truck. "A bit, yeah," she said. "I don't even know what that was… the house, the ritual—I don't know what I expected, but it felt wrong."

Mac nodded slowly. Something had to have gone wrong. That sort of reaction… certainly John would have warned him.

"Yeah, the house definitely didn't appreciate that," he said. "But you got something—some memories. That's a start." He exhaled audibly, running his hand over his face.

"I saw the Front 9 in there," he said, turning his head toward Lyndsay.

"You want to go back there?" she asked.

"Not especially, no," he admitted. "But it feels important. It keeps coming up."

She nodded. "And the cemetery," she added softly. "It felt familiar. Like somewhere I've been a lot."

"It looked like Resthaven," Mac said after a long pause. "I go there every Satur… day…"

He trailed off as a thought struck him. His stomach tightened as he thought of the flowers—fresh, unexpected—left at Josie's grave. What if they were from Joanne?

Lyndsay's hand, or what would have been her hand, drifted slightly toward him before stopping short, as if she'd forgotten she couldn't offer the comfort of touch. The gesture was small, but Mac felt it.

"Hang on." Mac grabbed his cell phone out of his jacket and swiped until he found Maureen's number on speed dial. As the phone rang, Lyndsay turned to him again, her brows raised in curiosity.

"Have you heard anything?" Maureen answered, her voice hurried and anxious. "Did you find Jo?"

His heart sank, realizing he had nothing good to tell her. He'd called on instinct, chasing a clue, and hadn't considered how his next question might affect her.

"Nothing yet," he replied. "But I'm working on something."

He hesitated, his grip tightening on the phone. This question was going to be hard. Not only was he about to bring up Joanne, but to do so, he had to remind Maureen about Josie. Tying the fates of her two daughters together… he realized too late that he shouldn't have called. But now, he had to ask.

"Have any of you been to see Josie recently? I saw some flowers there on Saturday."

Maureen didn't respond right away, and Mac could hear her breath hitching on the line. "Jo said she was going to visit last week. But I don't know if she ever made it. I haven't been in a while, so I'm guessing—" Her sentence cut off mid-word, and muffled sobbing filled the line.

"I'm so sorry," Mac said. "And I promise, I'm working every angle. I will bring her home to you."

The call ended abruptly, the screen flashing *Call Ended*. Mac stared at it and sighed. She'd hung up, and he couldn't blame her.

"Fuck."

"You think the cemetery's connected?"

Mac shook his head and gripped the phone.

"I don't know. But it's another place you've both been. It's worth looking into."

He shoved the phone back into his pocket and put the truck into gear.

"Well… the bar ain't open yet, so I guess we hit the cemetery first." He turned to glance at the house one last time before driving away. It was quiet now, as if recovering from the ritual with them.

The cemetery was quiet, even for the middle of a weekday. Mac scanned the area. He couldn't quite put his finger on what, but something felt off as his eyes swept across the rows of gravestones.

Lyndsay drifted ahead of him and paused at the entrance, gazing over the cemetery with a focused intensity, like she was trying to pin down a memory that sat just out of reach.

"You okay?" Mac asked.

She nodded, though she didn't turn around.

"Yeah," she sighed. "I just need to look around."

He waited, allowing her to search the cemetery on her own.

"Don't go too far," he yelled out. He glanced around, making sure no one was nearby to witness him yelling at himself.

She waved a hand in acknowledgment and kept walking.

As she disappeared down the path, Mac looked around at the gravestones near him. He couldn't shake the gnawing feeling that something wasn't right. It was too quiet, empty, and it finally hit him—where were all the ghosts?

John had tried to explain it to him once—the dead don't rest in cemeteries. They cling to the living and wander like moths to a streetlight. It was their nature, though standing there, there was nothing. Only Lyndsay—a solitary echo of the dead in a place meant to host thousands.

He shook the thought from his head. Those ghosts weren't his concern, and if he was being honest, he considered the peace and quiet a blessing. Still, he couldn't help but wonder if something had chased them off.

He started walking toward Josie's grave, the path so familiar he could probably get there blindfolded. The flowers he'd found during his last visit were still there, wilted and browning. He crouched down and tossed them aside.

"Hi, baby. Sorry, I didn't bring anything with me this time," he said softly.

As he stood there, talking to his wife, movement caught his eye. At the end of the row of headstones, atop a small hill, a man stood near one of the mausoleums, overlooking the graves. He was watching Mac.

He froze as an unease crawled up his spine. The man stood still, watching. Mac shielded his eyes from the sun, but all he could make out was a silhouette.

Then the man turned, climbed into a maintenance cart, and drove toward one of the sheds.

Mac let out a breath he hadn't realized he'd been holding and shook his head. "Paranoid."

He turned his attention back to the cemetery, scanning for Lyndsay. She stood a few rows away, frozen in place, her gaze fixed on a headstone. She wasn't moving, so Mac started toward her. When he reached her, she didn't look up. Her focus remained locked on the name etched into the stone.

"What is it?" he asked.

"I know this grave," she replied softly. "It's hers."

"Who?"

"A friend," she said, her voice trailing off.

Mac stared down at the small, flat stone nestled in the earth. It wasn't as ornate as Josie's—it was simple, understated, with the woman's name taking up most of the space. But it was the smaller print below that grabbed his attention. *Gone too soon.*

"We grew up together. Did everything together… she was like a sister to me," she said as she brushed her fingers over the engraved letters. "We were camping when she slipped into the river. It was weeks before they found her."

He stood silently, listening to her story, and it occurred to him that this was the sister she remembered before, and the more she spoke, the rawer her words became, the more human she seemed to him.

"I came here a lot," she said. "I'd sit and talk to her. It helped… I think. It helped me remember better times."

Mac nodded, understanding. He thought about all the Saturdays he spent with Josie, talking, bringing her things, holding on to the memories they'd shared. Though sad, most of the time it was peaceful. "I'm sorry," he said—the only sentiment that made sense.

Lyndsay turned to him, her expression shifting to one of determination. "I was here that day. I know it now. But there's something else…"

"Do you want to keep looking around?"

Before she could answer, her attention snapped to something in the distance. Her translucent form tensed like a tightly coiled spring as her eyes locked onto the wooded area behind the cemetery.

"What is it?" Mac asked, stepping forward to see what she was seeing. But all he saw were trees.

She didn't answer. Her eyes darted back and forth, as though following something. Mac watched her, then the woods, waiting to understand what was happening. And then she bolted.

"Shit."

He took off after her as she disappeared into the dense cluster of trees behind the cemetery.

"Lyndsay!"

⬧

His heart pounded as he broke into a jog, struggling to keep up. He weaved through the gravestones, desperate to keep her in sight, but she was fast, and he wasn't as young as he used to be. Her form became a blur as she reached the outer section of the cemetery, disappearing into the shadows of the woods.

When he reached the tree line, he stopped to pant for a few moments, bending over, focusing on not having a full-on heart attack. "Lyndsay!" he yelled as he scanned the trees for any sign of her. Though he couldn't see her, he could feel her presence… like a strange pull dragging him along through the woods.

He walked deeper into the trees, calling out her name, but she was gone. The farther he went, the quieter and eerier it became, and the more it felt like a bad idea.

When he finally caught sight of her, she stood motionless near a small clearing with her back to him. Her form was brighter and steadier than it had been since the ritual, and she was staring at something just ahead of her with her hands clenched to her sides.

"Hey," he said as he caught up to her. "What happened? What'd you see?"

"I remember something," she said simply, quietly.

Mac looked out, following her gaze. The clearing stretched out in front of them, the ground littered with fallen branches. Across the way was a small but well-maintained hiking trail that wound through the trees. Though he didn't know why, something about that spot sent a chill through him.

"This is it," she said. "This is the last thing I remember before waking up in the trunk of that car."

"This clearing?" Mac asked, looking for clarification.

"I was walking that path over there, heading home, I think."

She paused and furrowed her brow while she seemed to strain to recall the details. "This is where it all went dark."

Mac stepped forward, looking around but not entirely sure what he was looking for. "You're sure? This is where you were kidnapped?"

She nodded. "I'm sure."

Mac walked farther into the clearing toward the trail, still trying to find something that might help them discover what happened, but there wasn't much to find. The trail was well-used but also well-maintained, so it must get a lot of traffic. The clearing felt forgotten—once used, now left for nature to reclaim.

"Let's look around," he said, moving closer to the trail.

As they left the clearing, heading back into the trees, Mac's boot caught on something buried beneath the dirt and leaves. He crouched and brushed some debris away with his hand, uncovering a mound of dirt just a few inches above the forest floor.

He knew right away what he'd stumbled on and scrambled to move the remaining debris, exposing a mound just big enough to fit a person. The earth had been recently disturbed and covered again. Something, or more likely someone, was buried there.

"Lyndsay," he called out. "Come look at this."

She came up beside him, and they both stood in silence, staring at the grave. He assumed she was going through the same thoughts he was having, ultimately leading to the big question. Could this be *her* grave? Would they find her body lying there if they dug it up?

"What if it's me?" Lyndsay said.

"We don't know what's down there. It could be a dog for all we know."

"But the timing, the place—it's too close," she said. "The last thing I remember is that trail. What if… what if this is where he left me?"

Mac's throat tightened. He didn't want to admit it, but she was probably right—it all seemed to fit.

"What do we do?" she asked.

The fear in her voice was palpable. He grabbed a nearby branch and shoved it into the dirt. "We mark it," he said. "I'm not about to dig this up and find out we just disturbed… whatever it could be."

Lyndsay nodded, but he could see her hesitation.

He grabbed his phone from his jacket pocket. "I'm calling Jason."

CHAPTER 14

THE CRIME SCENE

The once-quiet clearing had been transformed into a flurry of activity. Radios hummed, boots stomped through the overgrowth, and voices barked orders as officers worked the scene.

Yellow police tape crisscrossed the area, marking the grave as the center of a growing crime scene. Uniformed officers and plainclothes workers were everywhere, some digging into the disturbed earth while other canvassed the surrounding area, looking for anything else they could find.

Mac stood out of the way at the scene with Lyndsay hovering close beside him, both watching as the chaos unfolded in front of them. Her tension and impatience radiated off in waves, sharp and insistent.

Jason approached them, lifting the yellow tape to get through. His usual easygoing demeanor had been replaced with a sharp, focused energy. He pulled his sunglasses from his face and placed them in his shirt pocket as he stopped in front of them.

"Hello, Mac," he said. "You want to tell me how you found this?"

"Does it matter?"

Jason pursed his lips and squinted. "Yeah, Mac, it matters. It's not every day someone stumbles on a body while on an afternoon stroll through the woods."

He stopped and looked around at the people working the scene before returning his attention to Mac. "Look, half these people already think it's you. So yes, damn it, it matters."

Mac thought long and hard about how to answer him, and he knew that "does it matter?" wouldn't cut it, and he wasn't even sure why he'd said it. He could feel Lyndsay beside him, staring, waiting to see how he answered, and he could feel Jason's frustration.

"Look," Mac said, his tone cautious. "I was visiting Josie and… and thought I'd take a walk."

Jason raised an eyebrow, his expression unamused. "A walk, huh? You're not out here investigating, right? This has nothing to do with Joanne… You know what? I know you weren't just hiking the trail, Mac. Out with it."

Mac exhaled heavily, bracing himself. "All right," he said. "I found it because of her." He motioned to Lyndsay standing beside him.

Jason's eyes followed Mac's hands as they pointed at nothing, just an empty space filled with nothing more than air. He looked back at Mac, as if trying to determine whether it was truth, fantasy, or crazy. They stared at each for what felt like an eternity until Jason broke the silence. "Lyndsay?" he asked. "That's your ghost, right?"

Mac nodded but stayed silent, waiting for whatever accusation or patronization was coming next.

Jason nodded and pressed his lips into a thin line as he surveyed the scene once more. "Okay," he said. "Go on, tell me everything."

Mac hesitated as the awkward nervousness set in. He hated this part. He scrunched up his face and took a deep breath before finally answering with a rapid-fire summation of the important bits.

"She showed up at my house last week. No memory of who she was or what happened to her. We've been trying to piece it all together, bit by bit. She's what led me to the cemetery, and then to this clearing. She said it was the last place she remembered before everything went dark."

Jason stood there silent, dazed by all the information he'd just received. Mac held his breath, waiting for his response.

"Okay," he finally responded. "So, she led you right to the grave."

"Yeah, that's what I'm saying."

Jason stood silent for a moment, processing the information. His face gave nothing away, but something in his stance softened. He seemed less skeptical, more thoughtful. Finally, a slow breath left his nose.

"All right," he said. "Let's say I believe you."

"You do?"

"Hypothetically," Jason said quickly. "Look, I don't understand how all this ghost stuff works, but I know you. I can't imagine you would make this up, and you sure as hell didn't kill anyone."

Jason peered at the space next to Mac. "So, like, she's here now?" he asked.

"Yeah," Mac replied, jerking his head to the left to point her out. "She's right here next to me."

The confused officer tilted his head slightly, like he thought it would help him see something invisible. "What's she like? What does she look like? Sound like?"

Before either of them could say more, someone shouted from the gravesite—"She's coming up!"—and both men turned to see the officers carefully exhuming the body and setting it on the ground next to the hole. The medical examiner leaned down beside the woman, motioning for Jason to come over.

"Stay put."

As Jason headed down to the M.E., Lyndsay drifted closer, staring down at the girl they just pulled out of the earth. "Do you think it's me?"

"I don't know," he said. "But if it is, we'll figure it out."

Lyndsay nodded, and Mac noticed her fists clenching tight at her waist. After a moment of silence, waiting to hear what they found, she moved forward. "I have to see," she said as she darted off toward the body.

"Wait," Mac called after her quietly, trying to avoid anyone around them hearing him. He wanted to be there for her, if it was her body. He didn't want her to have to see that on her own. But she left anyway.

As he watched her, potentially staring at her own corpse, Jason approached again with a grim expression on his face. "It's a young woman," he said. "Late twenties, early thirties. The M.E. thinks she's been there at least a month, but they'll know better after the autopsy."

Mac took a deep breath and sighed. "A month?" he repeated, still watching Lyndsay.

Jason nodded. "Does that fit your timeline? For Lyndsay?"

Mac shook his head. "No. Pretty sure Lyndsay's only been dead a week. At most."

Jason's expression darkened, and he glanced back toward the grave. "Then we've got another victim," he said grimly.

Mac's mind swirled with emotions. It wasn't Joanne, and he was grateful for that. As much as he knew Lyndsay was dead, seeing her in that grave would have made it real. Too real.

He looked back down to the gravesite where Lyndsay was still standing, staring at the body. Her form flickered again—stronger this time, more erratic—just like during the ritual, and her head tilted. He felt the hairs on his arms stand up, like an electric charge building in the air.

In the distance, a sob broke through the noise at the scene. He turned, startled by it, and found one officer standing near the perimeter of the tape. He was older, with gray streaking the sides of his dark hair, and he had his back to the grave. His shoulders were shaking as he tried in vain to keep his emotions in check.

"What's going on now?" Jason muttered under his breath as he stepped toward the officer, who was wiping tears from his face with the back of his hand. The man was clearly distressed.

His voice cracked as he spoke to no one in particular, choked with emotion. "She didn't deserve this," he cried out. "None of them do. It's just... it's too much."

Jason and another officer approached him, each placing a hand on his shoulders, murmuring something that Mac couldn't hear but sounded vaguely reassuring. The man shook his head as he clenched his hands at sides. "I've seen too many of these," he sobbed. "You think you can handle it, but then..."

Mac couldn't help but think it odd. These were seasoned professionals—Jason always boasted how his team could keep it together under pressure. And here was this man, falling apart at a crime scene they had only started processing.

As Jason tended to the man, Mac looked back over to Lyndsay, who hadn't moved. Her shimmering form was flickering more intensely than he had ever seen. She was still staring at the body, and each pulse of the flicker seemed to glow brighter and brighter.

He swapped his attention between the distraught officer and Lyndsay, and noticed that as her form flickered brighter, the intensity of his distress also grew. He remembered the bar, while she stood staring at her own picture, and the couple arguing next to her… out of nowhere. And the moment with Jason at the station, where he had his own minor breakdown. *What the hell is happening?*

He snapped his attention back to Lyndsay as alarm bells fired off in his mind. He once again noticed the electricity in the air as he put it all together. Could she be causing this?

Her form was more solid now. The light hazy blue hue she normally carried was crystal clear and brightly pulsing. Suddenly, a chorus of sobs broke out around him, and several of the officers fell to the ground, some crying and others screaming curses.

He tried to call out to Lyndsay, but instead of answering him, her form instantaneously expanded, and a bright light erupted outward. Mac instinctively winced, raising his arm to shield himself as the light enveloped the clearing in an instant of searing brilliance.

As quickly as it had appeared, the flash dissipated. Mac blinked, trying to shake the remnants of the flash from his retinas. He lowered his arm, and she was gone. Lyndsay had disappeared again.

He looked around for her but found that all the previously affected officers were finding their way back to their feet. Even the officer that began it all seemed to have come back to normal—exclaiming to those around him he was fine and he didn't know what came over him.

Jason, still tending to the older officer, shot Mac a look, watching him react to whatever had just happened. The look was a question, one Mac had no answer for, so he shrugged.

Jason walked back toward him, though his focus was split between Mac and the scene around them. "Dan seems fine now," he said. "But that was weird, right?"

"Yeah… Maybe the stress is getting to him," Mac said, keeping the focus off Lyndsay.

"Okay, you… two should go home. We got a lot to do here, and we'll call you if we have questions. And we'll need an official statement at some point."

Mac nodded and watched as Jason headed back down to the body. Now, once again, Mac needed to find Lyndsay and find out what just happened.

CHAPTER 15

A BREAKTHROUGH

From the edge of the crime scene, Mac watched the officers process the area—searching for any new clues the trail might offer up. As he paced the perimeter, he worried about Lyndsay. He could hardly imagine what she'd just gone through—her memories of this place, the dead body, whatever happened to her. And he couldn't blame her for disappearing, but he had so many new questions.

He waited until no one was watching and slipped away, heading toward an older section of the cemetery where weather and time had given the headstones an eerie sort of age. Even the trees were creepier there… taller, their gnarled branches reaching farther.

Far enough away from the bustling crime scene, it was the quiet that set his nerves most on edge—just the sounds of his breath and the muted crunch of his boots against the pebbly path. He retraced their steps, working back toward her friend's grave, hoping she'd gone somewhere familiar to find some comfort.

"Lyndsay," he murmured.

Every flash of movement or shifting shadow he caught out of the corners of his eyes would snap his attention as he continued searching, but nothing came of it. It was just him and the oppressive stillness of the cemetery.

He headed toward the newer section, and as he got closer, his body started to react in a more familiar way—tiny goose bumps crawling up his arms, a little prickle at the back of his neck, and his eyes darting around more, like it knew on its own that he needed to be more alert.

As he walked deeper in, he felt the familiar prickle crawling up his neck. At first, he thought it might be Lyndsay coming back, but there was still no sign of her. And then it hit him—the ghosts were back.

They meandered around the graveyard as though they'd never left, wandering aimlessly between the graves.

They hadn't been there earlier; he was sure of it. It was like something had scared them off. But there they were, and somehow, he was glad for it. It felt like a bit of normalcy returning.

He stopped and looked around, scanning each spirit he could see, hopeful that one of them might be her.

"Damn it, Lyndsay. Where are you?"

The ghosts paid no attention to him as he passed by on his way to her friend's grave, and in return, he ignored them as well. He kept moving, weaving between the stones until he got to it.

"If you can hear me… come back," he said to the air.

He waited a few more minutes, watching the spirits, and then let out a deep sigh. It felt like they'd made a serious step in the right direction. But now, without her, he didn't know where to go… or what to do.

It wasn't just about finding Joanne. He needed to know if Lyndsay was okay.

He drove for hours, scouring every place he could think of to find her—his home, the stretch of road where they first met, even the liquor store where she came to him the second night. In each place, all he found was silence.

He pulled off to the side of the road and stared out at the horizon. The sun was low, and while it was turning into a gorgeous Colorado sunset, he struggled to notice. He felt frustrated and useless. So much depended on figuring out the next step, and he couldn't even find Lyndsay.

The bar! Of course. It was the one place he hadn't looked yet.

He didn't relish the idea of going back there. His last visit had left scars he hadn't dared to probe too deeply. The weight, the unease—the suffocating feeling of something unseen digging into him. It was too much. But now, with Lyndsay missing, he couldn't keep ignoring the connection.

"It was probably just more of what happened at the graveyard," he muttered. "Lyndsay messin' with people's emotions."

Regardless of the rationalization, the pit in his stomach only grew. The ritual had given them two places: the cemetery and the bar. The cemetery had some answers, but if she was still searching, the bar was the only lead left.

He sat a few moments longer, wrestling with his hesitation as the anxiety clawed up from his gut. A little reminder of what he might experience if he went back.

"Right, then," he muttered, reaching for the shifter. "Only way out is through."

But just as he moved to put the truck into drive, his phone buzzed in his pocket. He pulled out the phone and saw Jason's private number flash across his screen.

"Crap," he muttered as he swiped to answer the call.

"Hey, Mac. I need you to come down to the station to give your statement, and I have some things I want to show you."

A flood of relief rushed over Mac. Somewhere to go that wasn't the bar. Fantastic. "I'll be right there."

***

Mac rolled into the station lot just as the last light of the day was fading. The building was quieter than before. Mac climbed out, shutting the door with just a tad more force than necessary, and strode toward the entrance.

Inside, Jason was waiting for him near the bullpen. He waved Mac over, and his expression was tense but determined.

"Good, you're here," Jason said, motioning for Mac to follow him. "I pulled what I could on the missing persons cases and the other victims. Not sure if it will help, but I thought we could go over it and see if... your friend...?" His voice trailed off with hesitation.

Jason led him to the conference room. Cork and whiteboards covered in photos, maps, and notes lined the walls. The table in the center overflowed with files, papers spilling out in a chaotic spread.

"Actually, she's not here at the moment," he said, taking it all in.

"Okay," Jason said, blinking, disappointed and surprised. "Well, this is everyone we've connected to the killer so far. We're still working out the timeline, but this is what we know."

He pointed to a cluster of photos pinned to the center of one board. Each was a smiling face, young women in their twenties or early thirties. Below each photo were details: names, ages, dates of disappearance, and, in some far sadder instances, dates of death.

"All women," Jason continued. "All of similar build and appearance—most of them reported missing within a fifty-mile radius over the past two years."

Mac studied the photos. At a quick glance, any of them could have been Joanne or Lyndsay.

Jason hesitated, his eyes flicking to a photo on the board. It was Joanne, at the end of a row of photos. Mac knew right away by her signature picture smile—like she was reluctant to pose. Hers was the last in a long line of photos, and next to hers was Lyndsay.

"We've recovered five bodies so far," Jason continued.

"Only five?" Mac asked, shocked by the low number. "There are at least fifteen women on this board."

Jason nodded grimly. "Yeah. The rest are still missing." He sighed, gesturing vaguely at the board. "We don't know yet. He doesn't… leave them in the same places."

Mac couldn't take his eyes off the photos. His stomach churned as he listened to Jason break down what they did and didn't know.

There were fifteen women on that board staring back at him, each one a life cut short or left hanging in uncertainty. They had families and friends who loved them, missed them, were wondering what happened to them. It was overwhelming.

Joanne's and Lyndsay's photos seemed to anchor him, but also provided a painful reminder of how close to home this was hitting.

"What about the ones you have found?" Mac asked. "Do they give you anything to work with?"

"They give us a time frame," Jason answered quickly, proudly. "Each of the five we have recovered… we've been able to determine that he keeps them for approximately four weeks before he… well, you know."

Mac's heart sank deeper the more he listened to Jason.

Jason's tone darkened. "We also know that those four weeks are brutal. Layers upon layers of abuse and starvation."

The grip he had on the table tightened as those words sank in. The timeline was horrifying—four weeks of hell before the inevitable. Joanne's face stared back at him from the board, as if begging him to help her. He felt a rage building, and his face flushed.

"This is what Lyndsay went through?" he asked, not really expecting an answer to something he already knew. "This is what Joanne is going through right now."

He tightened his jaw and pursed his lips, trying to keep his emotions in check. Lyndsay's flickering presence and fragmented memories had only hinted at the horrors she'd endured, but now, seeing the faces on the board, learning what those last few weeks of her life must have been like, it all became painfully real.

Jason cleared his throat, letting Mac know there was more. "We also found signs of restraints on the bodies," he said. "Bruising around the wrists and ankles."

"He has to be holding them somewhere close," Mac suggested. "I can't imagine he's driving across the country with a dead body in his trunk."

Jason nodded in agreement. "Right. The dump sites are within ten miles of where they were last seen. It gives a search radius, but outside of that, we can't find a pattern."

"And it's a lot of ground to cover."

"Exactly."

Mac stared at the map, tracing the pins. Yellow pins showed areas where the women were last seen, and red pins marked the five they'd recovered. He thought about what Lyndsay had said, how the trail was the last thing she remembered before the abduction.

"Where's Lyndsay's pin?"

Jason shot Mac a quizzical look before answering. "Here," he said, pointing at one pin on the board. "At her parents' house. Why?"

Mac reached up, snatched the pin out of the cork, and moved it, placing it directly next to the red pin near the cemetery—where they'd just found the body. He caught Jason looking around, presumably ensuring no one saw him touching the board.

"What are you doing?" Jason asked.

"This is where she was taken. The exact spot."

Mac watched as Jason processed what he had just said, shifting his focus between Mac and the pin's new home on the board. Jason nodded, like he was understanding something, then reached over and moved the pin back to its original location.

"Got it," Jason said. "That's good information… definitely gives me a new angle. He might be dumping the bodies near where he's finding his next victims. For now, though… I don't have a way to explain how I know that. But I promise I'll dig into it."

Mac continued to scan the board, hopeful that something else would jump out and make it all make sense, but everything else just seemed so random. There was some piece everyone was missing, some key that would tie it all together, something no one had found yet. But even as he studied the board, something tugged at him. The bar. It was there in Lyndsay's memory. In Joanne's timeline. Why hadn't he pushed hard on it?

"Any of these women have any connection to the bar?" he asked suddenly.

"Front 9?" Jason asked. "I don't think so… Well, aside from Joanne, of course."

"Lyndsay was there just before she was taken."

Jason flipped through his personal notes on the cases, like he was double-checking. "No, I'm not seeing anything, but it's the only bar in the city. It's possible." He grabbed a pencil and flipped to a clean page in his notebook, writing the words *Front 9 Connection?* in big letters. "I'll look into it."

"Already on it," Mac told him plainly. "I was actually on my way when you called."

"Let's make it an official visit. I'll come with you."

"I don't think you should, not yet anyway," Mac insisted. "I just want to talk to Caleb again. Press him a bit and see how he responds. If it's only me there, it's just a concerned friend. If you show up and the killer is there, it changes everything. I'll go in, check it out. If I think there's something, I'll call."

The look on Jason's face was enough for Mac to know he didn't like the idea, but strangely, he didn't argue. "All right," he said. "But Mac, if you think the guy's there, you don't play the hero. Actually call. Understood?"

"Jason. You know I'm not the hero type."

"Just be careful. I don't wanna add you to the list of people I'm searching for."

Mac appreciated Jason's concern, and it matched his own. Ghosts, vengeful spirits, poltergeists… he could handle the paranormal, but serial killers?

He turned toward the door, his mind entirely locked on Caleb and the bar. He could feel it. It was the last piece of the puzzle. Something was waiting for him at Front 9. Lyndsay, the killer, something else. Whatever it was, it was time to face it.

CHAPTER 16

KARAOKE AND ANXIETY

Cars lined both sides of the street—more than usual. The bar was already buzzing, even though it was only 7:30. He checked his watch again, surprised. Bit early for this kind of crowd.

Circling around to the back lot, he found only the drugstore spaces still open and pulled in. He climbed out, shut the door, and made his way toward the bar's rear entrance.

He walked down the hallway, past the bathrooms that opened up to the bar near the stage area, which was packed with patrons.

Shit. Karaoke night.

He already dreaded the clamor—drunken renditions of songs he didn't know or classics butchered beyond repair. His nerves were still frayed, and knowing what was coming wasn't helping.

He made his way to the bar, avoiding the people as best he could, weaving between folks too lost in their festivities to care about avoiding collisions. They milled about, most hovering near the stage, flipping through song menus. Others staked out tables at the back, overpriced beers in hand. It was a night of young, careless fun—a revelry at odds with the reality Mac knew: a serial killer was potentially lurking out there.

As he pushed through the crowd and found a spot at the bar, he scanned every face, every corner, looking for any sign of Lyndsay but finding only patrons. The bartender, a young woman he'd never seen there before, looked up and saw Mac.

"What ya havin'?" she asked, which meant she was definitely new. Everyone at Front 9 had known for months not to serve him. Oddly for Mac, the question didn't even register.

"Hey, you seen Caleb?" he asked, leaning against the counter.

She shook her head tightly. "Not yet. He gets here a bit later on Thursdays. You want something while you wait?"

The question hit him the second time, and his eyes darted to the lower shelf of whiskeys. For a fleeting moment, he considered it. *One or two shots wouldn't hurt*, he thought, but he ultimately shook it off. "Just a Coke," he said.

As he waited, he felt a tension building—slow and insidious, just like the last time. Like someone was watching him. He tapped his fingers lightly against the bar as he looked around again, hoping he'd find Lyndsay and that it was her affecting him this way, but she still wasn't there.

After about fifteen minutes of waiting, and the self-diagnosed paranoia building, the front door swung open and Caleb walked in. Mac watched as he exchanged nods and hellos with a few of the regulars, who reacted to him like someone famous had just walked in. It was a small town, and when you own the only bar, you get real important to the locals.

He finally noticed Mac and immediately walked over to him, smirking. "That better be soda in that glass," he said, looking down at an untouched glass of Coke next to Mac.

"Still not here for drinks, Caleb," he replied, keeping his tone serious on purpose. "I need to ask you a few more questions about Joanne."

Caleb's smirk faded. "I still haven't seen her."

Mac motioned for Caleb to follow him to a quieter corner of the room in the back, away from all the would-be rock stars.

"You were here the last night she worked, right?" Mac asked.

He nodded and held his hands up like he was answering the dumbest of questions. "Yeah, Mac. I'm here every night. I own the place."

"You notice anything unusual? Anyone hangin' around? Paying her too much attention?"

"Honestly, everyone pays her too much attention. She works for tips… she kinda likes it that way, ya know? But no, nothing out of the ordinary. She seemed fine when she left."

Mac wanted to press further—there was something there, something he knew would help—but before he could speak, his chest exploded with pressure, cutting him off.

The anxiety was back, stronger than before. It coiled around him like a vise, cutting his breaths in half, his heart pounding in his chest and ears. It came on suddenly, like getting hit in the chest with a baseball bat, and he doubled over, wrapping his arms around his stomach.

"You okay?" Caleb asked with sincere concern in his voice, but Mac couldn't respond. He swept the room, looking for Lyndsay or anything that could explain the way he was feeling.

"You're… like, really pale, Mac."

Mac's gaze finally locked on to a small grouping of tables near the front of the bar. A man, unremarkable at first, sat with his back to the bar—bald, jeans, and a worn jacket—but something about him prickled at Mac's senses. Dread, fear, and anxiety all washed over him like a waterfall as the pressure inside his chest sharpened, centered on this man.

He felt Caleb's hand press against his back.

"Mac?"

He stepped back, keeping his focus tight on the man as he stood and pushed back his chair. Every movement the man took sent a surge of energy through the room—a disturbance that dropped the temperature and thickened the air.

Then it happened.

A shadow burst out of the man—thick, black, unnatural, twisting and writhing around the man as it emerged, blotting out the light and filling the bar with darkness. Its shape was monstrous—jagged, shifting, its molten eyes burning with an intensity that seared the very air.

In all the years dealing with the supernatural, Mac had seen nothing like it. His eyes blurred as the shadow coiled around the man, obscuring him from view. The bar faded into darkness, and the noise from the patrons became a distant hum. The spirit—if that's what it was—fixed its many eyes on Mac, and it was like it was reaching in and yanking the anxiety up through his chest. It was suffocating and deliberate.

He stumbled back, bumping into Caleb, who grabbed him by the arm to steady him. "Mac, what the hell's going on?"

The fear was intense, like nothing he'd ever felt before, but he couldn't look away. It moved no closer to him, but its presence was overwhelming—a smothering force that pulsed with malevolence.

The man, and his shadowy cloak, turned and began walking toward the door, moving with an unsettling calm. Mac tried to follow, but his legs wouldn't move. The spirit lingered, blocking Mac's view of the man, as if intentionally protecting his anonymity.

"Mac!" Caleb yelled, cutting through the haze and grounding him. The spirit wavered and dissolved into nothingness as the man left the bar, and instantly, everything was back to normal. No shadow, no sign of the man—just a room full of people enjoying their evenings. No one else saw what Mac had seen.

He blinked as his pulse and breathing slowed back to normal. *What the fuck was that?*

Caleb stood over him, a strained worry in his eyes, waiting for an explanation. But Mac had nothing to offer him. He was still processing everything himself, and his mind was racing as he looked back toward the door. He felt exposed, like the thing had just shined a light directly on him as all the other lights dimmed.

"You okay?"

Mac brushed past him, ignoring the question. "I need air," he muttered.

His legs shook as he rushed out of the bar, like he'd just run a marathon. He nodded absently at the familiar faces he passed, in a desperate attempt to seem normal. It was over, but there was an echo lingering in his chest, like something had reached in and touched his very soul.

The crisp air outside slapped him in the face, jolting his senses back to normal. The door shut behind him, muting the sounds of the bar, and he took a few deep, deliberate breaths. It helped a little—the pressure in his chest eased, but his mind was still swimming.

He caught some movement out of the corner of his eye and turned just in time to see the man rounding the corner of the drugstore. A sane man might have let it go, but Mac pushed forward. He had to know. The need for answers wrestled with the fear of facing whatever that shadow was, and it won the fight.

He hurried around the corner, unsure of what he would find when he caught up, but there was no sign of him—just an empty alley lined with dumpsters and lit by a single flickering bulb. A chill ran through him as he scanned the shadows, his breath misting in the cold air. He felt the pressure in his chest again—not as strong as before, but enough to set his nerves on edge. He didn't feel alone in that alley.

"Jesus," he muttered under his breath as he backed out of the alley, clenching his fists at his sides. Whatever was out there, he wasn't ready to face it—not yet, not without a plan.

Back in the parking lot, he looked over at the bar, where Caleb was watching him from the back door. Mac had no explanation to give for what just happened—not one that would make sense to Caleb.

He climbed into his truck, still shaking from the encounter, and gripped the steering wheel. Sitting there for a moment, staring out over the lot, he churned through everything he'd just experienced.

That wasn't just another spirit. It was something worse. Something dangerous. There was no way it wasn't tied to Joanne and Lyndsay. He gripped the wheel and exhaled, forcing himself to focus.

He needed answers, and there was only one person who might have them.

CHAPTER 17

CONFRONTING DOE

The long drive to Denver did nothing to calm him down after his encounter at the bar. If anything, it had given him time to find a million ways to blame John for all the things going on. He flung open the door, slamming it into one of the display cases in the shop, and screamed, "John!"

John rushed out of the back office, visibly rattled by the commotion. "What the hell, Mac?"

John walked toward him, seething. "Yeah, that's the question," Mac said as he weaved aggressively through the displays and tables, closing the distance between them. "What the hell?"

John stopped and stepped back instinctively. He furrowed his brow with a look of shock and concern as Mac loomed closer. "All right, calm down. What happened?"

"Calm down?" Mac shot back, his voice cracking with fury. "Don't you dare tell me to calm down, John. Do you have any idea what I've been through… what you've put me through?"

John softened his tone and put his hands up in a placating gesture. "Mac, I don't know what you're talking about… but I'm listening. Just—start at the beginning."

"Oh, you want me to start from the beginning?" he said, letting out a bitter laugh. "You mean, Josie? My wife? The beginning is when she died, John. When you killed her. When you showed up with your cryptic warnings and your goddamned ghosts. Before you, there was none of this shit. No poltergeists, no shadow monsters—none of it."

"Mac…" John's voice wavered. "Josie's death—"

"Don't!" Mac snapped. "Don't you say her name, and don't you *dare* say it wasn't your fault," he roared as he took another step forward. "This all starts with you. Josie, Lyndsay, Joanne, my pathetic life. All of it. You brought this into my life. You brought this into the world."

John's jaw tightened, and Mac saw a hint of guilt flickering behind his eyes, but the man held his ground. "I am not the enemy here, Mac. Whatever happened—whatever you saw—it's not something I brought. Please, just tell me what happened so I can help you."

"You don't help. You never help. It's always some cryptic bullshit or backhanded promise that ends up biting me in the ass. You think you've helped me? You've ruined everything, and now Joanne…" Tears welled in his eyes as he fought to continue his sentence. His anger was giving way to sorrow, which was not a weakness he was willing to expose to John in that moment. He steeled himself and stood even straighter. "Joanne is going to die because of you."

They stared at each other for a moment while Mac caught his breath. John said nothing, which just made Mac even angrier—

although in truth, any word that came out of his mouth at that point would have done the same thing. "You've cursed me. I see them everywhere, every damned day, and now… the one time this stupid… gift… might be even remotely useful… Fuck you, John."

John's patience finally broke, and he'd had enough. His concern hardened to rage, and he straightened his posture, taking a step forward. "You think I wanted this for you? For anyone?" he asked in a way that made it clear it wasn't a question. "You don't know what you're talking about, Mitchel."

Mac refused to back down. He knew John was powerful, more powerful than even he knew. He was sure of it. But this was his time to let him have it. It had gone on for too long, and he had nothing to show for it.

"I know enough," Mac snarled back, matching John's forward step. "I know that you're the reason for all of it. All the pain, all the death—it's on you!"

Something shifted in John's stance. His calm, snobby, but approachable demeanor melted away, leaving something hard in its place, something otherworldly. His dark eyes locked on to Mac's with a new intensity that froze him mid-step.

"Mac, listen to me." His voice resonated, almost reverberating through the air. "I understand you are angry, but you need to stop. Right now."

"Or what?" Mac challenged. "You'll sic another shadow monster on me? Another ghost? What, John? What else are you hiding?"

"Hiding?" John shook his head as his patience finally snapped. With a sharp, fluid motion, he raised his hand, and the air around them surged. A gust of wind whipped through the shop, rattling shelves and scattering small items onto the floor as it passed through. Mac froze as he watched the display and the gust turn into a forceful, invisible grip against his chest, slamming him back against the wall. His shoulders pressed against the wooden planks, and he struggled to break free, but the harder he fought, the stronger the unseen force held him in place.

"What the hell, John?" he shouted, still struggling against the pressure.

"I warned you," John replied, keeping his voice steady, as if it was all too easy for him. "You're not listening, so now I am going to make you listen."

Mac gritted his teeth and allowed his anger to swell against his better judgment. He knew John could end him. It would be simple for him, and he probably wouldn't give it a second thought, but Mac was tired and beginning to not care. John must have seen it coming as Mac opened his mouth to retort because before he could speak again, John raised his other hand.

The flickering candlelight scattered through the shop dimmed as the flames began bending and stretching toward him, as if he was drawing them in. One by one, the candles extinguished, and Mac could only watch as their light was siphoned into a glowing ember in John's palm. Quickly it grew, twisting and stretching into a slender, fiery dagger that hovered just above his hand, its edges razor sharp and shimmering with heat.

Mac's eyes widened. He'd seen John do some crazy things in the past, but this was new. The dagger turned, still floating in the air, the tip aimed directly at him.

"John…" Mac said, now pleading as his earlier bravado faltered. "What are you doing?"

He didn't answer immediately, and with a flick of his fingers, the dagger flew through the air, stopping short of Mac's throat. He could feel the heat on his neck, forcing him to push his head back against the wall to avoid it.

"You need to calm down, Mac," he huffed. "Because if you don't, you're going to keep making mistakes. Mistakes get people killed… do you understand?"

Mac's chest heaved, his eyes darting between the blade and John's unyielding expression, and he felt the grip on his shoulders tighten briefly before easing again—a reminder from John about the power he held.

He slowly stepped closer to Mac, the dagger flickering a tiny bit as he moved. "This isn't a game, and I am not out to hurt you. Whatever happened, this shadow monster you keep talking about—if you keep letting your anger blind you, you're going to lose everything."

Mac knew he was right, even before all of this started. He'd been angry every day of his life since Josie died. No matter how hard he tried, he couldn't get rid of it, and most days he just wanted to scream at everyone or anyone who crossed his path. He had filled the bottle, and it was finally spilling over. There was a lot of blame that belonged to John, but he had no real reason to believe most of what he'd been saying.

John must have seen that he was coming down from his rage because he reached out to the fiery blade and dissolved it back into a tiny ember in his hand before a bunch of tiny pieces broke off, shooting back to the candles they came from. The room again lit up, the pressure holding him against the wall diminished, and Mac staggered forward.

"I'll let you down," John said evenly, "but only if you promise to calm down and talk to me like a rational human being. Can you do that?"

Mac hesitated, out of pride more than anything else, but eventually gave him a terse nod. "Fine."

John's hand subtly flicked, and the wind dissipated fully, freeing Mac from its grip. He glared at John, his anger still simmering beneath the surface, but for now, the unease John's display of power had planted in him kept it in check.

John crossed his arms and sighed. "Good," he said in a more friendly tone. "Now. What happened?"

John walked into the back office, and Mac followed, plopping down on an old, worn couch, its cushions sagging under his weight. The air in the room was thick with the musty scent of aged wood, incense, and old dusty books. He leaned forward, putting his elbows on his knees, and ran a hand through his hair as he processed the events of the day.

John didn't sit and instead leaned against the edge of his desk, his arms still crossed while he watched Mac patiently. The tension in the room was palpable, and Mac wasn't sure how to begin, embarrassed about the way he entered the shop.

"Just start from the beginning," John said again.

Mac leaned back on the couch, staring up at the ceiling while he figured out where to begin. "There's… something about Lyndsay," he said. "I'm thinking she can affect people… like, emotionally. I first noticed it at the police station. My friend Jason was practically in tears while we were there. Then there was this couple arguing at the bar—happened right as she was remembering something from before she died. And then again at the crime scene—"

"Crime scene?" John interrupted. "What crime scene?"

"We… sorta found this unmarked grave and thought it was her. When they pulled out the body, she kind of went weird… angry… I don't know. But it affected everyone there. And when she disappeared, it all stopped, like nothing had happened."

John frowned. "What about you? Does she affect you?"

"I dunno, I thought so, maybe, but now I think it's something else."

"This shadow monster you mentioned?"

Mac held his breath for a moment, trying to keep himself calm, and then let out a big sigh. "I don't even know how to describe it," he admitted, his voice still raw. "This guy at the bar—he looked normal at first, just some dude sitting near the pool tables, then… this thing came out of him. A shadow, but like alive. It looked right at me like it knew me."

John scratched at his stubble while he thought, and his eyes narrowed. "Could you feel anything?"

"Yeah… It didn't, like, touch me or anything, but it might as well have," Mac said as his hands balled into fists. "The entire bar went dark, like it swallowed the light. It had at least fifty eyes. And the pressure, my god, it felt like it was crushing my chest. Then, just like that, it was gone. The guy walked out like nothing happened."

"Anything else?"

"Yeah, it completely obscured the man, like it was trying to hide him from me as he walked out."

John nodded, like he knew what Mac was talking about. He pushed off the desk and walked over to a tall, dusty bookcase lining the back wall. His fingers traced the spines of the books, searching until he pulled out a thick leatherbound tome with faded gold lettering: *The Elementalist's Guide to Ghosts and Spirits.*

He turned back to Mac, holding the book and smiling. "The *EGGS*," he said, the levity in his voice not quite masking the seriousness in his eyes.

Mac stared at him. "The… egg?"

"E-G-G-S, Mac. Plural," he replied while flipping the book open and thumbing through the pages. "If what you are describing is what I think it is, you've encountered something far worse than a ghost."

"Yeah, I kinda picked up on that," Mac shot back. "What was it?"

He stopped on a page and set the book down on the coffee table in front of the couch, showing Mac an illustration of a shadowy humanoid figure surrounded by jagged, chaotic lines, four heads, and hundreds of eyes. Beneath it, intricate symbols and scribbled annotations described its nature.

"A phantom," he said. "They aren't your ordinary spirits. It's not even a singular ghost, really. They're born out of extreme negative emotions like fear, rage, despair. The more traumatic, the better."

"Kind of sounds like a poltergeist?"

John nodded. "Not quite the same… they're like cousins. They're both born the same way, but poltergeists bind to objects—like your house—and feed on anything that comes across 'em. Phantoms attach to people."

"People? Anyone?"

"No, not just anyone," John clarified, his expression getting darker. "They choose hosts who have the capacity to kill… When someone dies at the hands of a phantom's host, it feeds on the newly created spirit. It feeds off the trauma, the fear, the death, and it grows stronger each time."

"So… what?" Mac asked, his mind racing. "This guy at the bar was… what? A murderer? The serial killer?"

"If a phantom was attached to the guy." He nodded. "It's likely. Serial killers are ideal hosts. The torment and torture, the way the person dies—it all comes together to create powerful ghosts. And the stronger the ghost, the better the meal, and the more power the phantom gets from it."

Mac thought of Lyndsay's spirit, the pain and desperation in their first encounters still vivid in his mind. "Lyndsay," he muttered. "Is that why she was so… different?"

John's eyes turned up, like he was considering something new that had struck him, and his fingers began tapping the pages of the book. "You know. It shouldn't be possible for a ghost to escape a phantom. That kind of grip, that power… it's absolute. Unless… unless she's something more."

"More?" Mac asked, wondering what other fun things John was about to reveal. "Like what? What does that mean?"

"No clue," John admitted plainly. "We should figure that out."

"So… what do we do?"

"Well, first we figure out how to track it. Then, we deal with the phantom—and its host."

"We?" Mac asked, skeptical. "You don't usually get involved."

John's expression turned hard. "If what you are dealing with truly is a phantom, you can't do this on your own. It isn't some wayward ghost you can chant at until it moves on, or even just some killer you can track down and apprehend. It's both. They feed on each other. The phantom and its host are one thing, and it gets stronger with every kill."

Mac swallowed hard. "But… you can kill it, right?"

John smirked, and Mac assumed his normal bravado was about to spill forth, but it wasn't anything nearly as assuring. "Honestly? I've never faced a phantom before."

Mac, unimpressed by John's admission yet grudgingly impressed that he would admit it, stood up from the couch and took a step toward him. "Look, it's great that you want to help, and trust me, I'm not about to turn that down. But he's seen me. He knows I'm looking for him. What do I do if you aren't there when one of us finds the other?"

John didn't respond right away. Maybe because he didn't have an answer. Maybe because he wasn't ready to fully commit. Either way, it was clear to Mac that he needed to be prepared to fight without John.

"Teach me," Mac said firmly. "All this time, you've let me fumble through this on my own, figuring out bits and pieces as I go." He gestured toward the front of the shop. "I've seen what you can do. Teach me to do it."

"Mac…" John interjected, pushing off the desk to stand. "We are not the same."

Mac frowned but didn't interrupt as John continued. "What I do—it's not something you can just… learn. It's part of who I am and where I come from. I was born with it. I brought it with me to this place."

John rounded the desk and sat in his chair, his tone growing more reflective. He pulled the *EGGS* back toward him, flipping through the pages until he reached an entry near the end, handwritten and newer than the rest. After a moment of hesitation, he slid the book across the desk and turned it to face Mac.

"The night I met you, Mac…" John began, his voice quieter now. "I was battling a necromancer… *the* necromancer, really. Anyway, the blast you and your wife got caught up in? That was because I wasn't strong enough to win a fight like that yet. I had to set off what was basically a psychic nuke to stop him."

Mac's eyes flicked to the page in front of him. Scrawled at the top was a word that made his brow furrow. "Threshwalker?" he read aloud, glancing back up at John.

John nodded slowly. "You were like nothing I'd ever seen before—not in my world, or this one."

Mac caught the phrasing and shot John a sharp look.

"What does that mean, exactly… 'your world'?"

"That might be a story I could tell you another time, Mac," John continued. "It's my belief that the necromancy in that battle, combined with your overwhelming desire to be with your wife after her final moments, caused you to… step across—one foot into the veil. And you've been walking that threshold ever since."

Mac's breath hitched as he let that sink in. "So, I'm… what? This 'Threshwalker' thing in your book? If it's never happened before, why does it even have a name?"

John leaned back in his chair. "I wrote that after we met. You're the first… maybe the only one of your kind. You don't just see spirits; you interact with them because you live partially in the world, just like they do in ours."

He stared at John, his thoughts connecting as the pieces clicked into place, though for every answer, there were three more questions.

"So what does that mean for me?" he asked quietly. "What do I do with that?"

"I wish I had more answers for you, Mac. This is uncharted territory for both of us."

"Figures. So here I am, one foot in, but I can't really do anything."

Mac could see a thought forming in John's face as he stared off across the room. "What is it?"

"I think we should speak with Lyndsay," he said, bringing his attention back to the conversation.

"I haven't seen her since she vanished from the crime scene."

John smirked. "That's okay. I can fix that."

Mac watched, out of the way, as John carefully poured soil from a small cloth bag, forming a circle in the middle of the room just large enough for a single person to stand in. Once the circle was complete, he kneeled at the edge, smoothing it out with his hand, meticulously perfecting it and ensuring there were no breaks.

"Why not salt?" Mac asked. After years of dealing with ghosts, he knew how effective salt was in these rituals.

John glanced up and smiled. "Salt is good for binding or repelling. Earth is connective. It's like a tether to our world—it's where we all come from, and where we all end up. This soil's consecrated. It will act as an anchor to draw her in."

He stood up and walked over to the sink in the adjoining room, then filled a shallow metal bowl with water before setting it carefully in the middle of the ring. "And this will act as a sort of resonance chamber," he continued. "It will amplify my call… whether she's flitting about here or buried deep in the veil, she'll hear it."

Mac continued watching in silence as he moved with a practiced precision. He pulled a small dagger from a cluttered cabinet and unsheathed it, pressing the blade hard against his palm.

They both winced as he sliced the blade across his skin, a thin line of blood welling up instantly. John clenched his fist, holding it over the bowl as drops of blood trickled into the water, spreading out like ink, forming curling little tendrils that sank unnaturally fast to the bottom.

Mac grimaced—he never really liked the sight of blood, and these sorts of witchy rituals always involved some form of bodily fluid, something he never got used to. "Is the blood really necessary?"

"Everything costs something," he replied matter-of-factly. "You want something brought back, you give something first. Blood is life—it's a fair trade for the dead."

Mac rolled his eyes. He could never tell if John was just messing with him or if he really believed the weird things he said. Either way, he usually got results, so he scoffed in silence. He watched as John took his place just outside the circle, closing his eyes, and began chanting. His voice dropped about two octaves as he spoke the strange words.

After a minute of chanting sounds and words Mac had never heard before, he began speaking English again. "Lyndsay, personification of sorrow and hope. We call you from beyond the veil. Come to us who seek you. The door is open, and the path is clear. Hear my voice and follow."

Personification of sorrow and hope? Mac groaned. Did he practice this stuff in a mirror?

There was no way in his mind that these theatrics were real. But as if on cue, the air thickened and the soil edges of the circle trembled. There was a slight ripple in the water, even though the room remained utterly still.

Mac stared down at the bowl, nervous about what could happen next, and then a faint mist rose from the water, curling upward in twisty tendrils that seemed to wriggle like a living thing. A glow formed from inside the bowl, and the ripples were starting from tiny fleeting patterns, like letters or symbols, before fading again.

He wanted to ask John if he was seeing the same thing but swallowed his questions down, assuming John knew what he was doing and shouldn't be interrupted. But the air inside the circle radiated cold. So cold he could feel it even from where he stood. Not a cool breeze—the air was still. More like what a campfire would feel like if it gave off cold instead of heat.

"This feels wrong," he muttered.

John chuckled but kept his attention on the ritual. "Yeah, it should," he answered. "Necromancy's about as dark as it gets."

He continued chanting, and the mist coalesced into a shape. It was faint and wavering but unmistakably human. Mac almost gasped as the outline sharpened in the circle.

"Lyndsay?" he whispered.

For a moment, nothing happened, and the shape didn't respond. Then, from behind him, Mac heard a soft voice, hesitant and fragile, bouncing off the wall behind him. "Help me."

He froze as he heard the words. It was the same thing Lyndsay had tried to say when they first met. He turned slowly, hoping to see her standing in the corner, his heart pounding the whole way, but there was nothing there, just the dim light from the shop. Then he heard it again, this time echoing through the entire office. "Help me."

The figure in the circle shifted as the mist curled tighter around it. "Help me," the voice repeated, this time coming from the circle, clearer and more precise. Mac squinted as he watched the details forming on the woman—the curve of a shoulder, the fall of her hair. It wasn't Lyndsay.

The figure was shorter than Lyndsay, nearly a foot. Her hair was long, curly, and reddish and fell in loose waves around a pale, youthful face. The spirit couldn't have been more than twenty years old, by the look of her. Mac stumbled back a step, unsure what they had just conjured.

"Interesting," John said, causing the spirit to snap her gaze directly at him. Her expression turned angry as she stared at him. "Okay…"

"Something… It feels like I know her," Mac said, though he didn't really recognize her. He'd never seen her before, but there seemed to be a connection that he couldn't quite pinpoint. A feeling just outside his comprehension. It wasn't just recognition; it was a deeper familiarity, a sense of belonging… almost familial, and it clawed at his chest. He couldn't look away.

The spirit looked back toward Mac, and her expression softened. "Mac," she said with a tremble in her voice. "Please… help me."

He took a step toward the circle. He didn't understand why, and he hadn't given his legs the command to do so. Something was tugging at him, and for whatever reason, he wasn't resisting.

"Who are you?" he asked, keeping his voice low and quiet. "How do I—"

"Stop!" John interrupted, but Mac barely registered it. The spirit's eyes had locked on to his, and the pull was growing stronger, overwhelming him.

"Mac, get back!" John's voice rose dramatically. "That is not Lyndsay!"

"It's not?" he replied, though even as the words left his mouth, he didn't care. He couldn't care. His feet moved him forward, drawn toward the circle, and the air around the spirit shimmered as her form grew more solid with each passing second.

John's expression hardened as he raised his hand, snapping his fingers. The sound cracked through the office like a thunderclap, and in an instant, the glow from the bowl extinguished and the mist evaporated, the spirit with it.

Mac instinctively lurched forward, grabbing at the air above the bowl as John kicked it, spilling water and breaking the circle of soil. The energy in the room dissipated all at once, leaving nothing but a heavy, suffocating silence.

"What the hell did you do?" Mac shouted, whirling around to John.

John stared at him, his jaw tight. "I saved your ass. Jesus, you're like a magnet for these things."

Mac, still coming down from the haze she'd created in him, shook his head, his anger rising again. "She needed help."

"I don't know what that was, Mac, but it wasn't Lyndsay—and it was about to pull you into the veil," he said, before pausing a moment. "I don't know that I would have been able to pull you back."

Mac understood what he was saying, but part of him was still enthralled. The cobwebs were clearing, but he wasn't quite there yet. Suddenly, a voice called from the doorway.

"What are you guys up to?"

They both snapped their attention toward Lyndsay, casually leaning against the doorframe, watching them with a mix of curiosity and amusement.

"You're both sweating. It's a little gross," she added, scrunching her nose.

A quiet tension filled the room as Mac and John processed Lyndsay's sudden appearance. John squinted at her incredulously as Mac hurried over. "Where have you been?" he demanded, his voice sharp with relief and frustration.

"I've been here," she said matter-of-factly, gesturing around the shop. "Watching you guys call that spirit. Who was she?"

"You were here the whole time?" Mac asked. "Watching us?"

"Yeah, I got here right as the chanting started, or whatever that was. It was kind of fun… then it felt weird. Like something was pressing down on me." She peered at the tipped-over bowl on the ground. "Then that woman showed up, and you started acting all weird. I didn't want to interrupt. That seemed… unwise."

John stared at her, flabbergasted. "You didn't think to say something when I was calling your name?"

"I was curious," she shot back defensively. "Figured you knew what you were doing. Clearly, I gave you too much credit."

John grumbled as he cleaned up the mess, scooping up the loose soil back into the bag.

"Who was that girl?" she asked, turning to Mac. "She seemed sad. She looked at you like you were the only thing that could help her."

Mac glanced over at John, who was still cleaning dirt up off the floor.

"Don't look at me like that," John said, defending his actions. "That thing was dangerous… no matter how sad she was."

"She was asking for help," Mac said. "And we just got her back. What if—"

"Yes, Mac, what if," John interrupted, standing straight with a bag of dirt in one hand and an empty bowl in the other. "What if she'd pulled you into the veil? That's what they do. You were literal seconds away from it, and you'd have cursed me for eternity for screwing up your life… again."

Mac stood there, smiling inwardly, enjoying the rant he just induced from John. His head was clear now, and he knew the situation was no good, but riling John up was a rare pleasure.

"Okay, so… what was she, then?"

John placed the bag and bowl back onto a shelf and turned to Lyndsay. "She's not the problem at hand," he said, regaining his seriousness. "It's you I'm curious about."

Mac stepped forward, putting himself between John and Lyndsay. "Where did you go? At the cemetery. You vanished. What happened?"

She started to answer and then stopped, dropping her arms to her sides as her confident facade faltered. She looked away, and for the first time since she returned, she was serious. "I didn't mean to."

"One minute you were there, then you, like, exploded. Did something happen?"

Lyndsay's face was contemplative as she moved farther into the room until she was side by side with Mac. "I… remembered," she said finally, her voice trembling. "When I saw that body, it was like a flood of memories coming back all at once. They just slammed into me."

Mac turned to face her. "What did you remember?"

Her expression darkened as she turned her head to face Mac. "Everything."

CHAPTER 18

EVERYTHING

Mac perched himself against the doorframe, and John sat in a chair near his desk. The air was thick with a tense stillness as they both watched and waited for Lyndsay to explain what she had remembered. She brushed her fingers above the arm of the couch, as if she was trying to find something solid to ground her, then she sat on the floor. Her casual confidence faded, replaced by a quiet, haunted look.

"What do you want to know?"

Mac leaned forward, trying to keep himself calm and collected for her, though he was eager to know. "Tell us, tell us everything."

"I'd just finished my shift at the bar," she started. "It was only my second night. It was quiet, nothing out of the ordinary. Joanne offered to give me a ride home, but she was closing up and I didn't want to wait. So I walked."

"Hold on," Mac interrupted. "You worked at Front 9? With Joanne?"

Lyndsay looked up, startled by the intensity in his voice. "Yeah," she said softly. "Joanne was training me. She was nice."

Mac shot a look at John, his frustration mounting. "That's where I saw the phantom," he said.

John nodded and gestured to Lyndsay, the look on his face telling Mac to let her finish. "Go on."

"I cut through the cemetery, like I always do. I like to stop and talk to my friend a bit. Anyway, I know it's not the smartest thing, but I usually take the path through the woods; it's faster. It was dark, but I had my phone. I didn't see anyone or hear anything—until I did."

Her hands trembled as she recounted the memory. Mac could see the humanity returning and the toll it took on her. Every instinct he had pushed him to move closer, comfort her, hold her hand. Actions he knew her shimmering form could not accept.

"It was faint at first—just footsteps. I assumed it was someone else cutting through, like I was, and didn't think too much of it, but then I felt it. You know, that feeling like someone's watching you? I turned around, but there was no one there. I started walking faster, and that's where everything went dark."

"You don't know what happened?" Mac pressed.

She shook her head. "No, not until I woke up."

John leaned forward. "Where?"

"In the trunk of a car," she said plainly. "My head was pounding, and I could barely move—I think he'd hit me. There was another girl in there with me, lying next to me. She looked… like me. It was dark, but I remember thinking we could be sisters. She wasn't moving."

"Did you recognize her?" Mac asked.

"Not then, no… but it was the woman we found in the woods."

"You remember anything else?" John pressed.

"Yes," she said as something hit her. "It smelled terrible, and the trunk lid had all these little trees hanging from it. You know, the pine-scented ones?"

Mac listened and processed as best he could. He thought about Joanne and wondered if her story would match Lyndsay's. It was hard to imagine the fear he put them through.

"He opened the trunk, and I stayed as quiet as I could, hoping he wouldn't notice I was awake. He grabbed her first, the other girl, and pulled her out. When he came back, he saw me watching. That's when he stuck a needle in my neck. It was so fast, I didn't even have time to scream. Everything went black until I woke up in that cell."

Everyone stayed quiet for a minute, letting everything sink in, until John broke the silence. "You didn't see his face?"

"Not then, no," Lyndsay said, shaking her head. "It was dark, and I think he kept it hidden on purpose. I don't know how long he kept me." She continued, "The room I was in was always dark. I tried counting every time I slept, to… you know, keep track of the days, but it all blurred together."

"You were in the dark the whole time?" Mac asked.

"He would come in every so often, either to feed me or to…" She paused, her voice catching as she tried to keep her composure. "Do other things. I remember the light filling the room when he'd open the door and becoming thankful for those moments."

Mac had grown increasingly uncomfortable, his jaw tightening. "My God," he whispered.

John leaned forward. "Lyndsay, I need to ask you something," he said carefully. "It may be hard, but it's important." He hesitated, as if choosing his next words carefully. "Do you remember being killed?"

She looked away, as though trying to hide from the question. "He talked about meeting another woman." Her voice shook as she spoke. She turned to Mac, her eyes filling with sorrow. "I know now it must have been Joanne. He said it was time for me to go home, to be with my family again… I knew he was lying, but I wanted so badly to believe it. I was… hopeful. Stupid, I guess."

"Your death," John repeated. "What happened?"

He seemed very keen on the specific detail. Mac didn't understand why it mattered, but he didn't interrupt.

"He dragged me to the room where he always took me to… do things, but this time was different. He was angry, and I knew it was the end."

Her hands clenched as she continued. She looked deep into Mac's eyes, and he could feel her desperation. "I couldn't let him kill me, Mac. I… broke free, and I did it for him."

Her entire form trembled as she released a sob. Mac moved in instinctively, kneeling down beside her and wrapping his arms around her. As he hugged her, he glanced over at John, who had a strange expression on his face, not sadness or understanding like he'd expected, but confusion.

"What is it?" Mac asked him, still holding his embrace with Lyndsay.

His eyes narrowed as he watched the two of them. "You don't realize you're touching her?"

Mac recoiled from her as he realized what John was saying. She was almost solid. He hesitated before reaching out again, letting his fingertips brush hers. It wasn't like touching skin—it was colder and softer, like the surrounding air had thickened into something tangible, but it was there. She was there.

John looked deep into Lyndsay's confused eyes. "I know what you are."

The tension John had just created with his cryptic revelation was palpable as Mac and Lyndsay waited to hear the rest. Before John could continue, Mac's phone rang, cutting through the silence and startling everyone. He fumbled to grab it from his pocket, expecting to send the caller to voicemail, but he saw it was Jason and answered.

"Hi, Jason, what is it?" he asked, bringing the phone to his ear.

Jason wasted even less time than Mac, skipping the pleasantries altogether. "We found another body," he said. "The feds… they brought in some cadaver dog. Turns out there are a few other bodies near the one you found."

Mac felt something drop into his stomach. A cold knot had formed as his thoughts spiraled to the name he dreaded hearing—Joanne.

"Mac… it's Lyndsay."

Though he was relieved not to hear Joanne's name, his chest tightened as he looked over to Lyndsay, now waiting to find out what Jason was telling him. It wasn't like he didn't know she was dead and that this moment was inevitable. But seeing her there, with her memories restored, kind of solid, almost alive—it made the news feel like a fresh loss. He drew in a sharp breath and forced himself to ask the question. "And Joanne?"

"No," Jason answered quickly. "Thankfully. Older cases. But there is something else."

Mac wanted to be glad that they hadn't found Joanne along with the other bodies. He wasn't ready for something else yet. "What is it?"

"The cause of death. All the other women were strangled, all of 'em, but Lyndsay…" He paused. "Her throat was cut. Everything else matches, but that's different."

Mac locked eyes with Lyndsay. Sadness flickered in his gaze as he processed Jason's words. "She killed herself," he mumbled, more to himself than Jason. "She didn't want him to win."

"What's he saying?" Lyndsay's voice rose, her tone demanding as she stood up from the couch. Her form flickered, faint and unstable, and Mac's grip on the phone tightened.

"Thanks, Jason," he said curtly and dropped the phone into his pocket before turning back to Lyndsay. "They found your body."

His words seemed to hit Lyndsay like a wave. He watched as her form flickered, growing more unstable. "What?" she said. "Where?"

"Not far from the other woman…"

She disappeared again, her form dissolving into nothing. He sighed, staring at the space where she'd just stood, wondering why he couldn't keep her in one place for long.

"Dammit," John said, slamming his hand on the desk. "That's not good."

"Yeah, it's an annoying habit."

He turned and saw something in John's face. It was more than just frustration about the untethered ghost. "You good?"

"No," John said as he stepped closer. "You don't understand what she is. We need to get her back before it's too late."

Mac stepped back, confused and a little concerned about the intensity in John's voice. "Too late for what?"

John shook his head as his expression hardened. "Lyndsay isn't a ghost. She's a sub seeker."

Mac nodded, trying to play along, but John's words meant about as much as a punchline to a joke he hadn't heard. "What the hell is a sub seeker?"

Mac listened as John told the story of spirits born from deaths shrouded in desperation—the kind that drives someone to take their own life. That act, literally choosing death in a moment of unbearable torment, anchors a spirit to the veil, unable to move on.

He glanced over at the spot she'd vanished from. "So she's stuck here?" Mac asked. "Forever?"

"The torment becomes a driving force for a sub seeker, their purpose. And it doesn't stop with them."

"What do you mean?"

John looked puzzled, with a concern on his face that Mac had never seen before. "They don't haunt people... they infect them. Their emotions bleed and pour out into anyone around them—sorrow, rage, desperation."

Mac thought back to all the times the people around him broke down while she was there. He knew she was probably the reason, but this sounded much worse.

"It manifests differently in different people, but it's always there, spreading like wildfire."

Mac swallowed, thinking back to Jason, the cop at the gravesite, and the couple at the bar. It all made sense.

"So we need to find her," Mac said, like it was the most obvious thing.

"We need to do more than find her, Mac. She's driven by one thing: passing her suffering on to someone else. To create a substitute, someone to take her place. Feed all that pain and desperation into someone else, recreating the events leading up to her death, but it never works. It's never exactly the same, and it just leads to the creation of a second sub seeker."

It was a lot of information, and he barely understood any of it. John was talking so fast and saying so much, he needed more time to process everything. "So you're saying she can create other spirits like her?"

"I'm saying, if she's not stopped, she will create hundreds, and those hundreds will create hundreds of their own, and that will just go on forever." John rubbed his hands together like he was trying to warm them up. "She's the match that lights the bomb that ends the world," he said, throwing his hands in the air like *he'd* just set off a bomb.

This was too much. Lyndsay wasn't some contagion—she was a person. "So, we do what, exactly?"

John sighed, deescalating himself as he glared at the spot where Lyndsay had just stood. "We have to stop her. Before she starts something we can't undo. If she succeeds, even once, she won't want to stop."

Mac could see that John took no pleasure in what he was saying, but it did little to temper the anger now building inside him. He'd grown too close to Lyndsay to give up on her now. She'd grown too much, become too human, to just be written off.

"She trusts us. She came to me for help. You want to stop her, fine, but we're finding a way that helps her move on."

"Helping her might mean stopping her for good. You need to make sure you understand that."

Mac's fists clenched as his chest heaved, and the frustration mounted in the long silence between them. He wanted to argue but saw no point. John always thought he knew everything, and no amount of reasoning would change that now.

"Mac, wait." John sighed. "If you want to help her, find her. Help her understand what she is and what's at stake." He paused before delivering one final warning. "But don't mistake this for hope. She can't fight what she is. Not forever."

Mac turned his head back to John. "Maybe long enough to find another way," he said sternly before continuing toward the door.

"She'll be where her body is," John yelled as Mac closed the shop door behind him.

CHAPTER 19

THE FUNERAL HOME

The air outside was sharp with the bite of the coming winter, though Mac barely noticed as he stepped into his truck. He gripped the wheel and twisted his hands over it, still reeling from the conversation with John. He understood the danger, but he couldn't believe that it was hopeless. There had to be some way to help Lyndsay.

He had a choice to make. He could trust John, who clearly understood more about the world of ghosts and spirits than he did, or he could trust his gut, which told him to do whatever he could to help her. John only saw the big picture—a macro view that was always black and white—but Mac understood you needed to chop down individual trees in order to clear a forest.

For Mac, there was no possibility of giving up.

He fumbled for his phone, dialing Jason again as he turned the engine to heat up the truck. He set it to speakerphone and set it on the dash. The line buzzed as he looked over at the seat next to him, which may as well have belonged to Lyndsay at this point.

"Mac?" Jason answered.

"I'm sorry, Jason, I don't have a lot of time. Can you tell me where they've taken Lyndsay?"

"Yeah… the body's at the funeral home, at the cemetery," he answered without hesitation. "The pathologist should be there now, doing her examination."

"The funeral home?" Mac repeated back.

"Yeah, you know how it is around here. Small town, no morgue, no hospital—everything goes through the funeral home."

Mac nodded to himself, already putting the truck in gear. "Thanks, Jason."

"Mac, wait. What's going on?" he pressed.

Mac hesitated and then remembered what Lyndsay said about working at the bar and changed the subject abruptly. "I think you should look into Caleb."

"Why? What do you mean?"

"I found out Lyndsay worked at his bar for a few days before she was taken." He paused, waiting to see if the information was enough to elicit a response on his own, but it didn't. "Caleb lied to me about knowing her. He said he'd never seen her before."

"We actually looked into Caleb," Jason said. "When Joanne went missing. He's clean. Always at that bar—solid alibis for all the missing women."

"It can't be just a coincidence, Jason. He's hiding something."

"It's weird, for sure, but it really can't be him. The timelines we know about… he couldn't have done it."

Mac held his frustration, though he wanted nothing more than to scream as loud as he could into the void. "Fine," he muttered. "I gotta take care of something. I'll call you back."

Before Jason could respond, Mac ended the call and slammed the phone down on the passenger seat. His truck roared as he pressed the accelerator, heading back to the cemetery. If John was right, he had to find her before she hurt someone.

Mac killed the engine and exited the truck. It was dark, and from the lot, the only thing he could see was the light from the funeral home front door. Even the windows were dark, and the stillness made the place feel abandoned.

He walked to the door and pushed it open, creating a long creak that echoed through the empty foyer. The thick scent of flowers and pine hit him and filled the space inside. The place was empty, no one at the front desk to greet him, and it was quiet, eerily so.

"Hello?" he called out, but no one answered.

He moved cautiously toward a staircase leading to the basement and started down. The air grew colder with each step he took, and the flowery scent faded, only to be replaced with antiseptic and the faint metallic tang of cold steel.

When he reached the bottom of the stairs, he stared down a long hallway, barely lit by the lights above, lined with windows and doors. At the other end, a figure slumped in the corner, her body folded in on itself as though she were trying to disappear.

He moved closer, carefully—unsure of what he was about to encounter. As he got closer to the person, his nerves lit up. It was like walking through some nightmarish scene in a horror movie. She was now rocking as she held her knees to her chest.

"Hello?" he called out quietly, but she just kept rocking.

Next to her on the floor, there was a white lab coat with an ID badge dangling from the pocket. *It must be the pathologist,* he thought. She didn't seem to notice him, but as he got closer, she began clawing at her own hair as a muffled sob broke from her lips.

"All I've seen," she whispered, her voice thick with anguish. "All I've done." Her breathing hitched and her words dissolved into a choked whimper. "It's… too much. Too much."

Her rocking came faster, as if ramping up to match her growing despair. Mac watched her, unsure how to help. Would he just make things worse?

"The faces… I can still see their faces…"

Mac kept moving, and he could feel the change in the air. Lyndsay was nearby, as if it weren't already obvious by the woman pulling out her hair in the corner.

He turned toward a door with the words COLD STORAGE etched into the window. *Seems like the right place,* he thought as he reached for the handle, hesitating before pushing it open.

Inside, the room was frigid, that cold steel smell even stronger than before. It was mostly empty, aside from a few tables and the rows of metal doors along one wall, but his eyes locked on her instantly.

She stood in the middle of the room, her back to him, staring at a single drawer. Her drawer. The faint blue spectral aura around her form surged outward in pulses, like a living, breathing thing, snapping and writhing with each pulse. She was heaving, like someone breathing hard, and each exhale created a mist in the cold air as if her rage had become as tangible as her.

"Lyndsay," Mac called out softly as he stepped inside.

She didn't respond, but she reached out her hand, trembling as it brushed the drawer's handle, like she was testing her newfound solidity.

"Lyndsay, stop," he said, a little louder this time. "You don't want to do this."

Her hand froze mid-reach, but she didn't turn around. Mac took a deep breath and took another step closer. "I know what you're feeling," he continued. He tried to keep his voice steady, but it strained from his fear, the anxiety giving a slight shake. "That rage. That sorrow. I know it's overwhelming. But it's not just yours anymore. That woman outside… you're doing this to her. You're hurting her."

Lyndsay's head tilted, just enough for Mac to see her profile. Her eyes were wide and unfocused, but there was a flicker of recognition in them. Her hand dropped slowly to her side, and the swirling aura around her dimmed.

Relief washed over him, and he exhaled. "Let me help you," he said. "We can figure this out together."

He moved closer, still walking slowly, trying to keep everything calm, but everything changed. Her aura snapped back into focus—brighter and more chaotic than before. She turned toward Mac, facing him head-on, and her face contorted.

"Help me?" she hissed. Her voice shook with an emotion Mac couldn't quite place—somewhere between sorrow and barely contained rage. "How are you going to help me, Mac?"

He froze and straightened himself as she took a step forward. Her aura was crackling like a lightning storm around her. He thought she might pass right through him, but she stopped, her eyes boring into his.

Her hand shot out, her finger jabbing into his chest. It was solid and deliberate, and the force of it pushed him back a step. The sudden impact was a subtle but specific reminder that she wasn't just a ghostly presence anymore—she was real, dangerous.

"Lyndsay," he breathed, trying not to provoke her further. "This isn't you. You don't want this."

She jabbed him again, harder this time, her face twisting with frustration. "You don't know what I want," she yelled as her aura flared wildly around her. "You don't know what I need."

He raised his hands, holding his palms open to show he wasn't a threat. "I know you don't want to hurt that woman out there. I know you don't want to hurt me."

Her eyes narrowed as she stepped closer, and Mac instinctively backed up toward the door. His heart pounded, and he worried he might not make it out of this alive. He was in it, though, to whatever end. He'd either help her or he would die trying.

"Lyndsay, please listen to me."

She followed him through the door, and as she entered the hallway, her aura seemed to grow even stronger. Tiny tendrils reached out and brushed the walls. As she grew, so did the effect she was having on the woman in the hall—her sobs growing louder the closer Lyndsay got.

"Make it stop," the woman cried out, her voice cracking with desperation. "Make them stop! Please, God!"

A bloodcurdling scream bellowed out of the woman, startling Mac and sending a chill through him. He flinched, glancing down at the woman, still slumped in the corner. She buried her face in her hands, and she was trembling violently. "They're everywhere," she wailed. "I can feel them… I can see them. Make it stop!"

Lyndsay froze, looking down at the woman as her aura flickered, like it was caught between fading and flaring brighter. The woman's screams clawed at the air, a raw and piercing sound ripping through the hallway. Lyndsay tilted her head, and her expression twisted between confusion and guilt.

Mac saw an opportunity. She was becoming aware of the effect she was having on someone who had nothing to do with what happened to her. He could see her shifting, fighting the rage that had taken over her.

"Lyndsay," he whispered. "Look at her. Look at what you're doing."

The longer she stared at the woman, the softer her aura became. The cries grew softer as well. She took a step back as the tendrils she'd created retreated into her. "I…" she whispered, her voice barely audible. "I didn't mean to…"

Mac took a careful step forward, keeping his movements slow and deliberate. "I know. You didn't mean to hurt her."

Her hands shook as she clutched at the air like she needed to pull her aura back into herself. "I just wanted to see," she said. "To know. I didn't think…" She trailed off, her spectral form dimming further, almost back to normal. Her shoulders sagged as the energy around her dissipated, like the effort of coming back had taken its toll.

"You can stop this," Mac said firmly. "You are stopping it. Just focus. Be you again."

They stood there together as she pulled herself together. She looked at the woman as they both recovered, like she was anchoring herself to the woman's humanity, waiting for her to be whole again.

As the pathologist stopped rocking, her cries softened into hiccupping breaths.

"I'm so sorry," Lyndsay said, though knowing the woman could never hear her.

"Ma'am, are you all right?" Mac asked, bending down to help the woman up from the floor.

She blinked, like she was waking from a nightmare, and let him help her to her feet. "What… what happened?" she asked, wiping the smeared tears from her face.

⬥

Mac sat in the driver's seat, resting his hands against the steering wheel, the engine off. They sat in silence, except for the faint sound of Mac's breath, something he was still struggling to control after that experience. Lyndsay stared out the window, barely moving aside from the subtle tremble in her hands.

"I didn't mean to scare her."

Her voice cut through the silence, sending a jolt through Mac's chest.

"I didn't want to… hurt her like that."

Mac glanced over at her, watching her deal with the realization of what she'd almost done. "I know," he said. "But it happened… and we need to make sure it doesn't happen again."

She shook her head and balled her fists in her lap. "I don't understand what's happening to me."

Mac let out a measured breath before answering. "I don't fully understand either," he admitted. "John thinks he knows… but before I met you, I didn't even know something like you existed. I thought ghosts were just… you know, ghosts."

"What does he think I am?"

He hesitated, not sure how to phrase what John had said without overwhelming her. "He thinks you're something he called a sub seeker," he began carefully. "It's… not just unfinished business keeping you here. It's like you're caught in something darker."

There was so much to explain. Mac leaned back in his seat, rubbing a hand across his face, trying to decide which details were the most important.

"There's something called a phantom," he explained. "Like you, it's not just a ghost—it's more like a parasite that attaches to people, usually people who… kill. They feed on the fear and violence, and every time someone dies, they get stronger. John thinks whoever did this to you, your killer, had one of those things attached to him."

Lyndsay sat frozen, her eyes wide and searching. "So I'm stuck here because of some… parasite?"

"It's more complicated than that," Mac said softly. "The phantom's a big part of it, but there's more. You're here because when you took your own life, you became something stronger, and I'm guessing the phantom wasn't prepared for it and allowed you to escape."

Lyndsay looked away, her jaw tightening. "I don't feel strong," she murmured. "I feel… broken. Like I can't even control myself anymore."

"That's what John's worried about, too," he said before leaning forward slightly, resting his hands back on the wheel. "I don't think you're broken," he said firmly. "I think we just need to figure it out. It's messy, yes. But look what you did in there," he said, gesturing to the funeral home.

She shot him a quizzical glance, obviously not understanding what he was getting at. "Not the bad part," he quickly expanded. "You pulled yourself out of it… whatever it was. You stopped yourself from hurting me and that woman."

Lyndsay's expression softened as she stared at the dashboard. "I don't even know how I did that. It didn't feel like me—like I had any control. I just… felt the anger, and it was like it took over."

Mac nodded. "And then you took it back. That's not nothing, Lyndsay. That's strength—whether you feel it or not."

Lyndsay kept quiet for a moment, then asked, "What does it mean, though? If I'm this… sub seeker or whatever John called me? What am I supposed to do with that?"

He tapped his fingers against the steering wheel as he searched for the right words, as if there was such a thing.

"I don't have all the answers. But this phantom… it's connected to what happened to you. If we can figure out a way to stop it, maybe… maybe that's how you move on."

"You really think that's possible? That you can stop this thing?"

"I don't know. But I'm damn sure gonna try."

Her lips curled into a faint, almost bitter smile. "You make it sound like I'm some big project."

"Of course not. You're someone who didn't deserve what happened to her. And you're stuck with me, so we're figuring it out together."

Lyndsay nodded, and her eyes drifted back to the windshield. "I remembered something else," she said after a pause.

Mac turned toward her slightly, his interest piqued. "Yeah? What's that?"

"Joanne," she said, hesitating a bit.

"Right. You said you worked together."

"Yeah," she said. "She was training me. I wasn't there long before… well, before everything happened, but we got along." She hesitated a moment before continuing. "She talked about Josie a lot."

Mac flinched. "Oh yeah? What'd she say?"

"She missed her," Lyndsay replied. "Said she was the glue that held everyone together. She talked about you, too. Called you her loony brother-in-law who thinks he sees ghosts."

Mac sighed and nearly chuckled. "Sounds like her."

"She never said it like it was a bad thing," Lyndsay added quickly. "She called you harmless. Different, but in a good way. She said Josie's death broke something inside you, and…" She paused a moment, and Mac could tell she was weighing her next words carefully. "I thought of you that night, the stories she told me about your 'gifts.' When I… ended it, I swear I heard someone whispering your name."

"That's why you came to me?"

"I don't recall 'coming to you,'" she said. "I still don't know how I ended up in your truck. But you were the last thing I remember thinking about before I died."

Mac leaned back in his seat, her words washing over him like a wave. The weight of them hung in the air, raw and unshakable. He stared out through the windshield, searching for what to say.

"I don't know how you ended up here either," he admitted. "But… maybe that's how it works. You thought about me, and maybe that was enough. Maybe that's what pulled you to me."

They were both quiet for a long moment. "You really think I can be fixed?" Lyndsay asked.

"I want to—" Before he could finish his sentence, a familiar unease welled up inside him. His chest tightened, and it became harder to breathe. His vision blurred at the edges, and his pulse thudded in his ears. The same suffocating dread he'd felt at the bar had returned, but there was no shadowy creature this time. It felt stronger but more distant.

He hunched over in his seat, clutching at his chest with both hands as his body trembled from the fear taking root inside him.

"Mac?" she asked. "What's happening? Talk to me."

He shook his head, eyes wide as he scanned the darkness outside the truck, looking for any sign of the phantom. "Do you feel that?" he asked.

"Feel what?" she asked, the desperation coming out strong. "Am I doing this?"

Mac pushed the door open and stumbled out of the truck. His legs shook under his weight as he failed to steady himself. He spun in circles, trying to find… anything that would explain how he was feeling. Lyndsay appeared next to him, concerned and confused.

She reached out and placed her hand on his back, trying to comfort him, but it didn't stop the anxiety clawing at his chest. It did, however, remind him he wasn't alone.

"It's here." His voice trembled as he checked every corner of the cemetery. "I don't know where, but it's here."

Mac caught a shadow moving at the edge of his vision, and he froze, snapping his head toward it, locking on to a figure walking briskly toward a storage barn behind the funeral home. It moved quickly, not unnaturally so, but there was purpose in its movements.

"There," Mac announced as he straightened himself. Lyndsay tried to follow his gaze, but she was still confused.

"What? I don't see anything," she said.

Mac ignored her and kept his focus locked on the figure. He watched as it opened the barn door and stepped inside, shutting the door firmly behind him. And then—silence.

He staggered, reaching out to catch himself on his truck. The pressure in his chest, the suffocating dread, and even the pounding in his ears all vanished in an instant, and the relief almost knocked him down. He stood there, stunned, as his lungs finally filled with air again.

"Mac?" Her voice cut through the torpor with its sharp urgency. "What just happened?"

"It's okay," he said. "It's gone."

"What's gone?" she demanded as she stepped closer to him. "You were falling apart a second ago."

Mac stood, staring at the barn, allowing his mind to run through the possibilities. He was in there. The source of these problems, the killer, Joanne's captor. He was in that barn, and maybe she was, too. He could end this right now. And then he bolted up the hill.

"Where are you going?" she yelled up after him before following him up the hill.

He skidded to a halt in front of the door and reached out to grab the handle, pausing with his hand hovering just an inch above it. A moment of doubt washed over him. If the man was in there, if this really was the killer… He hadn't thought this through. The moment he came face-to-face with this phantom, he'd coil into a ball of fear and panic. He needed help.

He reached into his pocket, fumbling for his phone, but found nothing. "Ugh," he muttered, realizing he'd left it in the truck.

He looked back toward the lot, his truck barely visible in the dim light. Lyndsay stepped closer to him and brushed her hands against the sides of his face, gently guiding his panicked gaze back to hers.

"Mac, I don't understand what's happening."

Her soft touch and gentle voice grounded him, and he locked his eyes with hers, forcing himself to take a deep breath. "I think your killer is inside," he said as he breathed out. "I don't know how, but that thing attached to him… it affects me. It's like it can sense me, and it's trying to break me."

She recoiled slightly, darting her eyes between Mac and the door. "And you want to go in there? Now?"

"No," he blurted. "I can't do it alone… not with the way it affects me." He looked back down at the truck and then back to Lyndsay. "I want you to go find John. Tell him what we found. I'm going to get my phone and call Jason."

Lyndsay stared at the door for a couple of seconds and looked at Mac, not hiding the worry on her face. "Mac—"

"I'll be fine," he interrupted. "I can feel when it's nearby." He smiled. "It's like a built-in early-warning system. The faster you find John, the better."

She nodded and vanished without another word, leaving Mac alone. He started down the hill toward the truck, his heart still pounding from the run up. With each step, he ran through scenarios in his head. He would stop this guy, and he'd come up with a hundred ways it was going to end.

He reached the lot and leaned into the driver's-side window, stretching to grab the phone off the dashboard. Just as his fingers brushed it, pain exploded in his skull and his vision went blurry. The truck, the cemetery, the gnarled trees all spun wildly before the ground came up to meet him. The last thing he felt was the cold gravel against his cheek before everything went dark.

CHAPTER 20
THE MORGUE

A sharp bang echoed through Mac's consciousness, dragging him out of the darkness. His head throbbed as the sound reverberated through his skull like a second heartbeat. He groaned and shifted against the strange pressure pinning his arms and legs.

His eyes fluttered, and the world around him opened up into a haze of smeared colors and shifting shadows. The cold air pricked at his skin and carried a metallic tang of blood and disinfectant—sterile but old, like a place that hadn't seen daylight in many years.

"Wha…" he said. His voice cracked, and he coughed, the motion pulling at his shoulders, letting him know he was bound. He glanced at the leather straps biting into his wrists and ankles, holding him firmly in place, and panic bloomed in his chest as he tried to wrench free.

"Mac… stop," an urgent voice said as he struggled against the restraints. A figure appeared, bending over above him, working the straps of the bindings. "It's okay. I've got you."

He couldn't see clearly enough yet to know who it was, but the voice, though barely a whisper, sounded familiar. "Who…"

"It's Jason," the figure said, sending a wave of relief through Mac's core as his familiar face emerged from the blur. He moved quickly to undo each of the straps holding him down. "We're getting you out of here."

One by one, the restraints fell away, and Mac slumped forward, nearly falling out of the chair. His legs wobbled under his weight and he nearly buckled, but Jason caught him, setting him back into the chair. "Easy," he said. "Take a minute."

Mac nodded, then winced as the pain seared in the back of his head. His hand naturally went to where the pain was, coming away wet with blood. "Ow."

His eyes focused, giving him a clearer picture of the room surrounding him, the cracked white tiles of the floor and walls and flickering fluorescents above, the rusted drain in the floor, and a row of metal cabinets adorned with various instruments that were either clinical or maniacal.

"Where…" Mac's voice rasped.

"Looks like the old morgue," he said, as his eyes darted to the door. "Some sort of sick setup."

He struggled to piece everything back together and closed his eyes tight to block out the surrounding distractions. "Last thing I remember… I was going to call you… How'd you find me?"

Jason glanced over at the corner of the room. "I followed Caleb," he said after a moment of thought. "After your call, I went to find him. When I got to the bar, he was running to his car, so I followed him. I guess you were right."

Mac's eyes followed Jason's and locked in on a crumpled figure in the corner. A man, lying motionless, twisted awkwardly over a puddle of blood and a pistol next to one hand. "Wait… That's Caleb?"

Jason nodded slowly, still staring at his body. "I didn't see him attack you, but when I got here, he was dragging something into the barn…" He turned and looked at Mac. "I didn't know it was you until I saw you in that chair."

Mac stared at the body. He dealt with death every day of his life, but usually long after the event had occurred. Ghosts were normal. He understood how to process that, but a dead body—especially someone he knew—he'd only ever had to deal with that one other time in his life. His pulse raced, pounding in his head and chest, and the air was suddenly thick with the stench of blood and damp rot. "What do we do now?"

"We need to get you out of here. Can you stand yet?"

"That's not him." Lyndsay's voice boomed from behind Mac, startling him. He snapped to look at her and found her staring at Caleb's body. "That's my old boss," she continued. "He's not the one that took me."

"What is it?" Jason asked, reacting to Mac's reaction to Lyndsay.

Mac looked down at Caleb and then back up to Lyndsay, whose face showed zero sign of doubt. "Caleb isn't the killer," Mac stated matter-of-factly.

Mac could feel the frustration rising in Jason as his eyes darted between Mac and Caleb's lifeless body. "What do you mean, he's not the killer?"

"Lyndsay's here. She says it's not him."

"That doesn't add up. If Caleb isn't the guy, then why the hell did he bring you here?"

"I don't know. I thought it was him, too, but she was there, Jason. She's seen the guy."

Jason stepped back and paced between the chair and the door. "Okay… Let's say Lyndsay really is here… talking to you. Let's say Caleb wasn't the one who took her. That still doesn't explain why you were strapped to that chair, why he pointed a gun at me… why he was here." He paused in utter frustration, looking around the room. "Or why this place looks like something out of a horror movie!"

Mac sat silently, watching Jason as he worked through the scene and then turned to Lyndsay, who was still staring at Caleb's body. "Lyndsay…" he whispered. "Do you recognize this place?"

She shook her head. "No… not exactly. It's familiar, but it's wrong." Her voice faltered as she looked away. "It's not him, Mac. I know that much. Caleb isn't the one."

Mac turned to Jason, who watched him intently and crossed his arms. "You're hearing her now? She's talking to you?"

"Yes," Mac said firmly.

Before Jason could ask any follow-up questions, Mac saw something move out of the corner of his eye. Lyndsay took a sharp step back, and her form flickered erratically. He turned as her face contorted from confusion to sheer terror.

"What is it?" he said, following her gaze to the hall behind Jason.

Something stirred in the dark corridor behind his friend. He squinted, trying to get a better view. His breath caught in his throat as a large man entered the frame just a few feet behind Jason, his imposing form filling the space like it was tailored for him. He was thick-necked. Large, like years of muscle had been buried beneath layers of fat, and his bald head gleamed faintly under the light. He wore dirty denim overalls over a grimy white shirt that was stained with dark smudges that may have been dirt—or something worse. His face was a mask of fury, and his eyes blazed with a wild, unhinged rage.

Mac tried to yell out, but the air in his throat wouldn't cooperate. He snapped his attention to the man's right hand, gripping a machete. He pushed harder as the man raised the long blade high into the air. "JASON!"

He barely had time to turn before the man brought the blade down in a brutal arc, striking Jason with a sickening thunk and burying it deep into his shoulder. It cleaved through the flesh and bone like it wasn't even there, lodging deep in his chest.

Jason's eyes went wide with shock, and his mouth opened to release a silent gasp as blood splattered across the floor. Mac could only watch as his friend buckled, collapsing forward as the massive man yanked the blade free.

"No!" Mac screamed and lunged forward instinctively before stumbling to the ground.

Jason fell to his knees and clutched at his chest as blood pooled beneath him. He turned his head, his wide, shocked eyes meeting Mac's before his body finally sagged and collapsed onto the tile.

The man stood over Jason's body and looked over to Caleb. His chest heaved with labored breaths as his face twisted into a grotesque snarl before returning his eyes back to Mac.

Mac's heart hammered in his chest as he scrambled against the floor, trying to push himself upright. "Who the hell are you?" he screamed through the fear and anger.

The man didn't answer, but took a step forward. His boots squeaked across the blood-soaked floor as he raised the machete once again.

Mac continued trying to get to his feet while also retreating as the man approached. "Stay back!" he yelled.

He took another deliberate, predatory step forward. His eyes were locked on Mac, but there was something off about the way they looked. Empty, like he wasn't entirely there. Then, something changed.

Mac froze. A deep chill swept through the room that felt like ice water washing over him. The lights flickered violently, and a low, guttural sound thundered through the space.

"No…" Mac whispered as he realized what was happening. The man tilted his head slightly, like he was listening to something only he could hear, and the air around him seemed to bend and distort as a dark shape coalesced behind him.

It was just like the bar. He felt every movement as if it were happening to him. The same shifting, writhing darkness casting a shadow through the room that seemed to move with a will of its own. It rose up behind the man, towering over him in a form that was both jagged and fluid at the same time. The void where a face should have been swirled in a mass of blackness that seemed to pulse with malevolence, and twenty or thirty eyes all fixed on Mac.

He couldn't move. Fear took over, and the anxiety shot through the roof. It was exactly as he feared—face-to-face with the killer and he crumbled. Whatever this thing was doing to him, he had no way out of it. He was about to fail, spectacularly. But then Lyndsay's voice broke through.

"Mac! Get up!" she shouted, her form casting a blue haze over his face. "That's him!"

Mac blinked rapidly as he took his first successful breath since the phantom emerged. The fear was still present, crippling, but the anxiety that kept taking him over had completely washed away.

The man advanced again, his movements changing as the shadow enveloped him. His muscles tensed unnaturally, and his breathing grew heavier, more monstrous. He let out another roar and swung the machete down toward Mac.

He rolled to the side just in time, and the blade struck the floor with a deafening clang, just missing him. Sparks flew as the machete hit the tiles, the force of it sending tremors through the ground. Mac scrambled backward, bumping into Lyndsay, who stood watching the man, paralyzed in fear.

The man, now completely enshrouded by the phantom, raised the machete again, and the room seemed to shrink, the walls pressing in under the oppressive shadow filling the space. But before the machete could descend, Jason let out a strangled gurgle from where he'd crumpled to the ground. His body convulsed, one or two last twitches of life, and the phantom's attention broke.

"Jason," Mac whispered, his voice cracking.

His body went still as his chest rose in one last defiant breath before falling, and then nothing.

Time slowed as Mac watched a faint, shimmering outline form above Jason's body. It was hardly noticeable at first, like smoke curling in the air, but it quickly coalesced into a figure—Jason's figure. His ghost.

His new form flickered, and his confused expression flipped to horror as he looked down at his lifeless body. Mac's eyes stung as the sorrow welled up inside him. He watched as his friend processed what had just happened to him. "I'm so sorry" was the only thing he could think to say in that moment.

But the phantom wasted no time. It turned its shapeless head toward the newly formed ghost, its jagged edges quivering with hunger. Mac shook as the air got colder and watched as the phantom's focus shifted entirely from Mac to Jason's spirit.

"Mac." Lyndsay's whisper cut through the suffocating dread. "Get up. Now."

He scrambled to his feet, powered by a renewed instinct to survive, and stared in horror as the phantom surged forward, stretching unnaturally as it enveloped Jason's ghost.

"Get away from him," Mac shouted, but the phantom's otherworldly growl swallowed his words up.

"What are you saying?" Lyndsay asked insistently. "You need to run."

He ignored her, unable to look away as Jason's form flickered wildly while the phantom dragged his essence apart inch by inch, devouring him.

His knees threatened to buckle as he staggered back, watching as the phantom's jagged form twisted and pulsed with hunger, its shadowy edges clawing at the last flickers of Jason's spirit. The sight was horrifying, but Mac couldn't tear his eyes away.

"Mac!" Lyndsay demanded once again. "Why aren't you running?"

He realized Lyndsay could only see the man, not the spirit, and had no idea what was unfolding in front of them. His voice trembled as he finally spoke. "Jason... his ghost. The phantom's feeding on him."

Lyndsay snapped her attention to the man, her face twisting with confusion. "I can't see it. I can't…" Her voice faltered, but something in her posture changed. She straightened and squared her shoulders. Her gaze leveled. "I won't let him kill you."

She stepped between Mac and the man, and her translucent form shimmered with volatile energy. "I won't let it," she repeated.

"No—wait," he said, reaching toward her. "Don't—"

But she had already changed. A low hum filled the room, vibrating through Mac's chest like a distant roll of thunder and her hands curled into fists. Her form shifted—unraveling and reknitting into something jagged and monstrous—echoing the specter he'd seen in cold storage. Her edges flared with anger, her outline expanding as power surged through her.

"Lyndsay, please," Mac begged. "You don't know what it's doing—"

But the phantom had noticed her. It turned from Jason's fading spirit and faced her head-on, drawn to the fury storm she was becoming.

"It feeds on power," Mac said, his voice raw. "It wants you."

She turned her head just enough to look at him, and for the first time since the change began, her face was calm. Not cold. Not afraid. Just calm.

"Run," she said.

Mac hesitated. Every logical thing in him screamed to listen to her, but every instinct told him to stay, to fight and pull her back. But the look in her eyes was clear. She had made her choice, and if he stayed, it would be for nothing.

He backed away, watching as the two powers collided. Her blue aura shot out across the room, the nightmarish specter filling every space that wasn't already occupied by the phantom's shadow. The two forces pushed against each other, each taking their turns in the ebb and flow.

Lyndsay reached out with her hands and grabbed both sides of the man's face, pulsing her energy through her arms and into him. He winced with each pulse as she poured her rage and sorrow into the man, and a smirk tugged at Mac's lips. *She's winning*, he thought.

But as he watched, the unease twisted tighter inside him, threatening to snuff out the brief spark of relief. The man reacted, writhing and recoiling with every pulse, but something wasn't right. He glanced past the man—at the looming shadow just behind—and the dread came rushing back. The phantom hadn't budged.

Its jagged edges thickened, and the tendrils widened as each of Lyndsay's pulses rippled through it, stealing a bit more of the space she occupied with every jolt. The man was suffering, but the parasite was thriving.

Everything slowed around him as the truth clawed its way to the surface. He had been watching the wrong thing. Lyndsay wasn't pushing it back; she was feeding it.

Lyndsay must have felt it, too, because right at that moment, she turned her head toward Mac. Her eyes were softer—no anger or hate, only sadness and resignation. She smiled, just a little, and then mouthed the words, *I'm sorry.*

With one final push, the phantom filled the room. As its tendrils retreated into the man, it enveloped Lyndsay and dragged her in with it. It was finally claiming its lost prey.

"No!" he screamed as he staggered forward, reaching out as if he could bring her back, but it was too late. Lyndsay's form dissolved into the phantom's shadowy mass, her energy absorbed in an instant, and the room fell silent except for Mac's ragged breathing.

He turned and ran. Up the stairs and through the door in the barn floor. He could feel the phantom rising up behind him like a wave ready to break, but he dared not turn to look. The barn doors burst open as he pushed his way into the dark night and slammed shut behind him as he tore off down the hill. He slipped as he ran and stumbled at the bottom of the hill, falling onto the gravel lot.

He hit the ground hard—the pain flaring in his shoulder as he rolled onto his back and froze. The barn doors had opened again.

The man stepped out, silhouetted against a single light spilling from inside the barn. His phantom was wrapped around him now, full and ready for its next meal, like it had been waiting for this moment.

He scrambled back, head and shoulder aching, panic surging, and slammed into something solid. A hand gripped his arm, steadying him.

"Back," someone said, low and forceful.

Mac turned and looked up.

John stood just behind him with his other hand raised. He stepped forward, weaving his fingers through the air in intricate patterns as sparks of blue and golden light shot to life at his fingertips. He traced runes in the air that shimmered and burned as they coalesced into a fiery circle.

The phantom roared and thrashed its shadowy limbs, like it sensed the magic taking shape. It lunged at him, surging forward with murderous intent, but John's hands moved faster, weaving through the ritual like he'd done it a hundred times.

"Hold," John commanded, startling Mac with a voice that seemed to layer atop itself, like there were seven of him, all saying the word at the same time.

The runes spun into place and formed a blazing golden ring around the phantom's host. The man stopped, but the phantom didn't. It pressed forward, testing the edge of something unseen, and for a second, it held. Just long enough for Mac to feel the moment breaking.

"They're pushing through," John muttered as he raised both hands to the air.

Wind picked up around them, swirling into a tight spiral and lifting dust and gravel in a ring. Overhead, the lights buzzed and popped as stray sparks leaped into the night, arcing toward John's outstretched finger. He clenched them into a fist, pulling the energy down and shaping it into a crackling shell around them.

The barrier snapped into place, and there was a sudden, deafening silence.

The man stood just outside it, breathing hard, but it was the phantom that held Mac's attention. It hovered behind the man like smoke coiling up from a fire, its body shifting and pulsing and its gaze entirely fixed on Mac.

"I see you."

The gnarled voice belonged to the creature, but somehow it came from inside Mac's head, louder than his own thoughts. It didn't lunge or roar—it was like it knew there was no way through whatever John had conjured. It simply withdrew, slow and deliberate, as the man stepped back into the dark.

John didn't move until the air stilled and the man and creature had long since passed out of view.

"You all right?" he asked.

Mac shook his head. Jason's lifeless eyes. Lyndsay's final smile. The weight of both losses hit him like a physical blow. There were no words strong enough for his answer.

John set his hand on Mac's shoulder, grounding him. "Come on," he said, helping Mac off the ground. "Tell me what happened."

Mac leaned against the hood of John's car, staring at the barn in the distance as the weight of all that had happened sank in. Lyndsay was gone. Jason was gone. His fists tightened until his hands ached, but it wasn't enough to ground him. He felt like a failure. The hollow ache rising from his gut threatened to swallow him whole.

John emerged from the barn and shook his head. Joanne was somewhere else. It was all for nothing. Jason's last moments replayed in his mind—his shocked face, the blood pooling beneath him, the sound he made just before the phantom devoured him. And Lyndsay… trying to protect him. There must have been something he could have done to stop all of it, but no matter how he turned the events over in his mind, he couldn't find it.

John ended his call and approached the car. He looked different. His usual cockiness and detachment were gone, replaced by a somber expression that almost made it seem like he cared. He slipped the phone into his pocket and leaned next to Mac.

"I'm sorry," he said softly.

Mac let out a sharp breath. The words seemed hollow, meaningless. He wanted to snap back and blame John for everything. All his cryptic warnings, half-truths, and failed experiments. If he'd ever been honest about anything, maybe they would have been better prepared. But the words never came. He was too tired to summon that anger.

"They're gone," he muttered. "Jason… Lyndsay… Caleb… I did nothing. I just… sat there."

John didn't say anything right away. He followed Mac's gaze up to the barn. "This isn't your fault," he said.

"Isn't it? I dragged Jason into this. Lyndsay, too. And for what? They're dead because I couldn't protect either of them."

"You didn't drag anyone into anything, Mac. This was Jason's job, something he devoted his life to—"

"If I hadn't run up that hill all half-cocked," he interrupted. "If I'd simply thought it through—"

"Both of them fought for you, not because you dragged them into anything… They did it because they thought you were worth fighting for."

Mac blinked a few times, sighed, and shook his head. "It doesn't make it feel better."

John glanced over to him, his eyes softening. "Because you're human. You're not used to this world—the weight of it all. You see every loss as your failure because you think it's your job to fix everything." He paused, then added, "If you keep carrying every loss, every mistake like this, you'll break. And then you won't be able to save anyone."

"Save anyone?" he said, rejecting the premise. "I'm completely useless. If you hadn't shown up, I'd be dead in there, too."

John sighed. "You just weren't ready. A week ago, you thought dealing with ghosts meant taking them to AA meetings or chanting away the things that went bump in the night. I…"

John paused, looking up at the night sky as Mac waited. "I simply didn't know what to make of you. What you were becoming. I spent so much of my life fighting… I should have helped you more. You weren't prepared, and that is my fault."

Mac snapped his head at John, shocked to hear anything remotely apologetic coming out of his mouth. No platitudes, no sideways shifts of fault, just something real.

John placed his hand on Mac's shoulder. "No more gloves, no more waiting. I don't have all the answers about you, or your gift, but starting tonight… I'm in this with you to the end. We're going to find Joanne, and we are going to stop him."

Mac was shocked, but he managed to nod as the faintest spark of resolve ignited in his chest. He still didn't know if he could trust John, not fully, but right then, he needed him in his corner.

John opened the car door and motioned for Mac to get in. "Come on. I'll drive you home. We can get your truck in the morning."

As they pulled away, Mac took one last look at the barn. The fight wasn't over—not by a long shot.

CHAPTER 21

REGROUP

The ride home was mostly quiet, both of them reflecting on the events in the bunker as John's car thumped over the washboard dirt road. Mac pressed his fingers onto the tender spot where either the killer or Caleb's attack left its mark. His head, throbbing a little less now, still ached, and he winced at his touch.

"Stop poking at it," John said.

Mac dropped his hand quickly, like a child caught doing something he knew he shouldn't have. "Feels like my skull's cracked," he muttered, letting his head fall back against the seat with a groan.

He exhaled and let his thoughts churn, trying to piece together everything that had happened. Jason was dead, Lyndsay was gone, and Caleb's role in the nightmare still loomed over it all. The killer was out there somewhere, and now he knew Mac was onto him. What would that mean for Joanne? For himself?

"It was a brave thing she did," John blurted out of nowhere. "Foolhardy... but brave."

Mac turned his head slightly, still lying against the seat back, and stared at him. "Look where it got her."

John kept his eyes ahead of him, white-knuckling the wheel as the road threatened to jostle his tiny car right off the road. "Most spirits… they hide when dealing with something like that."

He sounded like he was dealing with regret. If Mac didn't know John better, he would assume he was torturing himself over judging her as quickly as he did. It didn't matter much. Either way, she was gone.

For most of the remaining drive back to the house, John focused on not allowing the road to destroy his car, while Mac focused on his throbbing head. And neither of them knew what to say. For ten glorious minutes, there was silence.

John turned the last corner leading home. "I hope this house of yours is as safe as you think it is."

"It's never let me down before," he replied. "If there's any place we can safely regroup, it's there."

The headlights cut through the fog as the house came into view. Mac smiled as John marveled at the ghostly Victorian sentinel. He slowed the car to a stop in the long driveway and let his hands rest on the wheel while he cocked his head, trying to get the complete house in one view.

"What is it?" Mac asked.

John shook his head, letting out a slow whistle. "This house isn't just haunted. It's alive."

"It's a poltergeist." Mac shrugged. "A big one."

"No," John said firmly. "It's not just big. This thing… it's old. I've seen poltergeists… but this," he said, gesturing at the house. "I've never felt anything like this."

"Feels like home to me," he said as he unbuckled his seat belt.

John didn't move. He sat there staring at the house, his hand still gripping the steering wheel. "How long have you lived here?"

"Long enough to know it doesn't bite," he said as he pushed his door open and climbed out of the car. "Not me, anyway. You comin'?"

John took a moment before following Mac out of the car and up the drive. They walked up the porch steps, and Mac could feel John's nervous energy radiating off him. A low hum rumbled beneath the boards in the floor. Once again, John paused. The house obviously made him nervous, and Mac enjoyed that a bit.

"It's just welcoming us home," he said as he reached for the door.

The door groaned as he pushed it open and walked inside, John following cautiously behind. His eyes widened as he entered, noticing the contrasting modernization of the room against the older, weathered architecture of the exterior.

Mac tossed his jacket onto the couch and then collapsed against the cushions, wincing as he leaned back. John lingered in the entryway, his eyes now taking in the cluttered, mismatched state of the family room.

"This house…" he said, pausing while he looked around. "It's got a nice foyer."

Mac snorted. "Yeah, someday I'll get around to finishing it."

John studied him for a moment before walking over to the window and looking out, his own reflection staring back at him. "Mac," he said quietly, "I think your house might be the most dangerous thing in this town... including that phantom. And I think you know that."

Mac didn't respond right away. The house never felt dangerous to him, only to the wayward ghosts that made the mistake of crossing the property line. "What I know..." he scoffed as he pushed himself up from the couch, "I need a drink."

On the way to the kitchen, he tapped an empty bottle on the floor with his foot and continued past when it was evident that it was empty. John called after him, his tone suddenly became sharper. "No, Mac. You need to call the police."

He froze for a second and rolled his eyes, then with a deliberate slowness pulled open the fridge door. He bent down and rummaged through the mostly empty shelves and answered. "And tell them what?" he snapped. "Oh, hey, just thought you'd like to know... there are a couple of dead bodies rotting in a murder bunker under the barn."

He slammed the fridge door shut, rattling the condiment bottles inside, and paced before deciding on checking the pantry.

"Oh, and by the way, one of the bodies is a cop. Don't worry, though," he continued as he opened the pantry door. "It totally wasn't me. Nope, it was some backwoods psycho possessed by a phantom the size of a Mack truck. You should go arrest him... I'm sure that will go over great."

"Mac..."

Mac let out a hollow laugh while he leaned on the pantry door, scanning the shelves. "Right, because that's exactly what they want to hear from the town freak." He paused, standing upright. "Shit. I'm definitely getting arrested," he muttered to himself.

Just then it hit him, a tiny flicker of a memory. "Fireball."

He grabbed a chair from the dining room and scraped it across the floor. He climbed up and opened the small cupboard above the fridge and reached for the dusty bottle hidden in the back.

"Gross, but it'll do the trick," he muttered as he gave the bottle a quick shake.

John rounded the corner and leaned against the wall at the entrance of the kitchen, watching Mac struggle to twist the cap off the bottle. "They don't need to know about the phantom," he said. "To them, he's just… the backwoods psycho."

Mac, still struggling to open the cap, paused for a moment. "And what about me?" he asked, his voice barely above a whisper. "What am I to them?"

"You're the guy with answers they don't want to hear, and yeah, calling them will put you on their radar—"

Mac's grunt interrupted as he gripped the bottle, his knuckles whitening as he strained to untwist the cap.

"There's a dead cop, Mac. They're going to find them eventually, and if you aren't the one to call it in…" he continued, his frustration coming out in his tone. "They'll find your truck, or some fiber from your clothes, a drop of your blood…"

Mac sighed. He knew John was right; he just didn't have it in him to deal with it in that moment.

"They'll look at you," John added, lowering his voice. "And you'll be the one that looks guilty."

"Fine. I'll call…" Mac said as he stormed into the family room, pressing the bottle into John's chest as he passed by. "But not until I've had at least half that bottle. So if you wouldn't mind… figure out why it won't open."

CHAPTER 22

A PLAN

The faint clacking of a keyboard in the distance woke Mac from his deep sleep. His eyes fluttered open as the morning light filtered through the partially closed curtains in the family room. His head throbbed, a reminder of the previous day's chaos, along with the overly sugared Fireball he downed before passing out.

The continued clatter of keys drew his attention to the dining room, where John was hunched over Mac's laptop, his fingers flying across the keyboard.

"You didn't sleep," he muttered as he rubbed the sleep from his eyes.

"Rarely do," John responded without looking up.

Mac pulled himself upright and winced as he worked to stretch all of his sore muscles. "What are you doing?" he asked, before noticing a coffee mug beside the laptop. "And where's mine?"

John finally looked up, raising one eyebrow. "Didn't think you'd be up before noon."

Mac grunted as he dragged himself off the couch, getting in one more large stretch before heading into the kitchen. He poured a cup of coffee and took a long sip before leaning against the counter. "So? What are you doing?"

John stopped and leaned back against his chair. "Working on a way to help us find the killer… and Joanne."

"Come up with anything?"

John nodded, tapping on the trackpad before turning the laptop to face Mac.

Mac moved closer and set his cup down next to the computer, struggling to focus on the words on the screen. "You're not serious?"

"Dead serious," John replied. "No pun intended."

Before Mac could finish his eye roll, a loud knock at the door cut them off, and Mac's stomach sank, the blood rushing away from his face. "It's them," he whispered. "It's the cops. They're here to arrest me."

John stood and moved quietly over to the window, careful to keep out of sight. He peeked out through the curtains and whispered back, "It's just one car. Unmarked. And one guy in a suit."

"They wouldn't send just one guy to arrest me, right?" Mac paced the room, unsure how to proceed or what to think.

"I doubt it. I'd expect everyone: uniforms, cruisers, the whole circus—a bunch of folks waitin' for you do something to give 'em a reason to avenge the dead cop."

Mac inhaled deeply, forcing himself to remain calm, and shot John a look of distaste. "His name was Jason," he said as he exhaled. "Guess I better find out."

Mac opened the door slowly, letting the sun in and blinding himself for a moment. On the porch stood a man in his late forties, clean-cut and wearing a sharp black suit—and an air of authority. The man held up a badge with the words "FBI Special Agent Graham Kane" printed on it.

"Mitchel Crichton?" the man asked. His voice was calm but direct, and it made Mac nervous. He'd never had a fed show up at his door before.

He hesitated and turned to John over his shoulder, who gave him a subtle nod. "Yeah," he said. "That's me."

The man lowered his badge and slipped it back into his pocket. "I'm Special Agent Kane. Can I come in?"

"Sure… I guess," Mac said, standing aside to let the agent through, who had already started pushing his way in.

He stepped inside and looked around, first the foyer and then the family room, resting his attention on John for a moment, who stood near the dining room table. "You can call me Graham," he said, turning back to Mac. "This is a very nice house, Mitchel."

"Thanks," he replied as he shut the door and walked past the agent into the family room. "What can we do for you, Graham?"

"Well," Graham started, as his eyes darted through the room, taking in every detail, "you called in a double homicide last night. I imagine you knew someone would be stopping by."

Mac stood in one spot as the agent paced throughout the room, following him with his eyes. "Yeah, I figured."

The agent stopped pacing and turned, locking his attention on Mac. "Good, then we can skip through the…" He paused and sniffed the air, raising an eyebrow. "Is that coffee? You know… I can't operate more than twenty minutes without the stuff," he said, smiling. "Mind if I have a cup?"

"Sorry," John interjected from the other room. "Just ran out."

John didn't trust this guy. His entire demeanor changed as soon as he introduced himself, and Mac knew there was at least a half a pot of coffee sitting on that burner.

Graham's smile turned, and he nodded. "Pity," he said as he ran a finger across the desk by the living room window, inspecting the residue before leaning against it. "So… what happened last night?"

Mac stepped closer to the agent, keeping his movements slow and deliberate. "Like I told the dispatcher. Caleb attacked me and dragged me into that bunker. Jason…" He paused as his voice caught while saying his name. "Jason stopped him. Saved my life."

"Right." Graham said, pulling a small notepad from his jacket and flipping a couple of pages. "And then… correct me if I have this wrong—a 'giant hick' came out of nowhere and killed the officer. That about sum it up?"

Mac nodded but said nothing.

The agent looked over at John, who hadn't moved a muscle since the man entered the home. "And you? What's your role in all this?"

John didn't answer right away, and for a minute, the two just stared at each other like a battle was raging and the first to blink was the loser. "Nothing," he said finally. "I was there to meet Mac. Saw him stumbling out of that barn and gave him a ride home."

"I see. So you two were just… hanging out at a cemetery?"

"We were there visiting my wife," Mac cut in, his voice sharper, making it clear he didn't like the insinuation. "She's buried there."

"Ah," he said. There was a small shift in his tone, though it felt disingenuous—rehearsed. "I'm very sorry for your loss."

Mac couldn't get a read on Graham, and it was setting his nerves on fire. John, meanwhile, had been burning a hole through the guy's head with his eyes throughout the entire visit.

The agent pushed off the desk and stepped closer. "You have a bit of a reputation around here, Mitchel," he said, pulling a business card out of his jacket pocket.

"It's just Mac."

"You're kind of a local legend."

Mac took the card without looking at it, keeping his eyes locked in with Graham's. The agent took a deliberate, exaggerated step around him and headed back toward the door, pausing as he opened it. "I liked Jason," he said. "He was a good cop, great instincts."

Graham turned to Mac one last time. "He believed you, you know?" he said, his tone remorseful and genuine for the first time since he arrived. "If you think of anything else… anything at all… call me. I might believe you, too."

The door shut, and Mac stood there staring at it for a moment, the agent's words still hanging in the air. *He believed you.*

The sentence echoed in his mind and twisted in his chest. *If he hadn't, he might still be alive.*

He let out a slow breath, tightening his fingers around the business card before tossing it onto the entryway table. He turned to John, still standing in the dining room, watching him.

"Well, that was… weird," Mac said as he walked toward John.

"He only came here to let you know he knows about you."

"It's your turn to deal with the feds next time," Mac replied.

"You did fine," he said, turning back toward the laptop, gesturing for Mac to join him. "Now, let's talk about something we can actually control."

Mac grabbed his coffee and sat at the table. "What've you got?"

John looked directly into Mac's eyes. "I'm sending you into the veil."

CHAPTER 23

THE HEART OF THE HOUSE

The family room went dark as the curtains were drawn tightly against the early-afternoon light. John worked to set up the ritual, spreading salt in a precise circle around the coffee table and muttering words under his breath as he moved.

"I thought me going to the veil was a bad thing. You remember that whole 'don't help the ghost damsel' thing in your shop?"

John ignored him and continued working the circle.

"Looks like the same ritual you had me do for Lyndsay," Mac said as he watched the careful movements. He looked around the room, waiting for the house to come crashing down around him.

"Similar," John replied without looking up.

Remembering the last time, Mac shifted uncomfortably. "Maybe we should do this somewhere else? The house wasn't exactly thrilled the last time we did this here."

John stopped, stunned, and snapped his gaze to Mac. "You did that *here*? Inside the poltergeist?"

"Yes?" Mac answered, keeping his voice low as if testing if it was the correct answer.

He let a brief, incredulous smile tug at the corner of his mouth before allowing a short laugh to escape. "Yeah, that was probably not your best idea," he said as he turned back to the ritual.

"So… are we about to make the same mistake?"

John waved away the concern and kept his focus on the setup. "No. Last time, the house reacted because you were binding a spirit. It probably felt threatened, or maybe a little territorial. We're anchoring you this time, something living. I doubt it'll even notice."

"Okay… so you anchor me here. Then what?" Mac asked, eyeing the ritual circle uneasily.

John adjusted a few of the items, ensuring everything was perfectly placed and aligned. "In theory, once the anchor is set, I should be able to just give you a little shove."

Mac blinked, unimpressed by the lack of certainty in his voice. "In theory? You've done this before, right?"

He didn't look up, but Mac could see the crooked smirk on his face. "Nope. Just came up with it last night."

"You're making this up as you go?"

"Relax," John said, holding up a hand. "Nothing bad is going to happen. It will either work or not work." He paused, realizing that his words were doing nothing to calm Mac's nerves. "I told you before—you're a new thing to me. There aren't any instruction manuals for Threshwalkers."

Mac narrowed his eyes nearly to a squint. "You aren't filling me with an abundance of confidence."

John shook his head and chuckled. "That's why it should work. You already have one foot in. We're just… shifting your weight, so to speak."

Mac stared at John and John stared back—still arguing, only in silence. Finally, John had had enough. "Stop complaining and get in the circle."

He finished the final touches of the ritual and stepped back, inspecting his work. The symbols on the floor glowed and pulsed, casting a faint sheen onto the salt line. Mac stood just outside the circle, contemplating whether he should actually step in. "So what happens if I screw this up?"

"You won't," he said while adjusting one of the charms hanging from a chain on the table. "Just stay inside the circle and don't fight the process. The ritual will do the rest."

"Okay, but—"

"Dammit," John interrupted. "Stop stalling and get in the stupid circle."

Mac sighed and stepped inside, carefully avoiding the salt line. Once inside, he felt a faint vibration humming under his feet, like the air itself was alive. He shot a wary look at John. "Is it supposed to feel like that?"

"Probably." John smiled, enjoying Mac's anxiety a little too much. "Yes…" he said reassuringly. "It means it's working. Now listen. Once you're in, things will be different."

"Different how?"

"In our world, spirits are bound by their patterns—their death, places, emotions. They're echoes, mostly, replaying moments over and over because they can't let go." He grabbed a small vial of something dark and viscous and swirled it between his fingers. "But in there… they have agency… they're more like Lyndsay. They think, speak, and move with purpose. They aren't shackled by the same rules."

"That doesn't sound so bad," Mac said, thinking about how annoying it was that he had to play guessing games with ghosts all the time. It would be much easier if they could just tell him what they needed.

"It is, because they'll see you, and they'll see that you're different—not like them. Some may want your help, others might want to hurt you. Avoid them at all costs."

"Great," he said. "So I'm playing hide-and-seek with a bunch of needy, pissed-off ghosts."

"It's more like a minefield. Just stay focused and don't engage. You're not there for them."

Mac nodded. "Once I'm there, how will I know where to go?"

John leaned back and uncapped the vial, pouring a few drops of the liquid onto the crystal, and the faint scent of iron hit the air. "Entities like the phantom pulse with power, even in the veil. In an area like this… aside from your house, that phantom should be the biggest, baddest thing you'll feel. Just follow that," he said as he placed a couch cushion on the coffee table. "Now sit down."

As he lowered himself onto the cushion, he felt something prickling at his senses—maybe the ritual, maybe his nerves. He crossed his legs and placed his hands on his knees. "Once I find him, how do I get back?"

"I'm going to give you two hours. Get in, find it, and then I'll pull you out."

John closed his eyes and began muttering under his breath. His voice was low and guttural and resonated in a way that made the hairs on Mac's arms stand up. The air around him became colder, and the hum beneath him deepened as it settled into a slow, rhythmic pulse.

The glow of the symbols brightened, and a jolt of static shot through Mac's chest. He took a quick, deep breath as his vision blurred around the edges. "Should I be feeling this… um… weird?"

"Just relax," John said, pausing his low mumblings. "You're almost there."

He clenched his fists as the static running through him vibrated with the pulse coming from the floor. "What the hell is this—"

Before he could finish his question, John leaned forward and extended his hand, pressing his finger firmly against Mac's forehead. It felt gentle and also overwhelming, and with one deliberate push, the world shifted.

For a moment, Mac was weightless—like his entire body had been untethered from gravity—and the pulsing energy around him grew to a deafening buzz. A rushing wind seemed to come from nowhere and everywhere at once, and then, abruptly, it stopped.

He blinked a few times, disorientated, and then finally opened his eyes. He was still in his family room—or something that looked like his family room. The walls seemed to stretch higher, and everything was there but off—muted colors, blurred edges—as if they were painted from memory by someone who hadn't seen it all in years.

The air felt thick, heavy and hard to take in, and the light in the room was dimmer, though it pulsed faintly.

He glanced down at himself and let out a gasp. His body was faintly translucent and glowing at the edges. "What the…"

Even his voice sounded strange, and it echoed faintly, like the room swallowed up the sound and then spit it back fractured.

He turned, his pulse racing from a heart he no longer carried with him, and his eyes darted around the room, unsure of what he would find in the muted gray shadows. The salt circle he'd been sitting in was still there, glowing slightly, but John was gone, and the only thing Mac could hear was his own uneven breath and the constant hum of energy coming from every direction.

The veil was almost the same as his world, but the differences were enough to twist his stomach, and the more he tried to focus on them, the harder they became to articulate.

"Hi, Mac," a voice called out, low and faint.

Mac spun around to find the voice that had just called to him, and standing near the dining room was the woman he'd last seen in John's shop—the one he'd accidentally summoned. But there, in the veil, she was even more imposing, and her presence pressed against him with a tangible weight.

Her long red hair flowed as though it was carried by the mist of the veil curling around her. Her faintly glowing eyes were locked on to his. It felt like she was looking straight through him. She didn't glide like most ghosts did or step when she moved toward him; instead, her form flickered, appearing closer in an instant, like the space between them folded for her.

"It's good to see you," she said in a soft whisper that seemed to be carried by the air between them.

He stared at her, remembering what John said about avoiding the spirits, though too intrigued to heed his warning. "You…" he muttered. "You're the one from John's shop."

She tilted her head slightly, still staring deeply into Mac's eyes. "We've known each other a lot longer than that," she replied as her lips curved into the faintest hint of a smile. Once again, she disappeared, reappearing behind him.

He turned and backed up a step as she moved closer, leaning in almost as if she were trying to smell him. "What do you mean?" he asked, keeping his tone as neutral as he could, given the circumstances.

"For years, I've been your protector," she said, her voice dipping into something almost intimate. "The keeper of your secrets. Your pet."

He froze as the words settled over him and he realized what she was saying. "Protector?" he repeated. "You're the… poltergeist?"

She smiled wider and glided closer to him. "Protector. Heart. Keeper. Poltergeist. Call me what you will."

Her tone was soft, but he could sense an unmistakable edge to the words, as if she was testing him.

"I have watched over you. I have watched you grieve. I watch you fight… and drown yourself in whiskey. I've been with you all the years as you stumbled through this house as if it were your own."

"Is it not mine?"

For an almost imperceptibly brief moment, her expression went dark before her smile returned. "Maybe yours… or you might just be a tolerated guest? Or perhaps…" She paused. "Perhaps it's something else entirely."

Mac blinked while he tried to decipher whatever ominous thing she was implying. A familiar frustration surfaced as he lamented how everyone in his life was so damned cryptic. He kept that bit of frustration to himself, though. There was more to her than just some malevolent spirit rattling pipes and tormenting other ghosts, and his curiosity was piqued.

"I don't understand," he said carefully. "I thought poltergeists weren't spirits… well, like you."

Her smile faded slightly, turning into something more contemplative. "I am the heart of the house," she said quietly. "Where it started. I'm old, Mac—much older than this house or the wood that frames it."

She paused again, and her eyes narrowed slightly, like she was weighing her next words carefully. "When you pulled me into that quaint little store, you changed something. It was like waking from a long dream that wasn't mine. Where I was once part of a collective… a raging storm of pain, sorrow, and things you wouldn't dare imagine—now, I am… me. Something I haven't been in a very long time."

"What do you want?" he asked, still working hard to keep his voice low and neutral.

She smiled again. "I want to help you, Mac," she said simply. "I will always help you."

"What do you mean?"

"You're different," she replied, moving closer. "I felt it from that first moment you stepped inside and tried to rid the house of me so many years ago. I could sense you more clearly than any human who'd come before you."

"Sense me?" he asked.

She nodded. "You're there, but you're also here. You walk in both worlds, freely. Not bound as they are," she said as her voice softened with a reverent tone. "You are remarkable, Mac."

She studied him in silence, moving like she needed to see every inch of him as quickly as possible. "But that made you a target," she said, breaking the uncomfortable silence. "I made sure you had a sanctuary—a place where you could be free from the things that made you so angry… so sad."

"You kept the ghosts away," he said. "What about Lyndsay? Why'd you let her in?"

She kept smiling, but a more somber expression emerged. "She was helping you in ways that I couldn't."

Before he could press further, her form vanished and reappeared by the front door, the movement sending a chill through him. The jarring way she could move was something he wasn't sure he'd ever get used to.

"Your friend was right," she said, a new urgency resonating in her voice as she passed through the door. "You are in danger here."

He instinctively followed her onto the porch, immediately taken by the distorted gray light of the veil, a vision that stretched for miles in every direction, more clearly than what could be seen in his world. "Why am I in danger?" he said after a few moments of reflection.

She turned and faced him, her smile fully faded to a more grim expression. "Your presence here is like a beacon," she explained. "There are things here that will be drawn to you… drawn to your humanity—that connection you have with the world they no longer inhabit."

"Spirits, you mean."

"Among other things," she replied without explanation.

He glanced around, scanning the distorted landscape. Aside from the fog-like quality of the air and the strange, muted colors, everything looked the same. Houses, barns, trees, and bushes stretched out before him just as they were on his side. Though everything felt a bit darker.

He thought about what John had said, to look for a pulsing power that would lead him to the phantom, but he saw and felt nothing. No bright lights, nothing tugging him in any direction, just the gray mist.

"I don't feel anything," he muttered under his breath.

The woman turned sharply, her eyes narrowed with curiosity. "What do you mean?"

"John said I would feel something."

"Ah yes, the big power of the phantom," she said with a smirk.

"You know about that?"

Her smile returned, only this time it carried a hint of smugness with it. "John thinks he knows a lot more than he does," she said, with no shortage of amusement to her tone. "And yes, I heard everything. That phantom is powerful, but so are most things in the veil. If you were going to feel something, it would come from every direction… you'd drown in the weight of it."

"Fabulous," he muttered, allowing his frustration to mount. "I have two hours to figure this out, and that was my only lead."

She quietly studied him, something that made him more uncomfortable every time she did it. "I can help with that, too," she said after a few moments. "But I will need something in return."

There it was, he thought—the motive. He thought of John's words in the shop, *If you want something, you have to give something first,* and his warnings to avoid the spirits at all costs. There was work to do, and he thought about tearing off, but he had no clue where to start. He decided that hearing her out couldn't hurt… hopefully.

"What kind of something?"

"All I need is a promise," she said quickly. "You need help… finding your phantom. I will point you in the right direction, if you promise to do something in return."

"Promise?" he repeated back cautiously. "Promise what?"

"When it's all over, you will come back," she said, lowering her voice. "Come back and free me."

It was all too much to process. The house, the girl, the phantom… this promise. Free her—what did that even mean? It all felt like it should fit into a larger picture, but the edges were jagged, and nothing quite fell into place.

He took a quick but shaky breath, trying not to let his nerves become evident, though he heard in his voice that he was failing. "I… I'm not sure what that means. How would I free you?"

She didn't respond right away and instead turned, gazing out to a field across from the house. The mist seemed to be drawn to her and curled toward her. She stood, still focused on the field, contemplative.

Just before Mac was about to press and ask the question again, she turned back to him. "John has a book," she said with a steady, low voice. "I felt it when you summoned me. It has magic—strong magic, not of this world."

He assumed immediately which book she was referring to. "You mean that *EGGS* book? He said it was like an encyclopedia."

"He doesn't tell you everything," she said. "With that book, I believe you could exorcise me from the house."

Mac snapped his head. Her request was so far from anything he'd expected. "Exorcise?" he echoed back. "That sounds…" He didn't even know how to finish that sentence. Exorcisms were like a permanent death. He never really understood it fully—what happened to them once they were banished from his world, but it didn't seem like a good thing.

She had a resigned, tired look on her face. "It is freedom, Mac. I have been here longer than I can remember. I don't know what will happen to me, but I know I will no longer be stuck here." She paused, showing a moment of vulnerability. "I want to be free of it."

Those words—the same ones he told Daniel to help him end his haunting. He watched her while she spoke, the quiet sedation in her voice, the resolute firmness of her desire to be free. It reminded him of all the people he'd helped as they struggled through their hauntings and addictions. It was a longing he hadn't expected, and he didn't know what to say. So he said the only thing he could. "I'll try."

She immediately smiled again, and her expression lightened ever so slightly. "You will," she said softly before shifting her tone to a more direct command. "Swear by it, Mac. Swear, and I will help you find what you need."

He didn't know if he could do what she asked of him, but he wanted to help if he could, and he needed her help at that moment. He nodded firmly. "I swear."

Her smile widened as satisfaction flickered in her eyes. "Then let us begin."

"What do I call you?" he asked, figuring "hey, poltergeist" seemed rude. "Do you have a name?"

Her eyes softened, and she tilted her head. She seemed taken aback, as she appeared to be digging deep into her thoughts, reaching for something that had long been buried. "A name…" she murmured in a wistful tone. "It's been a long time since anyone asked me that."

He waited as she dug through her memories, watching as she seemed to struggle to find what she was looking for, and then suddenly, as if a light had turned on, her expression jumped. "Adaira," she said, like she was surprised it came to her. "That was my name… once."

"Adaira," he repeated, testing it out. "It suits you."

"You think so?" she asked earnestly.

"Better than Heart of the House," he muttered, earning a chuckle from them both.

"Well, Adaira," he said, flashing her a smile as he said her name. "I'm running out of time. What do I do?"

"Time works differently here. It doesn't mean the same thing it does in your world," she answered. "It stretches and folds. What feels like hours to you might only be minutes to the other side. Or it could be the opposite." She paused and looked back inside the house. "For John, only a few minutes have passed since you came here, but that won't always be the case. You probably have more time than you think, but either way, you should use it wisely."

"Okay, great," he said, eager to get started. "What do I do with this time?"

"You are looking for the phantom, but you are not ready to face it, not in this place. Instead, you need to find Caleb."

"Caleb? I assumed the phantom had him."

"He will still be in the place he died," she said simply. "The phantom only takes what belongs to it. And Caleb's belonged to your friend."

"Okay, so he's still here because Jason was the one who killed him? Even so, why would finding him help me?"

"Spirits in the veil are pure—freed from the distractions, goals, and pretenses of humanity. In this place, he will be stuck where he died, stricken with guilt over what he did—or allowed to be done."

Caleb, he thought as confusion and anger swelled inside him. Whatever role he played—with Joanne, with Lyndsay—he wasn't sure he was ready to face him. The broken trust, the lies, Jason's death... It never even occurred to him that he would get these answers here, and as the confusion turned to rage, he didn't care about the guilt Caleb might be feeling.

Adaira could see where his thoughts were heading. "This is how you get what you need. You will have to put all your anger aside. Treat him like any other ghost who desires to move on. Do that, and he will tell you everything he knows."

As he worked to temper himself, to keep his eye on the ultimate goal of finding Joanne, he glanced at Adaira, watching her as she moved. Sometimes she glided, as though carried along a conveyor, while other times she blinked out of existence entirely, reappearing somewhere else. "How do you do that?" he asked suddenly.

"Do what?"

"The way you move," he said, gesturing at her. "Sometimes it's like you're floating, and others it's like… I don't know, like you're teleporting."

She smiled. "The Shade," she said simply. "It is the essence of the veil. It binds everything together, like a web of shadow and memory. I can step in and emerge anywhere it touches… only limited to what binds me here."

"Useful trick," he said. "Could I do that? To cover more ground faster?"

She thought about it for a moment. "I am not exactly sure," she said. "You are not like us… but you aren't entirely unlike us either… and you're not bound to anything. If the Shade accepts you, you could theoretically go anywhere."

"How would I even try?" he asked.

She nodded and thought for a moment, like she was trying to remember the individual steps to a process she'd long since mastered. "Focus," she said. "See a spot where you wish to be and imagine yourself dissolving into the shadows. See yourself becoming one with the veil itself and take a step forward."

"And if it doesn't work?" he asked.

"Then it's a good thing you still have feet," she said with a big grin.

He turned, staring at a spot a few feet away, and squared his shoulders as if preparing for a fight. "All right," he muttered to himself. "Focus, dissolve into the shadows, become one with the veil, and… step."

He shut his eyes and imagined the shadows curling in around him like a mist pulling him in. For a brief moment, he felt something—just a tiny flicker of movement, like the world was tilting beneath him. An excitement surged through him, and he opened his eyes.

He groaned, seeing he was only one step ahead, the step he'd taken, and turned back to Adaira. "I guess that answers that."

"You felt it, though, didn't you?"

"I think so… for like a second," he shot back, frustrated. "And now I'm here. A whole six inches closer."

"It's not about force, Mac. It's about trust. Let it carry you."

"Trust…" he echoed, throwing his hands up. "Trust the shadowy web of supernatural… whatever. Cozy."

"You're overthinking it. You've spent too much time fighting the veil, resisting its influence in your life, hating your gifts. Just let go. Try again."

He took a deep breath, nodding his head as he planted his feet and shook out his arms like a runner about to take off. He closed his eyes again and envisioned the mist wrapping him up and tugging at him gently. The air around him shifted, and the ground beneath him felt less solid. It was working.

When his eyes opened, he looked down and found he was two steps ahead this time, which was a slight improvement, but his frustration was mounting. "I feel stupid," he snapped, turning back to Adaira. "I'm not going to get anywhere like this. It isn't working."

"Do you treat every new thing like this? Give up if it's even the slightest bit hard?" she asked, losing patience with his lack of it. "Just surrender. Stop trying so hard. You can't control the Shade."

"Surrender… right. Let the creepy ghost magic do whatever it wants with me. Got it."

"You are closer than you think," she insisted. "That you moved at all means you're capable. One more time."

He groaned but relented quickly. Focusing on a point farther ahead this time, he repeated the process and felt the faint pull from the Shade, the tilt of the air, but again, he was still only a few feet closer.

"Okay…" he said as he threw his hands up. "I'm done. It's not happening."

"You're giving up?"

"No, I'm accepting reality," he countered. "Which is that I have legs, and I'm going to use them. Thank you for trying, but like you said, I need to use my time wisely."

She regarded him for a moment and then nodded in agreement. "I understand," she said. "Remember what I said about your humanity? John was right about one thing… The other spirits here, avoid them if you can. Most will only want your help, but there are older, more terrible things in the veil—things that have no memory of ever being human."

Mac started walking toward the cemetery, eager to get started. "All right, great," he said. "Let's go."

When she didn't answer, he checked behind him and saw she wasn't moving, and her eyes were more sorrowful.

"I can't go with you, Mac."

"What?" He turned and walked back toward her. "You said you wanted to help?"

"If I could do more, I would," she replied as she gestured at the house behind her. "But I am bound here. Just like in your world, I cannot leave the property."

It was a disappointing revelation, but it made sense. He nodded and smiled. "Thank you, Adaira… for everything."

He turned and started walking down the driveway, stopping only to say one last goodbye. "See you on the other side," he said, grinning like a fool. He glanced back to see if she was smiling, too. "Get it? Because I'm literally on the—"

"Go, Mac," she said, dry but not unkind. "Before you waste any more of your *wise* time." She smiled, but there was sadness beneath it, like an old friend saying goodbye for the last time.

He chuckled softly as he continued toward the road, unsure and wary of what was ahead of him, her warnings replaying in his mind, along with the promise he had made.

CHAPTER 24

TRAVERSING THE VEIL

An eerie facsimile of the road he knew stretched out ahead of him as he made his way to the cemetery. The air around him felt thicker than it was at the house, though it was calm, and unnaturally so.

He reached a stretch of fenced land surrounding an old farmstead. The house near the end of a fenced yard seemed worn but sturdy. Barely visible through the thick mist, there was a barn and a few outbuildings that leaned in the distance. He paused, resting his hand against one of the posts of the wooden fence, and stared off into the expansive yard.

It was a long walk, and he kept thinking about Adaira's movements and her attempts at teaching him how to more easily traverse the veil. *What the hell, why not?*

He found a point just past where the fence ended and closed his eyes, focusing and imagining the shadows curling around him and pulling him. For a moment, the air shifted, and his body felt weightless, though when he opened his eyes, he was standing exactly where he'd been.

"Dammit," he muttered, instinctively reaching up to brush back his hair. But he wasn't ready to give up just yet. He stepped back and planted his feet, trying again. This time he felt the pulling sensation come on faster and stronger. The mist around him felt like it was thickening, and before he knew it, he stumbled forward, landing flat on his face in the dirt.

"Son of a…" He groaned as he pushed himself up, brushing the grit off his hands, and as he straightened, a voice behind him froze him in place.

"What are you?" it asked with a curious tone.

He whipped around and found himself staring at a man dressed in coveralls and a white shirt, standing on the other side of the fence. His form was shimmering, a little dimmer than Mac's, and the edges of it were blurred like smoke. His eyes were wide and hollow, and they locked on Mac with an intensity that made his skin crawl.

"What are you?" the man repeated, this time with a more desperate tone. "You feel… different."

Mac took a quick step back, away from the fence. "Just passing through," he said. "What are you doing here?"

Shit, he thought, as he was already breaking the one rule both John and Adaira warned him about. He should have kept walking, but for whatever reason, he'd engaged.

The spirit hesitated and then turned to the farmhouse. "I can't leave," he said. "I've been here since I died… Stuck."

Another good reason to not engage: Mac didn't know what to say to this man, and he really didn't have the time, but he continued anyway, in spite of himself. "Stuck?"

"I don't know why," the spirit admitted. "Maybe it's because of them," he said as he gestured toward the house. "My wife. My kids. They live there."

"So… you're haunting your family?"

The man snapped back to face him. "Haunting?" he repeated back. "Maybe. I wasn't a good husband… or father. I made their lives harder than they had to be." He paused and stepped closer to the fence. "If I could just… make her understand how sorry I am, I feel like I could be free of this. But they never hear me."

Mac nodded, pretending to understand, and resumed walking toward the cemetery. "I'm very sorry to hear that. I… I hope you can find closure."

The spirit followed from the other side of the fence line, and his voice rose in desperation as he kept pace with him. "You're different," the spirit said again. "Maybe she'll listen to you. Please. Tell her I'm sorry. Tell her I loved her, even if I couldn't show it."

"I'm sorry," Mac said as he quickened his pace. "I'm not sure she'd hear me either."

The man tried to move closer, almost crossing the fence before being forced back by something neither of them could see, startling Mac and forcing him into a jog. "Please," he cried. "You can help me. You have to!"

"I… I'm sorry. I have something I need to do," Mac called back as he broke into a sprint, putting distance between himself and the spirit.

As he reached the end of the property line, he glanced back and saw the old man stopped at the fence line, unable to follow. His cries were louder, though muffled by the distance, and Mac could still feel the despair radiating off him.

"Please," the spirit said again, unrelenting and full of anguish. "Help me!"

Mac forced himself to turn away and continue down the road, and the farther he got, the quieter the cries became—though they never left him completely. Part of him wanted to help, but time wasn't on his side, and he wasn't even sure how to help at this point.

The man's pleas echoed in his mind, and he realized how much worse his presence may have been for the man. He saw Mac as hope, a hope that hadn't existed until that encounter, a hope that Mac had just crushed. He should have listened to their warnings.

The cemetery. He finally made it. The expanse of twisted gravestones, monuments, and gnarled trees stretched out before him. In the living world, it was quiet and somber—a place for the living to come and remember, with only a handful of pesky ghosts milling about to annoy him during his visits. Here in the veil, it was alive.

Ghosts peppered the landscape, a horde like something out of a zombie movie. Some stood silently at their graves while others wandered aimlessly, and a few loomed near the edges, staring outward like they were keeping guard.

He froze at the sight and thought back to the spirit from the farm. The desperation and his never-ending pleas for help. He did the math with what he was seeing in that graveyard.

Between him and Caleb, who was somewhere in the bunker below the barn on the complete opposite side of the cemetery, stood hundreds of spirits. He imagined each of them as desperate and unstable as that poor man at the farm. The thought of trying to walk through that… There was just no way.

Traveling the Shade crossed his mind, but the memory of eating dirt was still fresh. If he tried and failed here, he'd be surrounded and vulnerable to a throng of spirits. No, that wasn't an option. Not yet anyway.

He turned to the woods skirting the cemetery. It was the long way, for sure, but it was his best option. He'd use the trees to stay hidden until he reached the barn.

The woods were quiet, eerily so, but it did exactly what he'd hoped. He kept to the shadows, hurrying, but cautiously, to avoid drawing any attention to himself, only looking back occasionally to ensure he wasn't followed.

The spirits in the cemetery never noticed him, and he could see the barn coming into view through the trees. His plan worked. Until it didn't.

Without warning, something slammed into him and knocked him to the ground. He hit the dirt hard, tearing the wind from his ghostly lungs as he scrambled to push himself back up. Standing about ten feet away from him was another spirit, and before he could say anything, it vanished and reappeared on top of him, knocking him down again—a furious, screaming blur of translucent light.

"What are you?" the spirit shrieked as he settled back to his mark. "Why are you here?"

Mac rolled to his side and tried to put some distance between them, but the spirit darted forward again, slamming him down when he tried to stand.

"I'm…" he gasped. "Just passing through!"

"Liar!" the spirit screamed as he circled Mac like a predator, looking for the right moment to pounce. "You're trespassing. This is our place. You don't belong here!"

Mac tried again to stand, but the spirit kept knocking him down. Its movements were erratic, violent, too quick to anticipate, and each blow felt like an icy wind cutting through him, leaving him gasping for air.

"Please," he said, raising a hand up to shield himself from the onslaught. "I don't mean any harm… I'm looking for someone."

"Lies!" the spirit howled. "You don't belong here."

Mac's eyes darted in every direction, desperate to find a way out. There was obviously no reasoning with this spirit. He didn't seem to care about anything other than knocking him to the ground, and he couldn't keep taking hits like this. He could feel it taking a toll, even if he didn't know what that meant.

In his desperation, he once again thought about the Shade. It wasn't reliable, but he had to try. Focusing through the pain and the spirit's incoherent shouting, he locked on the barn across the distance. He closed his eyes and pictured himself there, dissolving into the shadows just as Adaira tried to teach him. He felt the familiar pull and the shift in the air… but in the last moment, another thought crept in—home.

When he opened his eyes, he wasn't at the barn, not even close. He was back in his house, sitting cross-legged on his coffee table. The soft light replaced the gray haze of the veil, and his eyes needed a moment to refocus. As they did, he saw John sitting at the dining room table across the room, staring at him with a shocked look on his face.

"Why'd you pull me out? I was right there!" Mac yelled.

"I didn't," he snapped as he stood up from his chair. "Mac… You're glowing."

Mac looked down. John was right. A faint ripple of light danced across his exposed skin. He pulled his hand up in front of his face, turning it as the glow followed its movements. It felt like static but moved in ununiformed waves like a thick fluid.

"What the hell?"

John stepped back, grabbing the wall between the rooms to steady himself, only moments before the house groaned. Mac's body jerked, like someone grabbing his shirt from behind to pull him off the table. He tried to look behind him but the glow surrounding him began peeling away, stretching toward the ceiling.

The house was feeding.

He fought to keep his eyes open as the negative pressure threatened to siphon away his breath along with the aura. But when he could open them, he saw a figure taking form in the glow as it was forcefully detached from him. The spirit from the woods. Somehow, it hitched a ride through the Shade. And the house, Adaira, wasn't having any of it.

"Mac!" John yelled as he rushed to help. Before he could get to him, Mac felt the pull once again, harder this time. The warmth vanished, replaced by the icy chill of the Veil, as he landed back in the woods, flat on his back, with the angry spirit looming above him.

"What did you just do?" the spirit asked, looking around him, confused and even more angry than before.

With no time to think about what had just happened, Mac closed his eyes again, drawing in a long, shaky breath. He focused on the barn, and the pull of the Shade came almost instantly this time, and far stronger than before. The air shifted and folded around him, and he prayed silently that it would work before the spirit landed another blow.

A thud jolted him as his body hit something solid, the impact sending a sharp ache into his shoulder. It didn't feel like the spirit that time, and when he forced his eyes open, he was leaning against the side of the barn.

He stayed for a moment, still, as the realization sank in. Not only had he gotten it to work, but it had taken him exactly where he wanted it to. "Yes!" he yelled out before diminishing into embarrassment.

He looked around for any trace of the aggressive spirit that had ambushed him, but he'd escaped it. Just him and the barn, and below it—Caleb.

CHAPTER 25

MURDER BUNKER

Mac stepped into the barn, scanning the empty room before heading to the trapdoor he and John had escaped from the night before. He shoved aside some straw covering it and pulled it up, crouching to look down the staircase leading to the bunker below.

The memories of Lyndsay's and Jason's last moments were front and center, and he hesitated at the top of the stairs, taking one last breath to steady himself. He pushed through and forced himself to take that first step down.

He took one last look at the empty barn before descending, and brushed his hand over the rough stone wall, careful not to lose his footing. Fear gnawed at him and doubts whispered in his ears, growing louder with each step down. But he couldn't stop. He had to find Caleb.

It was just as he'd remembered, like an old black-and-white photo of the nightmare he'd just survived. The bolted chair sitting in the center, the straps dangling down, taunting him; the surgical tools and cold steel cabinets all remained.

A figure kneeled in the corner, hunched and rocking with their hands covering their ears. It felt like something was going to jump out at him at any moment, kicking his unease into overdrive.

"Caleb," Mac whispered, just in case they weren't the only ones down there.

The figure froze unnaturally fast and straightened itself, and Mac caught a glimpse of his face. It was him. He tilted his head as if straining to listen to something that Mac couldn't hear.

"Mac," he said with sharp surprise in his voice, and a slight edge of relief. "You're here, too?"

"Caleb," Mac said again, fighting the urge to explode on the man. Anger and bitterness swelled within him, but he fought to swallow it down. Caleb wasn't the enemy—not anymore. "I need your help."

Caleb stared at him, his surprise shifting to confusion. "I don't think we can help anyone anymore," he said as he gestured vaguely around the room. "The living don't hear the dead."

Mac stepped forward, careful to keep his movements and his eyes neutral. He knew now that spirits in this place could hurt him, and he had no desire for another round like the one in the woods. "I'm not dead, Caleb," he said. "I came here to find you."

Caleb's head snapped up as a look of defiance, or maybe fear, crossed his face. "Everything here is dead. Hopeless, alone, and dead."

"Look at me," Mac said in a slightly more demanding tone. "Really look. I'm not like you."

Caleb froze, then slowly tilted his head and squinted, like he was trying to focus on Mac in a way he hadn't before. Suddenly, he was no longer in the corner, and he appeared directly in front of Mac, sending a jolt through him that almost knocked him back. He could feel the cold radiating off him, tickling the tiny hairs on his arms.

Caleb was just inches away, scrutinizing him intensely. There was something almost primal about the way Caleb studied him, like he was seeing something new. "You are… different," he said finally. "Not like me, not like them… What are you?"

Mac took a deep breath and held his ground, despite the mix of fear and hatred the encounter provided him. "I'm alive," he said, keeping the calmness in his voice. "I found a way in so you could help me find Joanne."

Caleb's expression softened the moment her name left Mac's mouth, and he backed away a few steps, no longer interested in what made Mac different. "Joanne," he repeated like an old fond memory he hadn't considered in years. He turned his head as a look of shame fell over him. "Jeremiah has Joanne."

"Jeremiah?" Mac asked as he stepped forward, barely able to contain himself. "Who is Jeremiah?"

Caleb didn't answer and refused to face Mac, turning away as Mac tried to get in front of him. "Look," Mac said. "I need to know who he is, Caleb… and I think deep down, you want to make this right. Just tell me what I need to know so I can save her… Who is Jeremiah?"

Caleb stiffened, and he seemed to flinch whenever Mac said the name. "Caleb—"

"He's my brother," Caleb interrupted as his head dropped.

Mac stopped, thinking back on whether he knew Caleb had a brother. He knew Caleb well, had known him for years. How could he not know he had a brother? "What?"

Caleb nodded, though he didn't look up. "He wasn't always like this. He had it rough growing up, ya know… we both did." He hesitated, like he was trying to find a way to speak words he'd long buried.

"Our dad was a monster, Mac. A mean, abusive drunk who…" He finally looked up at Mac. "He used to lock our mom in the basement when they fought, like some… disobedient animal."

Mac kept quiet, sensing that this explanation was something Caleb needed and would ultimately lead to the information he needed. He listened in horror as Caleb told the story of his mother's death at the hands of his father.

"He choked her… and we just stood there, too scared to move. Then he made us help him hide her… bury her in a field. Told everyone she'd run off and left him. No one questioned it. No one cared."

Mac felt a twinge of sadness hearing the story, but it wasn't nearly enough to sweep away the anger about Joanne, Lyndsay, or the countless others that were kidnapped and murdered, but he kept his mouth and his rage shut.

"He never really got over it," Caleb continued, his voice trembling. "It broke something in him. He shut down… stopped talking. And the fits… he was so angry. I thought maybe, once the old bastard finally died, we could start over. Took the money he left, bought a house, the bar, everything. I thought I could give him a safe space. A way to heal."

"But it didn't work," Mac said.

"No," Caleb admitted as his voice shifted from sorrow to disgust. "He got much worse. I'd find dead animals in his room, and he'd become obsessed with women at the bar. I didn't know what to do." He paused and lowered his head for a moment before continuing. "Then one night… I came home and found him in the cellar, standing over a girl. A young woman I'd never seen before. He killed her, Mac. Choked her. Just like…"

His voice cracked, and he shook his head in shame. "I should have stopped it then. Called the cops," he continued. "But he was my brother. My baby broth… I thought if I helped him hide it… If I kept him safe… I could find a way to save him. It just kept happening, and I… I was a coward."

Mac inhaled, taking in a slow, measured breath before allowing himself to speak. He'd heard enough, and it was time to get the answer he was there to find. "Where's Joanne?"

"I don't know if she's still alive, Mac," he answered quickly. "If she is… if there's any chance at all, I'll help you."

"Just tell me where she is, and I'll do the rest."

Caleb hesitated, his shoulders slumping under the crushing weight of his guilt. "Go to the house… Country Road 26. Follow it past the reservoir. It's the only house off the road. Look for the storm cellar. That's where he keeps them."

He got it. It was unbelievable, and he struggled to maintain his composure. He knew who the man was, and he knew where to find her. He knew everything he needed to know. Without saying a word to Caleb, he turned toward the door with a new, singular, sharp focus. It was time to end this.

"Mac, wait… there's something else."

He stopped just before reaching the door but refused to face him. "What is it?"

"I saw him… when I got here," he said. "He's not my brother anymore… There's something wrong with him. He's something worse."

Mac turned his head and stared directly into Caleb's eyes, hard and unforgiving. "I know exactly what he is, Caleb… What you helped him become."

Just as the last syllable left his mouth, he felt a pull—a tugging force coming from every direction, like something was gripping him with invisible hands, dragging him upward. It wasn't gentle—it was relentless, disorienting, and raw. It felt like when he entered the Shade, but rougher—like someone was forcing it. He tried to fight it, whatever it was, but it was too strong.

The world around him faded into a blur, and suddenly, with a jarring, violent shift, he was slammed back into the world of the living. He gasped, filling his lungs like he'd just emerged from a deep pool. His senses returned all at once, and he was home, for good this time, with John standing over him.

"I got it, John," he said immediately. "I know where she is."

CHAPTER 26

EGGS AND A SIDE OF WTF

"We have to go," Mac said urgently as he paced across the room, pausing at the window to stare out at the darkened yard. Caleb's words looped in his head. *The storm cellar. That's where he keeps them.*

"I get it," John shot back, watching him from the entryway of the dining room. "But we need a plan."

"I have a plan. We go, we find her, and we bring her home."

John sighed, and Mac could feel the frustration coming off him. "That's not a plan," he said plainly. "It's a suicide mission. You tried that before. He's too strong."

Mac seethed. He was so close to ending this nightmare and getting Joanne back home where she belonged. He knew John was right. Hell, even he couldn't stop the thing. "What about that thing you did before? Can you like… trap him or something?"

"That only worked because he wasn't expecting it," he answered. "The phantom's smart. He'll be ready for it next time…" He paused and sighed again, and Mac could tell there was more.

"What is it?"

230

"He has Lyndsay in there with him now… I'm worried… she'll make him stronger."

"What do you mean?" he said, finally turning his attention from the yard.

"I think the phantom will have the ability to affect the real world… directly."

Mac stared at him, letting his words sink in before shaking his head. "Great… John. That is fantastic news…" Then a thought struck him—a wild, desperate thought—as he recalled the night of his accident. "What about that nuke? The thing you did the night we met?"

John stood up straight, the shocked look on his face telling Mac everything. "*You* want me to do that again?" he asked, his disbelief completely unhidden. "No, it's not possible, anyway. I had to destroy something very powerful to make that happen, something very rare."

"Christ, John, what, then? We just sit around here twiddling our thumbs?"

"Of course not. But we play it smart. We need a plan. If we screw this up, we all die. You know, if we could just get him to come here… This house would make short work of him."

Suddenly, Mac remembered the promise he made to Adaira. "John!" he said, turning and rushing toward him. "What about the book?"

"What book?"

"The book… the *EGGS* thing."

John squinted at him. He could tell that he was surprised Mac had even asked about it, and he could also see that he'd been hiding something.

"Adaira told me it had power," Mac continued.

John stiffened and reversed the step back he'd just taken, reclaiming the distance between them and resetting Mac's bravado. "Who… or what is an Adaira?"

Mac backed up. He knew he was about to get an earful once he explained, but it was worth it if it helped them get to Joanne. "She's… the heart of the house," he said reluctantly. "The poltergeist. She kind of spoke to me in the veil."

John closed his eyes and sighed. "You just had a leisurely chat with the poltergeist… and it gave you advice… and you think it was good advice?" he said as his tone elevated with each fractured question. "What the hell, Mac?"

"She helped," Mac said, defending himself. "I never would have gotten anywhere if she hadn't."

"There is no way she did it out of the kindness of her heart, Mac. What did you give her in return?"

"Nothing," he shouted before calming himself. "Yet… look, she asked me to exorcise her."

"What?"

"She said the book could do it, that it was more than just an encyclopedia."

John's stunned silence was answer enough for Mac. He looked like he was considering it, like it could be something.

"Is it true?" Mac pressed.

After a few more silent moments, John finally answered. "Sort of," he said, exhaling a long, sharp breath through his nose. "It's not some all-powerful weapon. Yes, it can absorb spirits that have been cataloged… but it's not nearly strong enough… And it's dangerous, a tool created by necromancers, and you don't trust tools created by necromancers," he said as his voice escalated. "Just like you don't take advice from a freaking poltergeist."

"And yet, you wrote me into it," Mac said, changing the subject to something he thought he could control.

John flinched and dropped his tone. "That's different," he said quietly. "I never would have… I didn't know what you were becoming. I had to prepare for the worst."

Once again, silence filled the space, both too heated to continue arguing. Finally, John broke first. "Did she happen to give you any clues about how to make it powerful enough to kill the phantom?"

Mac shook his head. "No, actually," he replied, more calm than before. "She didn't say to use it on the phantom… She wanted me to use it on her."

Something in John's eyes lit up, and his eyes narrowed as he stared past Mac, mumbling something he couldn't understand.

"What is it?"

"It's not powerful enough…" he said, trailing off before looking at Mac. "She would go willingly? No resistance? No fight?"

"That's what she said," Mac answered. "She made me promise."

A cold, calculating look flashed across his face as he walked toward the front door. "This could work," he said, almost to himself.

"Where are you going?" Mac demanded as he followed him to the door.

"We have a poltergeist to kill," he said as he stepped outside. "And we have our plan."

He followed John to the car, putting together the plan John had concocted in the house as he walked around to the passenger door. When he looked up, John was not getting in the car as he expected and instead was heading to the trunk.

"What are we doin'?" he asked as he met him at the rear of the car. "Don't we need to get the book?"

John smirked, his eyes gleaming with something close to satisfaction as he popped open the trunk.

As the lid opened, the light shone down, illuminating a chaotic treasure trove of arcane paraphernalia. It was like a mobile version of John's shop crammed into the tiny space, a sort of haphazard mix of dusty tomes, dried herbs, and vials of who knew what. At the center, surrounded by candles in various stages of melt and unmarked jars, he saw it: the book.

He let out a short laugh in disbelief. "You had it the whole…" And then the smell hit him like a freight train.

A foul, sulfuric stench poured out of the trunk, slamming hard into Mac's face. He gagged and staggered back as the acrid odor of rotten eggs and decay reached deep inside his nostrils. "What the hell is that?" he said through the coughs as he waved his hand in front of his face.

John glanced over, a small smirk of amusement threatening to burst out into full laughter as he reached into the trunk. "Asafetida," he said with a smug sort of satisfaction as he brushed aside a loose bundle of herbs to grab the book. "Dried sap. For banishing spirits."

"For banishing everything, you mean," Mac shot back, holding his nose.

John let out a rare chuckle and slammed the trunk lid shut, gesturing for Mac to follow him back into the house. "I hope she's as willing as you say. That's the only way this is going to work."

The house seemed to hold its breath as John set the book on the dining room table, the heavy thud echoing through the room. Mac watched, his eyes darting between the book and the empty space around him, half expecting Adaira to appear or the house to fall down in protest.

"I'm not sure I understand how this is going to help?" Mac said. "I thought you said the book wasn't powerful enough?"

"The book gets stronger with every spirit it collects. If this… Adaira really will go without a fight, it'll be a massive power-up."

"So it's like the phantom?"

"It's more like the poltergeist, really," he said as he thumbed through the pages. "The phantom collects spirits, and they become part of it, feeding it and making it stronger. The book only keeps the energy… nothing of the spirit remains."

"What happens to the spirit? It's just gone?"

"It's a true death, yes." John paused but didn't look up. "It's why we don't use it carelessly. If there is an afterlife, anything taken by the book will never see it."

"Jesus," Mac whispered as he thought about Adaira. Suddenly, it seemed wrong to use her sacrifice as a weapon. He looked around, hoping she understood what she had asked him to do. Hoping it was what she really wanted.

"So, what? No chanting… circles… candles?" Mac asked, trying to shake the weight of what they were doing from his head.

"Nope. The book doesn't need theatrics; it is the ritual." He stopped on a page near the middle and turned the book toward Mac. The text, though verbose and hard to read, clearly bore the title: *Poltergeist – Collective Entities.*

"Just out of curiosity. What happens if she doesn't go willingly… like she changes her mind at the last minute?"

John turned and looked him square in the face, with the most serious look Mac had ever seen. "That… would be very bad for both of us," he said before turning back to the book. "Best-case scenario, the book would explode and we'd die instantly."

"Do I want to know what the worst case is?"

"Probably not," John snapped back. "Look, it's your call. If you trust her… I'll trust you."

He stared at the page as a growing unease built up inside him. "That's it? Just open to the right page and… what? The book does the rest?"

"Not quite," John said as he reached into his pocket and pulled out a pocketknife, flicking it open.

"Ah… right," Mac said. "More blood."

John shot Mac a knowing smirk. "It requires a *little* blood," he continued. "A connection between the practitioner and the target spirit. Simple but effective."

Mac raised an eyebrow, his unease coming to the surface. "Simple? You're literally bleeding into a cursed book."

John shrugged. "Would you rather do the honors?"

Mac didn't answer, figuring his silence was answer enough.

He pressed the blade against his palm, a sight Mac was becoming far too comfortable seeing, and sliced quickly. A small bead of blood welled up, and he turned his hand over the book. "It's now or never. Make the call."

Mac wrestled with it in his head. It had to work. Why would she help him if she didn't want this? Was he ready to risk his life? Would Joanne survive without this? And that last thought was all he needed.

"Do it."

John slammed his hand down, pressing it firmly on the book, smearing his blood out across the page. The book responded immediately. The letters glowed as the blood seemed to be absorbed into them, pulsing in time with a new hum filling the room.

A tremble rolled through the floor and walls, and Mac grabbed the doorframe to stabilize him. Then the hum transformed into a low, guttural growl that rose into a deafening roar as a whirlwind of energy erupted out of nowhere and swirled through the room like a storm.

"Is this supposed to happen?" he yelled over the noise.

John didn't answer. His focus remained entirely on the book. His hand firmly pressed against the page, still feeding the book with his blood. The glowing letters pulsed faster, and Mac thought he could see tendrils of energy winding toward the book, drawn into the pages.

Then he saw her. Adaira's form appeared in the storm for a moment. She looked right at him. It seemed like she might resist, but then her lips turned up into the faintest smile. He thought he heard her say, "Thank you." She lowered her head, and just like that, she was gone.

The energy continued to surge as the last of the house's essence spiraled into the book. It drank it all in, and then it all stopped. The house was silent again, and the air felt lighter—empty.

John pulled his hand away from the book, and the cut was healed, as though it had never been there. The two stood there staring at each other, both kind of shocked that it worked.

"A lot smoother than I expected," John said quietly, looking like he was thrilled to still be breathing.

Mac nodded but didn't respond. He hoped he had done the right thing. He looked around the house, and it felt different, quieter. Like having lived with a hum in your ears your whole life and only noticing it when it stopped. He smiled and offered Adaira a quiet, "No, thank you."

He took a deep breath and straightened his shoulders. Whatever came next, he knew they were one step closer to facing the phantom—one step closer to finding Joanne.

John closed the book, sending another heavy thud echoing across the room, and ran a hand across the cover. "It's done," he said, almost to himself. "We're ready."

Mac watched, noticing some small hint of hesitation in his voice and a subtle furrow in his brow. Quite the contrast against the normal cocky arrogance he was so proud of. "You still don't think this will work, do you?"

John exhaled, and his hand lingered on the book. "I don't know," he admitted. "It could work… it could fail," he continued. "Or it could backfire spectacularly."

Mac nodded, wishing he'd had the luxury of doubt that John had. "Unless you've come up with something else in the last three seconds, it's all we got."

John tucked the book under his arm and turned toward the door. "I'll be in the car," he said, his voice wary from the ordeal. "Get your head right, Mac. It's about to get hairy, and we need you sharp."

He shot John a quick nod and shoved his hands in his pockets, looking around the now-quiet house. "Be there in a minute."

John hesitated, like he wanted to say more but thought better of it, and left without another word.

There was a faint click as the door shut behind him, and the silence that followed was deafening. Mac stared at the spot where he'd just said goodbye to Adaira as his mind churned. The noise was gone. That blanket of unease he'd felt for years had evaporated. He had become used to it, even appreciative of it. It kept him safe, alert, and made him feel less alone. And now it was gone.

He glanced around the room, half expecting to find Adaira's flickering form one last time, but he found nothing. It was just a house.

He sat in one of the dining room chairs and put his head in his hands as the image of Adaira's essence fading into nothing was seared into his mind. It wasn't just her, it was Lyndsay, too, the way the phantom had consumed her. The helplessness he'd felt watching her slip away all came crashing back like an avalanche of grief and guilt that started with Josie so many years ago.

"Josie," he whispered as he leaned back, staring at the ceiling as if all the ghosts from his past might be staring back at him. "I miss you. God, I miss you."

He closed his eyes and pictured all he had lost, one by one. Lyndsay, Jason, Adaira, Josie. And even Caleb, whom he'd once counted as a friend. "I'm sorry I couldn't save you. I'm sorry I couldn't… do better."

He took in the room one last time. The house that once groaned, whispered, and watched over him, now just a house—as empty as he felt inside.

His throat tightened as he nearly lost himself in his sorrow and self-pity and sat forward, refusing to let it consume him. "But I won't let Joanne end up like you. I won't let him win. I'll make this right, I swear it."

He pushed himself to his feet, shoving the chair loudly across the floor. "And John…" he added. "You're a colossal pain in my ass," he said, looking toward the door. "I'm sorry that I dragged you into this. I won't let you pay for my mistakes."

He straightened himself and rolled his shoulders to shake off the weight of his grief. He grabbed his jacket and headed to the door. Whatever was about to happen, it would end tonight, one way or another.

CHAPTER 27

ONE WAY OR ANOTHER

The drive to the farmhouse was a long one, and quiet—the only sounds coming from Mac nervously tapping his fingers against his thigh. His head was all over the place, bouncing from dread to sorrow to self-doubt to resolve. As they got closer, it became clearer to him that they were still underprepared.

"This is risky," he said, breaking the long silence.

John kept his eyes on the road ahead and tightened his hands around the wheel. "This was your idea."

"No, I know," Mac replied quickly. "I mean… maybe we get backup?"

John shot him a curious glance. "You mean like the police?" he asked. "You think sending a SWAT team in, guns blazing, makes this any less risky?"

Mac turned toward him for the first time since they left the house. "What about Special Agent… what's-his-face? At least he knows there's more going on here than just some psycho with a bunker."

He shook his head and pressed his lips into a tight line. "What do you think happens if we call him? He's going to bring backup. They show up, sirens blaring, and Jeremiah panics. Joanne's the first thing he'll take off the board."

"Okay, I get it," Mac fired back. "But even you said you didn't know if this was going to work. What if we fail, and we're the only ones who know…? We need a plan B."

"Fine. We call him when we get there," he said. "Should give us enough time to deal with the phantom before anyone else shows up. If they charge in too soon… it won't end the way we want it to." He paused for a moment before continuing. "You realize," he said, glancing sidelong, "plan B means we're dead."

The car fell silent again as the tension mounted. Mac stared at the windshield as his stomach twisted harder with each passing mile. After a few minutes, he broke the silence again. "What about a gun? Just, you know…" He made a crude gun shape with his fingers and clucked his tongue.

John snorted, though there wasn't any humor in it. "I wish it were that simple," he said. "He's not your run-of-the-mill psycho. That thing has its claws so deep in him… You shoot him, and best-case scenario, the phantom jumps to someone else and we're back to square one."

"Someone else? You expecting another serial killer host hangin' about?"

"It just needs to be someone with the capacity to kill." He paused and looked directly at Mac. "We all try to be good, Mac, but in the end, I don't think either of us can be sure we aren't vulnerable."

"Okay… Understood. And worst case?"

"If we're really lucky, it just keeps his corpse moving. Guns don't solve this problem."

Mac sighed. They had enough problems without adding psycho zombie hicks to the mix. "I should've grabbed a drink."

John looked over again, his expression softening. "You're sharper without it. We run in smart. We deal with the phantom first… then we deal with the man."

They rounded a bend in the road, and a solitary farmhouse came into focus. It was dark, like no one was home, but a single light near the side porch lit up the area, exposing the storm cellar door.

"This is it," John said quietly. "One way or another."

Mac nodded, though he struggled to push the anxiety down. He tilted his head toward his lap and took one long breath. "I'll call Graham."

The car came to a quiet stop along the side of the dirt road outside the front gate, and Mac peered out the window past John, scanning the darkened expanse of land beyond the fence. What must have once been a thriving farm, now just a seemingly never-ending plot of neglect, weeds, and a barely standing fence.

John killed the engine and leaned forward, squinting through the windshield. "I don't see any other cars," he muttered. "Doesn't mean no one's home, though, so stay sharp."

Mac shifted in his seat, trying to get a better look at the house at the other end of the driveway. Across from it stood a large barn that hadn't seen any real use or care in years. The red paint was chipped and peeled, and the weathered roof slumped in the middle, like it was just minutes from collapsing. Between the two buildings was the door to the storm cellar—their destination.

"He must be here. Why else would that light be on?"

"Or he left in a hurry," John countered, though Mac could sense the doubt in his voice.

Mac reached into the back seat and grabbed the book, handing it to John, hopeful he would take it, and he wouldn't be the one slicing his palm open to juice the thing up.

John looked at the book and then back up to Mac before reluctantly accepting it. "We're going to assume he's inside," he said, rolling his eyes. "We stay quiet. Focus on getting Joanne. If it goes south…" He trailed off, tapping the book's cover.

Mac nodded, but the tension was building, and he could feel himself grinding his teeth. "Right. We look for Joanne, not the phantom. No heroics," he said, trying to relax his jaw.

John stepped out first, tucking the book into a small bag strapped across his chest and gestured for Mac to follow as he approached the gate. The rusted hinges let out a whiny groan as he pushed it open. They both winced as the sound seemed ten times louder than it needed to be and went on ten times longer than it should have.

Each step toward the cellar felt heavier than the last, and the air became thick and cold. Mac heard every crunch his boots made on the gravel under his feet—the only time he wasn't focusing on his heart pounding in his ears.

As they passed the barn, his eyes darted to its dark, shadowy entrance. "You think he's in there?" Mac whispered, gesturing toward the open door.

John shook his head and gestured silently toward the cellar, as if to say, "It doesn't matter. Shut up. Focus."

As they got closer, the light above the cellar flickered once, sending a jolt of extra panic right into Mac's chest. He swallowed it down and sighed quietly, remembering to breathe. When they got to the door, John reached out and cupped the unhasped lock dangling from the wooden frame and shot Mac a look.

"That's not a good sign," Mac whispered.

John placed his hand on his bag, ensuring the book was still there. "It's now or never."

John held the doors open, and Mac descended first, taking slow, deliberate steps. The air was instantly warmer, and the faint scent of mildew and rust filled his nostrils as he made his way down. The cellar opened into a sprawling basement—much larger than Mac had expected—lined with shelves stacked with dusty jars, old tools, and forgotten storage containers. It was quiet, aside from a faint hum coming from something out of sight.

"Dark in here," John muttered as he followed behind.

Mac dragged his fingers along the edges of the wall, searching for a switch but not finding one. "There's gotta be a light somewhere."

"Here," John replied as he reached up, pulling a string dangling from the ceiling, and a bare bulb flickered to life, throwing shadows across the room as it swayed.

Mac spotted a massive metal door at the far end of the cellar, starkly contrasting the more earthy decor in the surrounding room. It had a large circular wheel-like handle in the center, and the edges were reinforced with thick steel. It looked old but sturdy, and it bore the unmistakable markings of an old fallout shelter.

John approached the door, carefully running his fingers over the surface. "I've never seen anything like this," he said. "It's like a giant safe."

"It's an old bomb shelter," he replied as he reached to open the door. As soon as he grabbed the wheel handle, the familiar weight of dread settled over him. At first, he thought it was just the anxiety of not knowing what they were walking into that caused it, but as the seconds passed, it grew stronger, sharper, and more suffocating. His breath hitched and then quickened, and he stumbled, reaching for the edge of a nearby shelf to steady himself.

"Mac?" John said, his voice leaving no room for doubt that he was concerned. "What's wrong?"

He didn't respond immediately, his focus split between the building pressure inside and scanning his surroundings, looking for the cause. His pulse hammered in his ears, and his vision blurred around the edges. "God," was all he managed to let out.

"Talk to me, Mac," John said, more urgently now. "What is it?"

"He's here," Mac muttered, gripping at his shirt, trying to lessen the tightening in his chest. And then the room exploded into chaos.

A shadow shifted in his periphery, and before he could say anything, an unseen force yanked John backward, throwing him across the cellar and slamming him onto a wooden shelf. Cans and jars toppled to the ground, shattering as they hit the floor, spilling their contents in every direction. "John!" he shouted as he stumbled forward.

He scanned the room, clenching his fists as he searched for the man or the phantom. The air became charged with electricity, sending the hairs on his arms to full attention and setting his nerves on fire.

John let out a groan, letting Mac know he was at least still breathing, and then pulled himself up from the debris. "Mac," he gasped. "We got company."

Mac's eyes darted around the room, still searching. The shadows along the edges of the cellar seemed to pulse and shift, writhing like something alive. They grew thicker and darker as they pressed in from all sides, and the air went heavy.

A low, guttural growl filled the space, vibrating his chest and rattling his already frayed nerves. It was unlike anything he'd heard before, a primal, otherworldly rumble. He tried desperately to steady himself, but the anxiety twisted in his gut. And then he appeared.

Out of the shadows, the massive figure loomed. He seemed impossibly tall and stood with an unnervingly still calm. Jeremiah. His features were distorted—more monstrous than their last meeting—and his hulking form exuded an unnatural menace.

Mac clutched his chest, still struggling to breathe as the man stepped closer. The growl deepened. It vibrated through him so hard he wasn't sure if it was coming from Jeremiah or something inside himself.

"Jeremiah," he whispered, hoping the sound of his name would calm him. It was desperate, he knew, but he wasn't sure what else to do.

He didn't respond, though his head tilted slightly, as if he were studying Mac, as if trying to decide how he knew his name. Then his lips curled into a faint, twisted smile.

Behind him, John got to his feet and wiped blood from the corner of his mouth. "Mac…" he called out. "Stay sharp."

But Mac couldn't look away. He could see it now—the phantom. It was there, wrapped around the man like a second skin—a malevolent energy swirling around him like a dark mist. The figure standing there wasn't just a man with something inside him—it was something far worse, and it was staring straight into his soul.

In the background, John didn't hesitate. He flipped open his pocketknife and sliced a clean line across his palm, then hissed through the pain, refusing to falter. He grabbed the book from his bag and flipped it straight to the marked page.

The movement caught the phantom's attention first, and its head turned unnaturally fast, followed quickly by Jeremiah's head, his deadened eyes locking onto John.

"Mac, move!" he barked as he pressed his bloodied hand down on the open page.

His hand was on the page for hardly a second before a shadowed tendril lashed out from the phantom, striking the book from John's hands with precision. Another shot out an instant later, slamming into John's chest like a battering ram, pinning him against the wall.

"John!" he shouted, lunging forward, but another tendril coiled toward him, stopping him short.

Suddenly, the phantom's face formed in the mass, staring directly into his eyes as it moved closer, still pinning John against the wall across the room. "What are you?"

Mac's eyes went wide as the low, growly voice reverberated through the room. It could speak, and it was curious about him.

He must have shown his shock on his face, because the monster spoke again as it gently slid its tendril down his cheek.

"Ah, yes, I learned a few tricks from your friend," it said. "I should thank you for the gift."

Mac thought of Lyndsay and her sacrifice as she tried to save him from his own mistake. The sorrow and guilt wanted to take over him, but his rage beat it down. He wanted to lash out, but his body felt like lead—the anxiety washing over him in waves.

"Mac!" John yelled, cutting through the haze. "He's got my hands. I can't cast. Get the book!"

Mac's eyes flicked over to the book lying across the room with its pages still open, and his heart pounded while his mind screamed at him to move.

"Go, Mac. Now!"

The phantom turned its attention back to John, pressing into his chest harder, forcing a quick grunt to escape. Mac watched as the phantom toyed with him, threatening to squeeze the life out of him as slowly as possible. He again thought of Lyndsay, and then Jason, and looked at John. He would not let it happen again, and he used that new determination to force himself to his feet.

With a growl, he pushed past the anxiety and ran. He took a step, then another, and the weight on his chest gradually lifted as the adrenaline surged through him.

The phantom snapped its attention back to the fleeing Mac, its hiss piercing through the cellar as it shot its tendrils toward him. He ducked just in time, and the shadowy limb whipped past his head, striking a shelf behind him with a crack.

Mac briefly looked up at the approaching Jeremiah before bolting toward the stairs, skidding slightly across the floor as he snatched up the book. Another tendril shot forward, grazing his shoulder as he dove, his hand closing around the book's cover. The pain seared through him, but he didn't stop.

The phantom roared, and its tendrils lashed out wildly. Mac staggered backward, narrowly dodging one of the flailing limbs as he rushed up the stairs.

"Get out of—" he heard John yell before he was cut off by another wave of crashing coming from behind him. He hoped he was okay, but he didn't have time to worry about that then.

His feet pounded against the steps as the shadows chased him out of the cellar, clawing at his heels as he pushed himself forward.

He burst through the cellar doors and gasped for air as he stumbled to the ground. For a moment, he allowed himself to pause, clutching the book to his chest as he turned to look back at the cellar, before forcing himself back to his feet. He darted forward to put some distance between him and the shadow following him out and then turned.

He stumbled back, his shoulder throbbing with each step as the phantom emerged first, then Jeremiah. Its tendrils of shadow spilled out as they hit the surface, filling the space around them. Jeremiah was barely visible behind the writhing darkness of the phantom's monstrous visage.

He clutched the book tightly in one hand and his wounded shoulder under the other. His breaths were labored, coming in shallow as the spirit's oppressive energy radiated toward him, making every movement feel heavier and more futile. He could feel it preparing to strike.

"Come on, then!" he yelled as he retreated. He searched for a way to escape, but the thing left no room for hope. The air crackled around it, and the shadows seemed to stretch out endlessly.

Suddenly, a gunshot rang out.

The phantom's approach paused, and its tendrils quivered slightly. Mac looked beyond it and saw another figure standing in the driveway. It was Agent Kane, his gun drawn—the smoke still curling from the barrel.

Jeremiah's head tilted, like he was hearing a distant sound, and the phantom's shadow pulled back, just enough for Mac to see the man clearly. Jeremiah looked down at his chest where a dark stain was spreading across his shirt around a gunshot wound, clean and precise, through and through.

Mac held his breath, and it was quiet, like the universe joined him. His heart thumped in his ears as he watched Jeremiah sway. For a brief, fleeting moment, the phantom's form seemed to falter, flickering like a dying flame.

"No..." Mac muttered, and watched in terror as the wound healed itself.

The shadow surged back with a vengeance, and it enveloped the man completely in an explosion of dark tendrils. It roared, shaking the air as one of the massive limbs lashed out, striking Graham squarely in the chest, throwing him to the ground with a bone-crunching force.

"Damn it," he yelled, looking over at Graham as the phantom advanced toward him. He was out of time and out of options. The thing was unstoppable.

His mind was spinning. He had the book, and he kind of knew what to do, but he didn't have a knife. As his shoulder throbbed, the realization struck him like a lightning bolt. He pulled his hand off the wound on his shoulder and looked down. Blood.

He gave the phantom one last, defiant look and flipped the book open, directly to the marked page. His fingers trembled as they landed on the title scrawled across the top: *Phantom: Amalgamate.*

The shadows surged toward him, but he didn't flinch and slammed his blood-soaked hand firmly on the page, looking up at the menace once again. "Gotcha."

It happened immediately. The power fired off from the book as it soaked in his blood. The blinding glow from the letters spread to the rest of the book and then outward like a ripple through a still pond.

It knew to be afraid of it. The phantom hesitated and recoiled, like it sensed the shift and what was about to happen. Mac steeled himself, certain that his victory was mere seconds away. But then the phantom did something Mac didn't expect.

It laughed.

Tendrils fired out in all directions, surging with a renewed strength and pressing against the glow from the book. It was just like the moment with Lyndsay. Mac's smile dropped as the glow faltered, and his heart sank as he felt the power from the book begin to fade.

"No," he hissed. "No, damn it. You are not winning this!"

But the glow continued to fade, and the symbols on the page dimmed until they were hardly visible. John was right. The phantom was too strong. The book was failing. He was failing.

The phantom surged forward, carrying Jeremiah with it as its darkness spread.

The weight of the phantom's energy pressed on him, suffocating and bearing down like a collapsing ceiling. He tightened his grip on the book, his last desperate hope, but even that had failed him. The glow that once pulsed with promise flickered weakly, dimming more with every passing second as the words on the page blurred and faded. The phantom's tendrils stretched farther, thickening and filling Mac's world with its void, pressing into every space, every breath, every thought, until nothing remained but shadow.

He closed his eyes tight, waiting for the inevitable. He could feel the phantom's approach—its presence beating down on him like pulses punching at his fear and anxiety. It reminded him of the spirit in the veil, slamming into him over and over, never giving him a moment to catch his breath.

Then, with a sudden, violent lurch, the world tilted. The shift came with no warning—no time to brace or understand what was happening. Something unseen, something deep inside him, twisted as gravity wrenched sideways like an invisible force had reached in and yanked him free.

The phantom's oppressive weight vanished in an instant, only to be replaced with something else, something familiar. The night blurred at the edges, and the colors bled into nothing, and then, with no resistance, he fell.

His knees hit the ground hard, shoving a gasp from his lungs. His hands pressed into something damp and unsteady as he scrambled to push himself up. The world around him was wrong, but in a familiar way that set his nerves on fire. He knew this place.

The veil.

He turned back toward the battle, toward the cellar, toward the monstrous thing that had nearly crushed him, but what he saw was far worse.

What he fought before, the towering mass of shadow wrapped around Jeremiah like a parasite, was exactly that—a shadow. Nothing more than an echo of what he was staring at in that moment. Here, in the veil, it was whole—a nightmare that Mac could never have conceived of.

More than just a shifting mass of darkness, it looked like a wound—a sort of tear in reality itself. A churning void, coiled and writhing—a vortex of consuming blackness that pulsed and shuddered. The tendrils that had lashed at him in the living world were mere fragments, and here the whole of it stretched endlessly, shifting in violent spasms. But it wasn't just darkness.

Faces bubbled up from within the mass, their forms stretching, mouths open in silent screams before being dragged back below the surface. He saw Lyndsay. Her expression twisted in terror and her hands clawed against the mass, as though she were trying to reach for something—for him. Jason surfaced only a moment later, his form flickering and his body writhing in the endless pull of the mass, his face contorting with shock and fury.

And there were others. So many others.

Dozens—maybe hundreds—of souls, torn from their lives and swallowed whole, trapped within the thing that had claimed them. They weren't gone like he'd assumed. Their suffering hadn't ended. It continued, trapped inside this monstrous entity, their endless torment feeding and sustaining it.

His breath hitched as the horror sank in. They weren't just ghosts; they were prisoners.

A tremor ran through the air, a shift he could feel in the way the veil moved around him. It knew he was there.

The churning darkness slowed for a moment, and then, as if the entire mass had turned its attention toward him, a single tendril reached out, slow and deliberate, like a curling finger beckoning him closer.

He tried to step back, but the moment he did, a chorus of desperate voices rose from the mass. They were calling him, begging, screaming in agony. The tendril twitched and shuddered unnaturally before curling back into itself.

And then the phantom spoke. Not in words or any language Mac had ever heard, but in a sound that crept into his bones.

I still see you.

The tendril shot back out and struck before he could react, sending him hurling backward. His body twisted violently before slamming to the ground, the impact crushing the air from his lungs. He gasped, rolling onto his hands and knees as he struggled to breathe.

He had to move, get back to the fight—to the book, John, Joanne. Everything that mattered was still in the living world, and without him, there was no one left to finish this. His body screamed in protest as he clenched his fists and forced himself to his feet. He had one way out, and it was time to use it.

He reached for the Shade, giving in, but also demanding it take him back. His eyes closed, and then suddenly, a hand clamped down on his arm, yanking him back.

He spun, expecting the phantom or one of the countless souls trying to drag him down, but instead found himself staring at Adaira—solid and shimmering, with a calm expression that made no sense with the chaos swirling around them. He froze, scrambling to process what he was seeing, because it wasn't possible. Not after what he'd done.

His voice came out hoarse, barely a whisper. "How are you here? We exorcised you."

Her lips twitched, like she found his disbelief amusing. "No, Mac. You set me free."

"So it was a trick?" he asked. "Never mind… What are you doing here?"

"I felt you when you entered the veil, and I told you before: I will always help you."

He didn't fully understand why, but it felt like a betrayal. Had she known the exorcism wouldn't affect her? If so, what were her true motivations? So many questions that couldn't be answered in this moment.

"I don't have time for this," he snapped. "I have to get back."

"You do," she said calmly, looking toward the phantom looming in the distance. "And I will buy you the time you need."

Mac's jaw clenched as he barely contained his frustration. "How?"

She stepped past him and locked her defiant eyes on the swirling mass of shadow. "I'll keep it busy."

He looked back at the phantom in the distance. It seemed stuck in place, but its tendrils were slowly stretching out toward him. As she moved toward it, panic surged as the memory of Lyndsay's sacrifice crashed into him. "No, wait…"

But she shook her head, never looking back. "If you don't make it, none of us do." And her voice softened. "I do this for you. Go. Win."

"Adaira, don't!" he yelled as the phantom's tendrils surged forward to meet her.

"Shit!" His heart pounded as the vision of Lyndsay's last moment replayed in front of him. He wouldn't let it happen again—he couldn't. He had to get back and find a way to stop this thing before it consumed her, and with a last surge of desperation, he reached deep into the Shade, tearing through the veil with raw emotion and urgency.

As the veil unraveled around him, something felt different. An unexpected weight and a subtle shift in the currents around him. It had never felt like this before, but he couldn't focus on that. He had to get back, and nothing else mattered. The veil collapsed around him, and for a moment, everything was nothing, until it suddenly wasn't.

He staggered as the cold of the real world shocked his system back to reality. He slammed back into his body right where he'd left off—facing Jeremiah, the book still clutched in his hand as though no time had passed at all. The phantom's presence still filled the air around him like a storm about to break.

He braced himself but then felt something strange—a surge of energy deep inside him, warm and powerful. Glancing down at his hand, his eyes widened when he saw a faint, ethereal glow pulsing around his fingers and wrist. He turned his hand, and the glow followed his movements, trailing imperceptibly behind, like a ghostly echo.

There was a power growing inside him, something he didn't recognize. He looked up at the phantom and then back down at his hand. *What the hell is this?*

And then he heard her. *Finish it, Mac. Now.*

It was Adaira, whispering to him clearly from inside his own mind. Calm and resolute, as though she knew what he needed to do. Before he could ask, she lifted his hand above the open book, and together, driven by urgency and hope, they slammed their joined essence down onto the page.

The pages flared to life, lighting up the symbols and igniting the letters to a blinding brilliance, and the shadow recoiled.

The glow fired out, pushing the phantom back as it let out a bloodcurdling shriek while its form unraveled in the light. Each of the tendrils snapped and dissolved as the mass of shadow retreated from the pulsing flashes. One by one, spirits were ejected from Jeremiah's body, each translucent form glowing faintly as they floated free, hesitating only a moment before dissolving into the veil.

He watched in awe as the phantom's power waned with each spirit released, and Jeremiah's body violently convulsed, his twisted form sagging as the last remnants of the phantom's energy were sucked into the book.

With a final, defiant roar, the phantom disintegrated, torn apart and devoured by the book's relentless pull. The man's body fell to the ground, limp and lifeless, as the oppressive weight of the phantom's energy was finally gone.

As the last remaining bits of the phantom's presence vanished, a gentle warmth spread outward from Mac's chest. His eyes blurred for hardly a second, and there was a strange pressure within him, pushing out just beneath his skin.

Then, with a quiet gasp, he felt something tugging away from him. A shimmering light emerged, separating from his body like a bright, glowing shadow being peeled away as it coalesced, kneeling beside him, her hand still pressed with his on the book.

He glanced over to Jeremiah and let out a slow breath he'd been holding since they pressed his hand down on the book. The air was clear for the first time in nearly a week. No oppressive weight, no gnawing dread, no anxiety. The glowing edges of the book faded beneath his hand. The battle was over.

A smile crept across his face as he turned to Adaira, still kneeling beside him, her hand firmly pressed over his. "You did it," he said softly, the relief dripping off his words.

Adaira looked back at him, and her lips curved and mirrored his faint smile, but there was something behind it—an emotion he couldn't quite place. "Yes," she murmured. "We did."

Mac snapped his attention to the cellar as its doors burst open and John stumbled out. He was battered—a little worse for wear—but he was upright, which was more than Mac could have hoped for. John's attention scattered around the scene, then back to Mac and Adaira, and his face contorted in alarm. "Mac!" he called out. "Get away from her... Now!"

"John," he exclaimed, his happiness at seeing him alive pushing past John's command. "It's over—"

"Damn it, Mac," he shouted as he rushed toward them. "Let go of the book!"

Adaira's hand flew back as she stood and retreated several steps. Her confused eyes bounced between John, Mac, and the book—wide, like she was searching for something.

Her expression changed quickly—regret, shock, maybe anger—Mac couldn't tell. She lingered only a moment longer before her form dissipated, her presence unraveling into the night air, leaving Mac and John staring at the space where she had stood.

John limped over and grabbed Mac by the arm. "You all right?" he asked, searching him for signs of harm.

"I… I think so," he muttered, still a little dazed from the fight. He glanced down at the book and then at his hand, still tingly from her touch. "Adaira…"

John looked around again, the area clear except for Jeremiah's body lying on the ground. "We'll have to figure that out later. Right now, we still have to find Joanne."

John suddenly stood, ready for another fight as a figure limped over. A bruised and bloody Agent Kane emerged from the shadows, cradling his chest and dangling a gun from one hand.

"What the hell was that?" he demanded, gesturing vaguely at the air. "Feel like I got hit by a truck."

He bent down, placing his fingers on Jeremiah's neck and noticing the hole in his shirt with no wound behind it. "I don't understand. No way that shot missed. He should be dead."

Mac and John exchanged a glance before John sighed and stepped toward the agent. "Short version," he said. "That truck was a phantom… a sort of parasitic entity that's been using him like a puppet."

Graham's eyes narrowed, like his skepticism and his intrigue were wrestling for dominance. "So… what? The killer was some supernatural thing wearing this guy like a suit?"

"Oh no, this guy's no innocent. He was certainly trash long before that thing showed up."

Graham rubbed his temple as he tried to process what John was telling him. "But it's… over now?"

"Not yet," Mac said, glancing toward the cellar. "Joanne's still down there somewhere."

Graham sighed heavily and pulled some zip ties from his jacket pocket, restraining Jeremiah. "Go," he said. "Backup should be here any minute. I'll make sure he doesn't go anywhere."

Mac nodded, grabbed the book, and handed it to John. The floodlight above the storm doors felt different now, more hope than shadows, and each step down the stairs felt like a promise— the same vow he'd made earlier. *Not one more loss. This ends now.*

CHAPTER 28

THE AFTERMATH

They stared at the heavy door that stood before them, the last obstacle standing between them and Joanne. He tried to open it and glanced over at John. "Locked," he said, like he knew it would be.

John nudged him out of the way and stepped in, studying the door. "It's very old. I think I can get it open."

Mac took a step back as John rolled up his sleeves and raised his hands, focusing entirely on the latch. He placed a palm on the door, just above the handle, and moved it around slowly, as if searching for the right spot. When his hand finally stopped, Mac heard a faint crackling sound and caught the slightest shimmer of a spark arcing between John's fingertips. The lock let out a low metallic groan before a satisfying click echoed through the room.

"That's a neat trick," Mac said as John pulled open the door, stepping aside to let Mac through.

They stepped in, and the view hit Mac like a gut punch. It was eerily familiar—an almost perfect recreation of the old morgue beneath the cemetery. The same bolted chair in the center, the same strange instruments, everything.

Mac shot a look at John, who seemed just as shocked as he was. "It's the same, right?"

"Not just similar," John said. "It looks deliberate."

He looked back, and his eyes landed on the chair, the memories surging to the surface—the loss of Jason and Lyndsay, his own crippling fear.

John must have seen it on his face because he gently put his hand on Mac's back. "Come on, focus."

He snapped out of it and forced himself to move, scanning the room for any sign of Joanne, though the room was empty. His chest tightened as his eyes landed on a dark hallway at the other end of the room, just as it was in the other bunker.

"This way," John said, nodding toward the hall.

Mac followed him, and he could feel his pulse racing faster with every step. As they entered, John found a light switch inside the corridor and flipped it, causing a row of fluorescent lights to flicker to life above them, revealing a series of identical steel doors lining both sides of the hall.

Mac moved to the nearest door, hesitating as his hand trembled over the handle, his heart threatening to burst out of his chest as the anxiety and anticipation grew with each passing second.

"Mac," John said quietly. "Whatever we find in there—"

"I know," he interrupted, keeping his voice low, and he gripped the handle, sliding the lock open.

The metallic scrape of the lock shattered the silence, yanking Mac out of his anxiety. He pushed the door open slowly, letting the soft light from the hall spill into the dark room.

Inside, the air was stale, stifling, and cold, and it smelled like damp stone, sweat, and despair. It was small and empty, aside from a mattress in the far corner, and there she was, huddled against the wall, shaking in fear. Joanne.

Her eyes squinted as the light hit her face. She was pale and gaunt, and her disheveled hair clung to her damp skin. She shook and shifted in her spot, as though she was preparing to defend herself.

He stepped inside, his shadow stretching across the room as the door creaked. He caught his silhouette cutting through the light and casting a looming figure against the wall. She flinched and retreated farther into the corner, still trembling, holding her hands close to her chest.

Her reaction sent a jolt through him as he realized how frightening this must be for her, and he froze, his words catching in his throat as he tried to speak. "Joanne," he said as softly as he could, the emotions cracking the word in two.

She didn't respond, and her eyes remained fixed on him. He remembered how Lyndsay spoke about her awakenings with Jeremiah and realized that to Joanne, this moment was just another visit from the monster coming to terrorize her. His heart twisted.

"Joanne," he repeated, slowly stepping closer. "It's me, Mac."

Her mouth opened slightly, but no sound came out, and her eyes shifted between his face and the doorway behind him.

He stopped a few steps away, trying to take it slow and careful, and lowered himself slightly to her level, holding his hands out, open and nonthreatening. "You're safe now," he whispered. "I'm here to take you home."

Her eyes locked on to his, and her expression shifted slightly. There was hesitation and doubt, but then the faintest flicker of recognition.

"Mac?" she rasped.

He nodded, and the emotion came flooding up to the surface, shaking every inch of him on the way up. "Yeah, it's me."

Her face crumpled, and her shaking body convulsed as a sob broke free. Relief and sorrow seemed to collide on her face as the weight of everything she'd endured came pouring out in a wave of emotion, and she wept. Her tense body relaxed into a slouch. "You found me," she said, choking the words out through her cries.

He moved closer, his own eyes burning from the tears, and extended his hand. "Come on. We're going to get you out of here," he promised, trying to keep his voice steady despite his own emotions threatening to overwhelm him. "I swear."

She hesitated for a long moment, crying and staring at her hands like she was willing them to move. Then, with a tentative movement, she reached out and took his hand. Her grip was weak and desperate. He grabbed her arm with his other hand to pull her up. She reached out, throwing her arms around his neck, and clung to him, and for the next few minutes he held her as she poured out the crushing weight of her pain, her fear, her exhaustion. But above all, he felt her trust.

As the sobs slowly subsided, Mac reached up and gripped her hand. "We have to go," he said.

"Mac," John called out softly from the doorway, with a hint of awe in his voice. "Look."

Mac looked up, letting out a small gasp when he saw her. Lyndsay stood in the corner, her form no longer shadowed or frail. Her glow was soft and golden and seemed to radiate warmth and hope. Her jagged edges were smooth, and her eyes, once burdened with sorrow and rage, now shimmered with a sense of purpose and peace.

"Lyndsay," he whispered as he slowly rose to his feet.

She looked at Joanne and then to Mac. The moment stretched, and the world seemed to stand still. There was no anger, no lingering pain—only gratitude.

"Thank you," was all she said before the light around her grew brighter, filling Mac's chest with a strange warmth.

Before he could respond, she turned her gaze upward, and her form began to dissolve. Small golden particles filled the room, swirling like fireflies as they rose, merging with the faint shimmer of the veil around them. And in an instant, she was gone.

He'd seen her leave a frustrating number of times, but this time felt different. There were things he wished he could have said to her, but his heart was strangely lighter after what he'd just witnessed, and he actually felt happy, which was a pleasant change.

John stepped closer, resting a hand on Mac's shoulder. "Looks like she got what she needed."

Mac nodded and finished helping Joanne to her feet. "She deserved it."

CHAPTER 29
THIRTY DAYS

It was a typical early November Saturday. The air was cold, but the early-morning sun shining over the cemetery held a small promise that it would warm up later. Mac leaned against the hood of his truck, watching as Agent Kane slowly made his way over. He still had a slight limp, but he seemed to have healed up nicely. He stopped ahead of Mac and stared out over the field of gravestones before turning to him.

"Graham," he said, greeting him as their eyes met.

"You ever wonder," he said, "how many of these folks didn't get justice before they ended up here?"

Mac followed his gaze across the field and nodded slowly. "It's come up a few times in the past few weeks."

The agent shifted, his shoulders sagging, like the weight of his cases was finally catching up with him. "You know we've closed fifteen cold cases since that night. Including the mother."

Mac shoved his hands in his jacket pockets and pushed out a quick breath, watching the mist form from his mouth. "Jeremiah and Caleb's mom?"

"Yep. Led us straight to her body," he said. "He's been very… forthcoming."

"I'm just glad it's over," Mac replied.

"Indeed," Graham said simply.

"How'd you know I'd be here?"

"Was told you come here every Saturday," he said. "Figured it'd be tough for you to duck me here."

Mac raised an eyebrow at him. "Did you need something?"

Graham looked down at the frosted gravel, kicking a small stone aside before looking back up at Mac. "I won't pretend to understand what you and John can do," he said. "But… I think there are ways we can help each other." He paused, waiting for Mac to say something before adding, "There are a lot of cases like this. Victims needing saving. Or justice. Skills like yours… we could do a lot of good together. Already spoke to John about it."

"Yeah?" Mac chuckled, already knowing the answer to his next question. "How'd that go?"

"He's a little rough around the edges, but I'll win him over."

Mac smiled as he nodded, thinking about that fiery dagger John once held inches from his throat. "Might not want to push too hard, Graham," he said as he prepared to walk away. "If you don't mind, I have a date with my wife, and she doesn't like it when I'm late."

He turned without giving the agent a chance to answer and started toward Josie's headstone, and he heard a soft laugh coming from Graham. "We'll talk again soon," the agent said.

"Hey, Josie," he whispered as he kneeled down in front of her headstone. "It's been a hell of a week."

He let the silence stretch while he thought about all the things he wanted to say. "Joanne's hanging in there," he continued. "She's… well, she's been through a lot. But I check in on her often. She's tough, like you. I can see it… she's starting to heal."

He paused and rubbed his hands together, blowing into them for warmth, while looking toward the horizon. "I've started working on the house. You'd probably laugh at me if you saw the mess I've made. Not really sure if I'm fixing it up for me or if I should just sell it. Either way, feels like something I gotta do."

He sighed as he brushed away a couple of stray leaves at the base of the headstone. "John wants me to go see him. Guess he thinks he's close to figuring out a way to fix me… make me normal again. But I don't know. I thought it was what I wanted… when it all started." He paused, thinking about it. "But now, I'm not so sure."

"Oh, yeah… When I was in the veil, I met this spirit. He was sad and stuck, and had the same story most of 'em have. I found his wife, told her what he wanted to say." He laughed. "She didn't believe a word of it, of course… but I guess it was enough to just have her hear it. He moved on." He shook his head and looked back at his truck. "Maybe Graham's right. Maybe I could do something with it."

He reached into his pocket, pulled out a small chip, turning it over in his hand. "Got this two days ago," he murmured as he rubbed his thumb over the embossed number *30*. "Thirty days. It's hard, Josie, especially this time of year. Some nights are worse than others, but I'm seeing things clearer than I have in years. Timothy always says, one day at a time."

He tucked the chip back into his pocket and looked down at the headstone one last time. "I miss you," he whispered. "Every damn day. But I think…" He nodded. "I think I'm figuring it out."

He stayed kneeling a moment longer, not quite ready to leave. The wind carried a fresh winter's bite to it, but he stayed anyway, digging into his pocket for his phone.

He scrolled through his playlist and found what he was looking for. He hesitated just a second before tapping play.

The soft, familiar melody of "Africa" poured out, but it wasn't the version Josie used to love. Though it was mostly the same, it had a rawer tone, with just enough edge to make it feel new again.

Mac smiled and set the phone down near the headstone. "Hope you don't mind the cover," he said. "Someone important to me… she told me about this one. Thought we could try it together."

He stayed as the song played, his arms resting on his thighs, letting the music spill out into the empty cemetery.

The bell above the door jingled softly as Mac stepped into the shop. The mixed-up smell of incense and old wood assaulted him as he walked in, and he groaned. He just knew it was going to cling to his clothes for the rest of the day. He looked around and found John hunched over the counter, intensely scribbling something in one of his old notebooks.

"Afternoon," he said as the door clicked shut behind him.

John glanced up, his dark eyes sharp but less unfriendly than usual. "You're late," he said, setting his pen down and stretching as he straightened up. He crossed his arms and leaned back against the counter. "Josie?"

"Yeah," Mac replied. "Seemed like the right way to start the day."

John nodded. "How's Joanne?"

"Better today than yesterday," he said, walking closer to the counter. "You said you were close to figuring it out?"

John sighed, pushed himself off the counter, and walked to a nearby shelf, pulling a thick book free and flipping to a specific page. "I think so," he said. "The way your... abilities work. It's similar to the tethering ritual we used when you entered the veil... but that tether is on the other side, always keeping you one foot in. I'm close to a ritual I think should be able to cut you loose... Make you normal again."

"By normal, you mean I won't be able to see ghosts, help people like I've been doing?"

John shot him a glance, probably picking up on the potential change of heart. "If that's still what you want."

Mac hesitated and thought about everything he'd done in the past month. Joanne, Lyndsay, Adaira, the farmer, all of it. "Maybe not as important as it once was."

John let a small smile escape briefly and then closed the book, setting it aside. "No rush, got it."

John reached under the counter and pulled out a familiar worn leather book. "In that case," he said, holding the book out toward Mac. "This might be more useful for you now."

Mac looked down at the worn book, its title shiny and bold: *The Elementalist's Guide to Ghosts and Spirits*. "You sure about this?"

John smirked. "Saving souls and stopping serial killers. Seems of better use in your hands than mine."

Mac chuckled and shook his head, though he accepted the book without hesitation.

"Just remember what I said. It's still dangerous. Don't screw it up, yeah?"

He nodded as he tucked the book under his arm. "I'll do my best."

As he turned to leave, John called out one last time. "Mac," he said, waiting for him to glance back. "You're sharper than you give yourself credit for. Don't forget that."

He nodded again, letting a tiny smile slip out before stepping out onto the busy street. As he looked around, for the first time, the street that had caused him so much pain and suffering, along with just about everything else, didn't feel so suffocating.

EPILOGUE

One Month Later

The house was filled with the scent of pine and coffee, a mix that somehow felt right for this time of year. Mac walked through his living room, dodging stacks of paint cans, tools, and patches of drywall along the way. There was tinsel and colored lights draped over every available surface, giving the space a cheerful yet cluttered charm. A tree stood in the corner of the family room, half decorated, its lower branches weighted down by an assortment of mismatched ornaments, while the top remained empty, the angel still sitting in its box nearby.

Mac adjusted the Santa hat on his head for the third time that morning and grumbled under his breath as the little white puff ball flopped in his face again. He swung it back a little too hard and stepped into the dining room with his steaming cup of coffee.

He sat at the table and looked out the window where giant fluffy flakes were falling, blanketing the yard with the season's first proper snow. It was almost Christmas, and only a few days from the anniversary of Josie's death, but for the first time in years, he felt… almost okay. The kind of okay that promised better days might finally be within reach.

He set his coffee down, opened the *EGGS*, and flipped to his page, lingering as he read the word scrawled at the top: *Threshwalker*. After a brief moment of reflection, he turned one more page, finding a new entry had been added: *The Heart of the House – Adaira*.

It was John's handwriting, but it was the title that stuck with him. "A whole section just for you," he murmured. "Guess we're both special."

Suddenly, the air in the room shifted, and a flicker of light drew his attention upward. Across the table, a familiar shimmer materialized. "Hello, Mac," she said.

Mac stiffened and tried to hide his concern before responding. "Adaira," he said.

She looked down at the book, still open to her page, and smiled. "You're reading about me," she said, gesturing at the book.

He nodded and gripped the edges of the table harder. "I have so many questions."

"I know you do," she replied. "But they'll have to wait."

He raised an eyebrow and leaned back slightly. "Why's that?"

Her eyes shifted back to the book. "That night we touched the book… something happened. Something I've been trying to understand ever since." She stepped closer, an actual step—not a glide or a shimmer. "The first time you summoned me, in your friend's shop, it cut me loose from the house. The second ritual, the exorcism… successful, yes… but instead of the book, I became trapped in the veil—until you pulled me out."

"Is this what you meant by free?" he said, still assuming that he'd been played.

Her eyes softened and flicked to his. "No, Mac. I really thought it would take me, too." She sighed and looked back at the book. "I don't know what I am anymore… something new, I think. But what I am sure about," she said, her voice growing more intense, "is that book… It's calling to me. It has been ever since that night."

She stepped closer, and the shimmer of her form brightened. Mac sat up straighter, preparing for whatever she was about to do. "What are you doing?"

"There's so much energy… almost too much for it to hold. Every ghost, the phantom, every spirit it's devoured… the energy's still there… It's about to crack, and it—"

Mac watched as she gazed into the book, almost like a trance had taken over her. "Adaira…"

She moved quickly, suddenly looming over him. Her eyes were locked tight onto his, and her hand shot forward, grabbing him by the wrist in an iron grip. "It's time," she whispered.

"Adaira, don't!" he said, struggling against her hold, but she was too strong. She forced his palm against the page with her name on it, and the ink glowed faintly under their touch. Energy pulsed through him, feeding back through his hand and into her. "Stop!" he shouted. "What are you doing?"

She didn't answer. Her eyes seemed distant, almost serene, as the energy continued to flow. Seconds passed, and the ink on the page faded, the letters unraveling into nothingness. He pushed as hard as he could, trying to get his hand free, but her grip tightened, anchoring him on the page.

"Adaira," he pleaded. "Please, let go."

The glow surrounding her intensified, and her form became a giant ball of blinding light. With one final pulse of energy, the page went blank as the ink itself vanished into his hand. Adaira released him and stepped back as she worked to steady her flickering form.

He slumped in his chair, trying to catch his breath as he stared down at the empty page. "What did you do?"

Her form pulsed one last time. "I'm sorry."

She dissolved into nothing, leaving behind only a faint static in the air.

Mac stared down at the blank page, then flipped through the rest of the now-empty book. "Shit," he muttered, as the puff ball from his hat flopped into his face again.

ACKNOWLEDGEMENTS

My deepest thanks to everyone who believed in this story long before I did. To Leslie for always pushing me forward and for your faith in Mac's ghosts; and to the early readers who saw something worth chasing through the streets of a haunted rural town.

To my Beloved Second Daughter. Even though this book "isn't really your kind of thing."

AUTHOR BIO

Timothy E. Jorgensen writes dark, character-driven thrillers that blur the line between crime, fantasy, and the supernatural. He lives in Colorado, where he divides his time between writing, technology, and trying to keep the ghosts in his stories from following him home.